MURDER
FLIES THE COOP

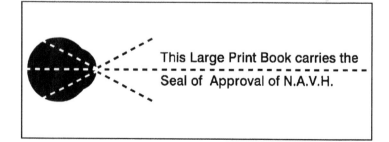

This Large Print Book carries the
Seal of Approval of N.A.V.H.

A BERYL AND EDWINA MYSTERY

MURDER FLIES THE COOP

JESSICA ELLICOTT

KENNEBEC LARGE PRINT
A part of Gale, a Cengage Company

Farmington Hills, Mich • San Francisco • New York • Waterville, Maine
Meriden, Conn • Mason, Ohio • Chicago

LIBRARY OF CONGRESS CIP DATA ON FILE.
CATALOGUING IN PUBLICATION FOR THIS BOOK
IS AVAILABLE FROM THE LIBRARY OF CONGRESS

ISBN-13: 978-1-4328-5716-5 (softcover)

Published in 2019 by arrangement with Kensington Books, an imprint of Kensington Publishing Corp.

Printed in Mexico
1 2 3 4 5 6 7 23 22 21 20 19

MURDER
FLIES THE COOP

CHAPTER 1

Beryl Helliwell watched as her friend Edwina Davenport capped her fountain pen and laid it on the desk in front of her. The morning post had yielded several pointed and chiding reminders from local merchants of accounts past due as well as a vexing dearth of alimony checks. Clearly the results of Edwina's calculations could not be considered good news.

"It's all here in black and white on the ledger page. Or perhaps it would be more accurate to say in red and white."

"Come on now, Ed, it can't be as bad as all that, can it?" Beryl asked. "After all, we were tediously careful with the funds all winter long."

"One can never be careful enough to make not enough go as far as one needs," Edwina said.

"Just last Sunday your dreary vicar was nattering on about some story or other from the Good Book about miracles and unending supplies of bread and fish or some such a thing. Can't you make the same thing work with the bookkeeping?" Beryl asked. Beryl noticed her friend looked shocked at the suggestion. But then, Edwina was easily shocked.

"The vicar is not the most prepossessing of men but I would hardly call him dreary. And the parable of the loaves and the fishes is not meant as a lesson in resource husbandry. It certainly isn't meant to encourage the congregation to tread all over the toes of the Almighty by assuming one can just as easily perform such miracles." Edwina shook her head at Beryl and delivered a severe look. "The only thing close to a miracle I've managed lately by way of stretching the comestibles is to water down your gin."

"I had wondered about my increased capacity for alcohol recently," Beryl said. "Rather a shortsighted approach, you know. I've only gone and consumed twice as much of it."

"But I haven't diluted it by half," Edwina said. "No wonder we are going behind each and every week."

"You should have told me and I would have cut down on my cocktail making,"

Beryl said.

"I didn't imagine you would have been willing to listen to reason about it. You've said as much in the past." Edwina gave the bookkeeping ledger another dour look.

Edwina was right, of course. Although Beryl had spent most of her forty-odd years rattling around the globe in an effort to complete one feat of derring-do or another, she had always returned to the States at the end of a journey. That is, until the outrageous passage of Prohibition. She had no intention whatsoever of stepping foot back on American soil until that nonsense had been repealed. Even finally granting women the right to vote had not changed her mind on the subject.

"I said nothing about reducing my consumption. You know quality gin is the reason for my glowing complexion and unflagging vivacity. I'd even go so far as to say it is responsible in large part for my youthful appearance. No, I would not stop imbibing, but would have stopped making cocktails."

"You aren't talking sense, Beryl. Not in the least."

"I mean to say I would have commenced to mooch. I would regale those at the pub with stories of my adventures in exchange

9

for the odd drink or two," Beryl said. Edwina gasped with a ferocity that put Beryl in mind of one of those newfangled carpet aspirating machines she had seen at a model home in London some months back. It really was extraordinary how well Ed mimicked the noise of the device.

"You mustn't spend your evenings in the pub. What would people say?" Edwina asked.

"I have never been concerned about what others say about me, Ed. You know that. It is only out of deference to your sense of decorum that I have not already staked out a favorite table at the village watering hole. Besides, I was quite sure you would not be willing to accompany me and I vastly prefer your companionship to that which I could find in the Dove and Duck."

"Despite my qualms and concerns for your reputation, I suppose if you wish to keep imbibing it may just come to that," Edwina said. "There are no two ways about it. Despite my very best efforts, and your own contribution to the coffers, our financial situation could conservatively be pronounced dire."

"Are you sure you have no piggy banks with a few pounds set aside for a rainy day? No unused silver knickknacks ready to sell floating around the place?" Beryl asked. But she already knew the answer. When she first arrived in Walmsley Parva a few months earlier she had been quick to note that all items of any value which Edwina's family home, the Beeches, had ever held, had already been discreetly sold off. As things stood, they were barely able to seat six for dinner with matching silverware. The income from Edwina's shares could generously be called paltry. The Great War had sent the English economy into a steep decline and she knew they weren't the only ones suffering. In fact, they were better off than many and she made sure to remind herself of that fact regularly.

"You know that there aren't. Despite all our efforts at economizing, we may yet be forced to take in a lodger." Edwina pursed her lips. "I just don't know what else we can do." Edwina threw her slim hands into the air.

"Something will turn up, Ed," Beryl said. "In my experience, it always does." Beryl could not help but notice Edwina did not appear soothed. At least she did not if her exit from her chair and commencement of pacing the long threadbare rug running the length of the Beeches' library was any indication of her state of mind.

"Your experience runs to reviving stalled engines and surviving crash landings, Beryl. Your knowledge of finance is limited to prying funds from former husbands and outrageous runs of luck at card games," Edwina said. Beryl did not see the trouble.

"I think that means I stay calm under duress," Beryl said.

"If we were plunging to our deaths whilst flying over the North Sea your expertise would be very welcome. As it is, I can't say I hold out much hope that your attitude is the right approach." Edwina chewed indelicately on the edge of her thumbnail. Her friend must be very worried indeed.

Beryl never did understand the concept of worry. Either something would happen or it wouldn't. She could see no point whatsoever in spending energy best suited to taking action and to having fun on fretting about possibilities that might never come to pass. But Beryl did recognize that not everyone shared her view of life. While she sometimes admired and even envied Edwina's rambunctious imagination she realized it came at a price far steeper than she herself would wish to pay. No, she felt quite sorry for Edwina as she watched her dear friend trying to keep her upper lip stiff as she snuck another glance at the bookkeeping ledger.

Something would have to be done and soon if Edwina were to keep from worrying herself to death.

Beryl took things in hand. She drew a deep breath and decided, yes simply decided, that all would be well. Then she sprang from her chair with as much vigor as her slightly stiff joints would allow and grasped Edwina by the arm, gently but persuasively.

"We shall take a turn about the garden and look at what has come into bloom today. Weren't you mentioning anticipating the unfurling of some peony buds just last night?" Beryl asked, drawing her agitated friend towards the library door. "I shouldn't be a bit surprised if a solution to all our troubles appears before we complete our tour."

Sure enough, by the time they reached the third garden bed on their walk, the roses were back in Edwina's cheeks. Beryl congratulated herself as she watched Edwina burying her nose in a fluffy pink peony blossom. While Beryl did not concern herself in the least with the garden, she was amazed at Edwina's intimate knowledge of all of her plants, their triumphs and their tribulations. Edwina leaned farther into the planting bed and inspected the underside of some glossy green leaves. She pulled a pair of secateurs from the pocket of her skirt and snipped off an offending branch.

Just then, Edwina's jobbing gardener, Simpkins, rounded the corner of the potting shed. Beryl wasn't certain but she thought she detected a slight wobble in Simpkins' gait. She suspected the privacy of the potting shed had provided him with the opportunity for a spot of tippling. Fortunately for Simpkins, Edwina was far less savvy about such things than Beryl was herself. Edwina found fault with her elderly employee's manner and work as a matter of course. Imbibing on the job would do little to improve her opinion of him. As he approached them, Simpkins slowed his pace and seemed to be having a care about putting one foot neatly in front of the other.

"Morning, ladies," Simpkins said. "I see you've noticed the fine glory of the peonies this day." He doffed his hat and made a slight bow. That clinched it. Beryl was certain that a cold-sober Simpkins would never bow to anyone. It was one of the things she liked best about him.

"The peonies are in fine form despite an infestation of aphids. I'm not sure how you call yourself a gardener at all," Edwina said, taking a step towards Simpkins and waving the leaf she had cut right under his nose. Beryl held her breath and wondered if Edwina was finally going to tumble to Simpkins' vice. Beryl could practically smell the fumes from where she stood several feet away. Perhaps a distraction was in order.

"Have you any news, Bert?" Beryl asked. "Any goings-on in the village we may have missed? Gossip down the pub you may have gleaned in your ramblings?" She winked at Simpkins as she uttered the word *pub,* hoping he would take the hint and do his best to look less disreputable. When Edwina had worries on her mind, she often was less tolerant of the foibles of others. In Beryl's opinion Simpkins was often just what Edwina needed and she would hate to see a breach develop between them.

"Indeed there is, miss," Simpkins said, drawing himself up to his full height. "There's been a bit of a hullabaloo with the local pigeon racing club. I thought of the two of you at once."

Edwina fanned herself vigorously with her leaf and scowled.

"The local pigeon racing club made you think of us, Simpkins," Edwina said. "I hardly dare to imagine how that could be."

"But there's been a scandal, miss," Simpkins said. "It put me in mind of the pair of you right quick like." Beryl shook her head slowly, wondering how Simpkins had managed to remain employed for as long as he had. Edwina most certainly did not prefer to truck with scandal.

"A scandal made you think of us?" Edwina asked, waving her cutting tool in front of her as she spoke.

"Now don't go getting yourself all hotted up, Miss Edwina," Simpkins said with only the slightest of slurs in his speech.

"What sort of a scandal?" Beryl asked before Edwina could say anything else.

"The pigeon club treasurer has gone missing," Simpkins said. Beryl laid a soothing hand on Edwina's arm, which had disturbingly reached out towards Simpkins while holding the secateurs.

"A missing person," Beryl said. "Of course you thought of us. After all, finding lost individuals seems to be something we are quite good at." Beryl turned towards Edwina and flashed her a brilliant and reassuring smile. She was gratified to see Edwina place the cutting tool back in her pocket.

"I suppose that's all right then," Edwina said. Edwina took a step closer to Simpkins, a sure sign her interest had been piqued. Simpkins directed a rheumy glance in Beryl's direction and cleared his throat. Beryl gave him the slightest of nods in encouragement.

"I'm not sure why the vicar would be so upset about a grown man who's gone missing, but he is right worked up about it," Simpkins said.

"Why would the vicar be interested in the comings and goings of someone in the pigeon club?" Beryl asked.

"The vicar is the president of the local pigeon club," Edwina said to Beryl. "It's a very popular pastime with many of the local gentlemen."

"Even though he was right cagey about the details, I told the vicar you'd be happy to give him a hand with his troubles," Simpkins said, swaying ever so slightly in the breeze. "He said he'd be happy for any assistance you might give."

"You told him what?" Edwina asked, her voice floating shrilly up into the treetops. Simpkins winced. Beryl wondered if this early in the day imbibing was to counteract the effects of a very long night of indulgence. She noticed him placing a gnarled hand over his stomach and decided the man was in fact hung over. She never had such troubles herself, a happy fact that left her feeling slightly superior as well as inordinately sympathetic towards those who did.

"Well, seeing as the two of you were such dab hands at solving the last mystery that came your way, I suggested to the vicar that you might look into this one," Simpkins said. "I see no reason why the two of you shouldn't start up your own private enquiry business."

And there it was. The solution to all their financial problems. Beryl was heartily ashamed she had not thought of it herself. Of course they ought to open their own private investigations agency. Beryl turned expectantly towards Edwina who, characteristically, did not seem to share her enthusiasm.

"Go into business?" Edwina said. "We haven't any idea whatsoever how to do such a thing." Beryl noticed Edwina did not cross her arms across her chest but rather began fussing with her collar and the cuffs of her cardigan. Beryl was encouraged to voice support for the suggestion.

"Is he willing to pay for our services?" Beryl asked.

"I'm sure that he would be. He seemed eager to have the problem taken care of quickly and quietly," Simpkins said. Beryl noticed the way Simpkins stressed the word *quietly.* "Of course he's a vicar so I wouldn't expect him to be a big spender."

"His willingness to pay does not make us more worthy of receiving payment," Edwina said. "We know nothing whatsoever about running an enquiry business. Or any other sort of business for that matter." Edwina's arms began to creep towards her chest. "It's one thing to look into criminal activities as a hobby. It is quite another to charge for one's services." This would require persuasion and quickly. Once Edwina had made up her mind she could be very difficult to budge. With an apologetic wink to Simpkins, Beryl took Edwina by the arm and drew her slightly out of his earshot.

"You recall our conversation this morning. I told you something would come up. This is precisely the answer to all our woes," Beryl said. "We would be foolish not to build upon our previous successes."

"Solving one mystery does not make us experts," Edwina said.

"If you recall, it turned out to be two mysteries in the end," Beryl said. "I would also point out we solved two crimes the local constable had determined were not crimes at all." Edwina took a deep breath and let out a long, loud exhale. If she had been a different sort of woman, Beryl

19

suspected Edwina would have allowed herself the indulgence of a profanity or two. As it was, Edwina simply sniffed extravagantly, as though she suffered from hay fever.

"But we haven't any capital even if we do have some measure of experience," Edwina said. "Surely one needs resources to set up any form of enterprise."

"We have absolutely everything we need to set up shop," Beryl said. She lifted her hand and counted off their assets one by one. "In addition to our experience and our gumption we have a telephone, an automobile, and a pistol."

Edwina gasped.

"A pistol," Edwina said. "You never mentioned that you have a pistol."

"I confess, I never thought to do so. I also never happened to mention I have a toothbrush. I find both of them to be absolute necessities."

"Have you ever fired it?" Edwina asked. Beryl was quite certain Edwina would have been embarrassed to realize her mouth was hanging open slackly like an adenoidal parlour maid finding herself in the presence of a member of the royal family.

"Only when absolutely necessary," Beryl said. "Unless you would like to be in the position of advertising for an additional lodger, I suggest we visit the vicar posthaste. Besides, I would have thought helping a vicar would be the Christian thing to do." Two spots of color appeared on Edwina's cheeks. Beryl felt grubby reminding her friend of her duty, but appealing to her sense of morality was the most expedient way to reach an agreement.

Edwina turned back towards Simpkins, lifted her chin, and squared her shoulders.

"Did the vicar happen to say when he would be available to meet with us?"

CHAPTER 2

It could not be said that Vicar Wilfred
Lowethorpe was a prepossessing man under
the best of circumstances. His sermons did
not inspire flights of spiritual ecstasy. His
singing voice cracked under the pressure of
leading the congregation in a closing hymn
at the end of Evensong. What few bits of
hair still clung to his head staunchly refused
to obey the laws of gravity. Edwina surmised
the vicar was not experiencing anything that
could be categorized as the best of circumstances if his agitated demeanor was anything to judge by.

He had been peering from behind the
vicarage's starched net curtains when she
and Beryl had arrived promptly at two in
the afternoon as Simpkins had indicated
they should do. Before Edwina had raised
her gloved hand to the gleaming brass
knocker, the vicar had yanked open the
front door and beckoned them in with a fur-

tive look up and down the street.

Even before she crossed the threshold, Edwina detected those dual scents of housekeeping virtue — cleaning solvent and laundry starch. The vicar's wife was sure to be somewhere about, ferociously upholding her usual tyrannical standards of cleanliness. Edwina liked a clean home herself, but as the sterility of the vicarage washed over her, she felt sorry for the untidy vicar and found herself more eager to help him with his troubles.

Beryl and Edwina followed the agitated man down a tight but spotless hallway and on into his study. He pointed to chairs for his guests to sit in, but rather than taking his own behind the desk, he paced the carpet with his hands clasped behind his back. Sunlight streamed through the long windows and Edwina noticed small puffs of dust lifting from the carpet with each step the vicar took. Clearly his wife's ministrations had not been allowed to extend to the vicar's private study. Beryl gave Edwina a significant look as if to say Edwina should take the lead in questioning their potential client.

"We understood from my gardener, Simpkins, that you had a matter you wish to speak with us about in a professional capacity," Edwina said with more authority in her voice than she felt. In fact, if she were to be honest, she was surprised her words were not drowned out by the sound of her loudly thumping heart. What would her mother say if she could see her now? Edwina was sure she already knew. Her mother had very strong opinions about the place of women in society, and running a private enquiry agency would certainly not have been something of which she would have approved.

In fact, if she had not already passed on to her eternal reward, surely the shock of seeing her daughter engaging in such a form of commerce, or any form of commerce for that manner, would have sent her to her grave. As she paused to consider it, Edwina realized it gave her enormous satisfaction to know she was taking exactly the sort of risks her mother would never have permitted. While she had been quite lonely after her mother's death and before Beryl's arrival, it was becoming most clear that there were advantages to being an orphan.

"I have a matter in mind that I would like sorted out but would not like to have the entire village speculating upon," the vicar said. "Are you able to go about the business of investigating whilst keeping to yourselves the exact nature of things?" Edwina noted a sheen of perspiration clinging to the grey stubble above the vicar's upper lip.

"Sensitivity and discretion are qualities for which our enquiry agency are best known," Edwina said.

"As well as guaranteed results," Beryl said with what Edwina assumed was meant to be a reassuring wink. The vicar halted his pacing. While Beryl was far more adept at handling most manner of gentlemen than Edwina ever hoped to be, she had much to learn about village vicars. At least those with wives as determinedly devoted as Mrs. Lowethorpe. The vicar would, quite correctly, find winks, especially from famous adventuresses like Beryl, utterly paralyzing. Not to mention, with only one successful case under their belts, she did not believe Beryl should offer any sort of guarantee.

"What Miss Helliwell means to say is that we can be relied upon to investigate thoroughly and discreetly. We also can be counted on to do so promptly and to make your difficulty our number one priority," Edwina said, sending Beryl a chastising look before slipping a notebook and a pencil from her handbag.

"How well you put things, Edwina," Beryl said. "We are utterly at your disposal."

25

Edwina was relieved to see Beryl refrained from following up that comment with another wink. She was even more pleased to see the vicar take his seat on the opposite side of the desk and lean back in his chair. "However, we will need a bit of information to go on if we are to make a start of an investigation."

"Simpkins will have told you one of the parishioners here in Walmsley Parva has gone missing," the vicar said. "He may even have mentioned that the man in question is Lionel Cunningham, a member of the pigeon racing club, of which I am the president." Edwina watched as several beads of perspiration collected between the vicar's eyebrows and threatened to race down the bridge of his hooked nose. He put her in mind of a pigeon himself.

"He did tell us that but nothing more," Edwina said. "I thought it very kind of you to take such an interest in your parishioners." Beryl nodded in agreement.

"While I am duty-bound to advocate for the safety of my flock it is not simply a matter of pastoral concern. I wish to speak with you in my capacity as president of the club. Lionel Cunningham is not only a member, he is also the club's treasurer. Which is where the difficulties arise." The vicar pulled a handkerchief from the depths of his tweed jacket and dabbed at his face.

"Do I sense some financial shenanigans?" Beryl asked.

"Unfortunately, that's it precisely. Lionel appears to have absconded with the club's entire treasury along with a number of other members' prize birds," the vicar said. Edwina watched as he gathered his handkerchief into a ball and squeezed it so tightly she thought she heard it squeak. Perhaps the vicar was not quite as mild-mannered as he seemed.

"Which members lost birds when Mr. Cunningham went missing?" Beryl asked.

"I did. So did Mr. Scott and the new fellow from the colliery," Vicar Lowethorpe said.

"And these birds were particularly valuable?" Beryl said.

"Indeed. Mr. Scott was especially distressed as his bird, Silver Streak, is the best racer he has ever flown," the vicar said.

"Are you quite certain that Mr. Cunningham is responsible for taking the funds and the birds?" Edwina asked. "Is there some possibility that someone else helped themselves to both?"

"I shouldn't imagine anyone else could be responsible. Lionel offered to take a basket of our best birds to a race. Frankly, I was grateful for his offer as my wife had requested my assistance that morning. According to the race officials Lionel never arrived at the starting point."

"A basket of birds?" Edwina said. "I thought that the birds simply flew from their roosts or some such a thing." Both the vicar and Beryl let out a muffled scoffing noise. The vicar looked at Beryl with new interest. It was no surprise to Edwina to discover that her friend was knowledgeable on the subject of pigeon racing. Beryl was knowledgeable about most forms of racing, from having been a participant herself or by having placed a wager upon the outcome of races at which she was simply an observer.

"I understand your confusion. You are thinking of short-distance pigeon racing, which is a pastime reserved for the working classes. People like myself race pigeons over long distances. Owners of long-distance racing birds converge upon in a previously agreed-upon site and at the starting gun release their birds. The first bird to reach their own loft is the winner," the vicar said.

"But isn't that unfair given that some pigeons must be closer to their roosts than others?" Edwina asked.

"Certainly that would be correct. I have

not made myself clear. The time is divided by the distance, and the bird which covers the distance in the fastest actual time is the winner. I had high hopes for one of my birds at that race," the vicar said. "And now I fear I shall never see Sunny Jack again." The vicar raised his handkerchief to his face once more but this time Edwina was sure he was dabbing at an unshed tear. She felt quite moved by the vicar's distress. She imagined how she would feel if someone had made off with her beloved dog, Crumpet. The notion was outrageous. If she had been a different sort of woman she would've reached forward and patted him on the back of his hand. As she was not, she contented herself with a quiet *tut-tut.*

"So you believe your treasurer made off with the money and your birds between Walmsley Parva and the start of the race?" Beryl asked. Edwina carefully wrote down the question in her notebook.

"I can't imagine what else may have happened," the vicar said. His voice rose an octave and he thumped his hand holding the handkerchief against his desk with enough vigor to make his inkwell jump. Edwina did her best not to jump, too. Emotional outbursts of that sort always made her nervous. "You can't mean to suggest that a grown man, a basket of pigeons, and the princely sum of ten pounds and four shillings have simply vanished into thin air."

"I should've thought that a man of the cloth would be more open to the idea of otherworldly occurrences," Beryl said, her voice pitched low. Edwina shot her a sharp glance before flicking her gaze towards the vicar, who fortunately seemed so caught up in his emotions as not to have heard Beryl's critical mutterings. Beryl folded her hands contritely in her lap. "I meant only to suggest that there was some possibility that your treasurer has met with foul play."

The vicar drew in a sharp breath and leaned against the leather back of his desk chair. He tented his fingers in front of his face and gazed heavenward. Edwina watched as his lips moved quickly without uttering an audible word.

"Perhaps I have been guilty of misjudging poor Lionel. It had simply not crossed my mind that he might have been as much a victim in all this as the rest of the pigeon racing club. I feel quite ashamed of myself," the vicar said.

"It is curious that a man of faith and filled with the milk of human kindness as you so clearly are would jump to such a hasty and unflattering conclusion," Edwina said. "It seems to me that perhaps your Mr. Cunningham had given you reason to mistrust him prior to his disappearance. Is that not the case?" She was quite gratified to see Beryl's eyebrows shoot up in surprise when the vicar slowly nodded his head.

"Indeed I did have reason to think perhaps Lionel was not a man of sterling character. But as I have only more unpleasant suspicions I would rather not taint your investigation by mentioning the cause of my concerns. I would much rather that the two of you went about this without the burden of my prejudices," the vicar said. "After all, I hadn't even considered that Lionel had not left Walmsley Parva with the intention of swindling the club. Clearly the two of you are far more experienced investigators than am I."

Edwina felt a rosy glow warm her cheeks. Perhaps Beryl had been right to insist they were adequately prepared to hang out their own shingle. She busied herself once again writing things in her notebook, hoping her blush would subside before the vicar noticed it. Beryl seemed to have sensed her distress and continued the questioning herself.

"Why have you chosen not to go to the police?" Beryl asked. "After all, the club's funds have disappeared. Constable Gibbs would provide assistance free of charge."

"Long-distance pigeon racing, whilst currently considered respectable, has not always been viewed as such. It took an interest on the part of the royal family to elevate the sport to its current position in society. It would not do to tarnish its reputation in any way. I certainly would not wish it to be seen on the same level as the working man's short-distance pigeon racing," the vicar said. "Any whiff of scandal might irreparably damage both our local club and the sport overall. To that end, despite the monetary cost, I decided to appeal to a private agency to retrieve our missing birds as well as the club funds."

Edwina felt Beryl stiffen beside her ever so slightly. Her friend was generally affronted by the notion of class distinctions. It wasn't her fault really as she had been burdened with the misfortune of being American. Edwina decided to jump in with a question, hoping to head off a tirade.

"Why is short-distance pigeon racing the purview of the working class?" Edwina asked. "I should think one sport would be very like another." The vicar snorted and shook his head from side to side slowly as if he pitied her lack of education.

"It all comes down to money, of course. One needs to have sufficient funds to travel by train to far-off points from which one releases one's birds. A workingman struggles to keep his birds fed let alone to find the extra money to transport them far from home," Vicar Lowethorpe said.

"Do you know anything about Mr. Cunningham's life outside of the pigeon racing club?" Edwina asked.

"He worked at the colliery in some sort of a professional capacity. I understood from Lionel that the owner relied upon him a good deal."

"Where does he keep his birds?" Edwina asked. "I assume he must have had some of his own if he was a member of your club."

"He most certainly does. He has a good-sized pigeon loft in the allotments," the vicar said. "He kept his own birds there."

"Where does Mr. Cunningham live?" Beryl asked.

"Last I knew he had a room at Mrs. Plumptree's boardinghouse. I believe he has lived there for as long as he has been in Walmsley Parva," the vicar said.

Edwina got to her feet and extended her hand towards the vicar who took it with a look of surprise. She shook it firmly and said, "Then the boardinghouse is where we will begin our investigation. Shall we go, Beryl?"

"We shall after the good vicar and I have come to an understanding on the small matter of our fee. As he is not a workingman I'm sure he will find the terms most reasonable," Beryl said. She gave Edwina what she could only describe as a devilish smile before announcing a sum that Edwina found difficult to hear without gasping in surprise. "We will of course require a retainer in the amount of two pounds." Much to her astonishment the vicar simply nodded morosely and opened a drawer in his desk. He withdrew a leather-bound check book and lifted a pen from its holder. He handed the check to Edwina who felt dizzy with excitement.

"We will be in touch as soon as we have something to report," Beryl said as she took Edwina by the arm and led her out the door.

CHAPTER 3

Beryl felt Edwina sag against her for support as they made their way down the hall and out the door of the vicarage. Beryl had always been of the mind that nothing ventured, nothing gained, and that extended to requests concerning money just as much as it did anything else. Edwina, of course, had not been raised to think of money as a topic a lady ever mentioned. Certainly not in mixed company or outside the walls of one's own domicile, if one could possibly manage to avoid it. Edwina couldn't help her reticence. After all, it was not her fault she had been born English. Beryl braced herself for the inevitable onslaught of recriminations and outraged questions from Edwina as soon as the vicarage door closed firmly behind them.

"Whatever were you thinking asking for such an outrageous sum?" Edwina said. "Two pounds simply as a retainer? I am still

light-headed simply even considering it."
Beryl felt a quiver running its way through
Edwina's thin frame. This would never do.
In Beryl's opinion Edwina's lack of confidence in terms of her worth was an even
greater impoverishment than her economic
state of affairs.

"The worst he could have said was no.
But he didn't, now, did he? We must endeavor to value ourselves at least as much
as others are willing to do," Beryl said. She
gave Edwina's arm a squeeze and steered
them both down the gravel path towards
the street. "Now, which way to the boardinghouse?"

Shady Rest Boardinghouse sat halfway
between the vicarage and the high street. It
appeared neither dispiritedly shabby nor ir-
reproachably well kept. It simply existed in
that anonymously respectable place somewhere in between. The two-story rectangular
building was utterly devoid of architectural
finery. Flat white clapboards covered the
outside. The windows were trimmed spar-
ingly by a budget-minded carpenter. Try as
she might, Beryl could not convince herself
to approve of such a modest undertaking. It
simply was not in her nature to endorse
such things either out loud or in the privacy

of her own mind. Still, despite its uninspiring appearance, as boardinghouses went, this one looked to be better than most.

"The name always puts me in mind of bereavement," Edwina said.

"Perhaps that is what sent Mr. Cunningham on his unexpected jaunt. With a name like Shady Rest, I shouldn't think it entirely out of the realm of possibility that residents are often found in the river with their pockets full of stones," Beryl said. She stepped up to the door and rapped firmly upon it with her gloved hand. She waited for a couple of minutes then knocked again but no one appeared. "Maybe this is a self-serve establishment." Beryl tried the knob and found it turned easily in her hand. She pushed it open and stepped across the threshold.

"Do you really think we ought to just let ourselves in?" Edwina asked. Beryl could tell Edwina was hesitant to enter the boardinghouse. But she wasn't sure if there was something about the place itself or simply an aversion to letting oneself in without an invitation that worried her friend. Either way, she was determined they would forge ahead.

"Of course I do. One mustn't worry too much about the niceties in the course of an investigation," Beryl said. The corridor was dimly lit and carpeted in a decidedly mangy brown runner that silently begged to be put out of its misery. A steep staircase filled the left side of the hall while a long narrow table clotted with souvenir spoons, ceramic figurines, and an unopened pile of post took up the right side. Beryl found herself in the unpleasant position of needing to turn sideways to continue along the corridor. She silently assured herself that she had not spent the winter becoming stout. It was surely the hallway that was sadly undersized.

The sound of a woman's voice issued forth from behind a closed door at the far end of the hallway. Despite the difficulties, Beryl squeezed doggedly towards the occupied room.

She knocked upon a wooden door, which even to her tolerant eye was in need of a fresh coat of paint, and waited for a response from within. Edwina stood just behind her, Beryl suspected hoping she would not be seen. The door opened and standing in front of them was a round dumpling of a woman well into her fifties and perhaps a bit older.

"Miss Helliwell, what brings you to my humble establishment?" the woman asked. Beryl was well acquainted with the experience of total strangers recognizing her wherever in the world she traveled. It did put one at a bit of a disadvantage much of the time. Especially considering Beryl had enormous difficulty remembering names. It rarely seemed worth the bother when one met so many people one would most likely never meet again.

Fortunately there were no strangers in Walmsley Parva, at least as far as Edwina was concerned. If asked, she likely could have reeled off not only the names of all her fellow villagers but the names of all their forebearers as well as their addresses and occupations. She likely even knew any grievances and grudges they clutched as jealously as dragons to their breasts. Yes, she had been right to name such a large figure when valuing the worth of Edwina's time.

"Hello, Mrs. Plumptree," Edwina said, stepping out from behind Beryl's shadow. "I hope we aren't disturbing you."

"Not in the least. In fact I am glad of the company. I was just having a bit of a chinwag with Cyril but his conversation tends to be rather limited. Although that's not to say I don't appreciate his companionship." Mrs. Plumptree took a step back and waved the newly minted pair of sleuths into the room beyond her. "Cyril, say hello to our guests." Beryl looked into the corner where a scarlet macaw with an even more disheveled appearance than the hallway carpet perched on a wooden swing hanging from the low ceiling by a thick brass chain.

"Quick, give me a kiss," the bird called out. Even for Beryl, a proposition of this sort was a first. The bird lurched forward and blinked lecherously. Edwina let out a tiny squeak Beryl interpreted as terror. Beryl did not dare to look at Edwina for fear she would burst out laughing. She was absolutely certain Edwina was not in the least amused by any of it.

"Did you teach him to talk yourself?" Beryl asked, taking a seat that placed her between the offensive bird and Edwina who had sensibly placed herself as far from the feathered menace as possible. Beryl could not fail to notice here and there, dolloped about, were traces of Cyril's flight path around the room. She discreetly eased herself into the chair, angling her backside to avoid contact with what Cyril had left behind. As she looked around the room it put her in mind of those parts of the world that had been bombed in the war.

"I can't teach him a thing. He belonged to Mr. Plumptree — at least he did before that husband of mine snuck off in the night leaving me to fend for myself in the world.

He left a note pinned to Cyril's perch telling me the bird would be a better companion for me than he had been. I've never seen hide nor hair of him since." Mrs. Plumptree clucked her tongue and sank down into the depths of the worn velvet settee facing her visitors. "At the time I was sad to see him go, but all things considered I'm happier left with the bird now that I've grown accustomed to him."

"Mr. Plumptree isn't the only bird-fancying gentleman you've had go missing from your boardinghouse though, is he?" Beryl asked. "You've had it happen quite recently, haven't you?"

"Imagine you knowing a thing like that. How could you possibly?" Mrs. Plumptree's face broke into a wide smile. "Is it some sort of a magic trick?"

"No magic but rather finely honed detective skills." Beryl lowered her voice and gingerly leaned forward in her creaking chair. "Miss Davenport and I have been asked to look into the disappearance of Mr. Lionel Cunningham."

"Well, you could just knock me down with one of Cyril's feathers," Mrs. Plumptree said. "Are you detectives now like some of those men I've seen in the pictures?"

"We are private enquiry agents," Edwina

41

said, with a darting glance at Cyril. "What we do is nothing whatsoever like the pictures." Beryl noticed that Mrs. Plumptree appeared disappointed by Edwina's proclamation.

"Perhaps it is a bit like the pictures. After all, we are trying to get to the bottom of a mysterious disappearance and that is something straight off the silver screen." She took another stab at eliciting information from their host.

"Why are you investigating instead of Constable Gibbs? Is it on account of your work for the king?" Mrs. Plumptree asked. Out of the corner of her eye Beryl noticed Edwina's impeccable posture stiffen to an even more irreproachable degree. Edwina had not approved of a rumor Beryl had put about Walmsley Parva when she had arrived back in the autumn implying that the two of them worked in His Majesty's service in a covert investigative agency. Clearly Mrs. Plumptree had been one of the many villagers to whom the deliciously outrageous tale had been carried. What was more, apparently she had believed it. Beryl knew an opportunity when one reared up on its hind legs to greet her.

"Our investigative work takes us along narrow country lanes just as frequently as it does broad city avenues. I am sure you will understand if we cannot share more details than that with members of the public," Beryl said. Mrs. Plumptree nodded and pantomimed locking her lips together with a tiny key. "I knew you were just the sort of person to understand such matters. I hope you will entrust us with all the information I feel certain you have concerning Mr. Cunningham." Beryl tugged off her ruby red kid gloves and laid them in her lap to signal she planned to stay for some time.

"I should say I did know him about as well as most here in the village. What is it you want to know?"

Cyril piped up with a comment of his own. "Lies, all lies," he said before tucking his head beneath his wing and appearing to drift off into a deep sleep.

"Do you know anything about what might have happened to Mr. Cunningham? Any reason he might have had for leaving without notice to anyone?" She noticed Edwina once again pulled a small notebook and pencil from her handbag. Beryl approved. She thought it gave their venture an air of credibility.

"I am as baffled as anyone. Unlike Mr. Plumptree, I never had a word of complaint from him. He was a model tenant. If I could have had a dozen more like him I wouldn't be up to my ears in work all day long, run right off my feet as I am now." Beryl noticed Edwina shooting a glance at Mrs. Plumptree's feet, which were tucked comfortably up on a small stool placed in front of the settee. From the look on Edwina's face it was easy to surmise she was decidedly unimpressed with the landlady's idea of hard work. While Beryl had recognized Edwina's superior knowledge of the clergy, she prided herself in being far more versed in the ways of rooming houses and their motley assortment of tenants, both human and avian. It was clear that Mrs. Plumptree, and Cyril, were best left to her.

"A likable man then, was he?" Beryl asked, hoping her tone would invite confidences from the landlady. Not that there was much to fear on that front. Mrs. Plumptree was starved for conversation if Cyril's dubious company was as valued as she claimed.

"That he was," Mrs. Plumptree said, patting her grey hair. "Never a cross word to anyone and always such a gentleman. I don't mind telling you that if he would have made me an offer of marriage I would not have thought twice about accepting. If I weren't still married, that is." Mrs. Plump-

44

tree crossed her hands over her bulging midsection and nodded sagely at Beryl. Edwina coughed discreetly into her gloved fist, a maneuver Beryl interpreted as an admonition to move things along before Mrs. Plumptree felt compelled to share any further intimate details of her wild imaginings. As the hopes and dreams of a boardinghouse landlady were not of interest to the investigation, Beryl resisted the urge to dig for details.

"I suppose the best thing to do would be to take a look at his room," Beryl said, getting to her feet. Edwina rose too and looked down at Mrs. Plumptree as she struggled up from the depths of the sagging settee. Cyril pulled his head from beneath his wing and let out another raucous comment.

"Give us a cuddle," he said. Edwina positively scurried towards the door. Beryl followed closely behind her, and Mrs. Plumptree, with an effort, brought up the rear. Edwina and Beryl pressed into the corner to allow the landlady to lead the way. The formidable woman grasped the banister at the base of the stairs and heaved herself upwards. Cyril swooped low over Beryl's and Edwina's head then flapped up the stairs ahead of them. By the time they reached the door to Mr. Cunningham's abandoned room Cyril was pacing the floor of the upstairs hallway.

"Now if I can just remember which of these keys fits this lock, we should be all set," Mrs. Plumptree said. Beryl noticed the landlady identified the correct key almost immediately. She wondered if Mrs. Plumptree had a habit of entering her lodgers' rooms when they were not at home. As she watched Mrs. Plumptree move about the spare space touching a penholder on the desk and smoothing the coverlet stretched across the bed almost unconsciously, she decided it likely that was her habit. "You know I did wonder if perhaps something bad had happened to him. He wasn't the sort of man to simply leave things behind like he was made of money. If he was he'd have no need of living in a boardinghouse." She gestured towards the dresser. A brush, a pair of nail scissors, and a shoeshine kit lined up across its surface.

"Do you know if there's anything he did take with him?" Edwina asked.

"Let's take a look," Mrs. Plumptree said. She opened the armoire and looked inside. A suit and an extra pair of trousers hung neatly inside along with five white shirts. A pair of brown leather shoes polished to a gleam sat on the floor of the armoire. On the top of the cupboard sat a hatbox, which Beryl reached up, pulled down, and opened. Inside she found nothing more than a wool hat in need of brushing.

Edwina stood at the windowsill running her finger along a stack of books placed there. Mrs. Plumptree joined her and bent over the stack and read the titles aloud.

"His pigeon rearing and pigeon racing books are not here where he kept them," Mrs. Plumptree said. She crossed the room to the desk and pulled open each of the drawers. "They're not in here either. Those were his prized possessions. Perhaps he left on purpose after all."

Beryl looked past Mrs. Plumptree at Edwina and arched an eyebrow. "I think we've seen enough for now. Thank you so much for your cooperation," Beryl said.

"Will you be sure to mention to the king how helpful I was?" Mrs. Plumptree said, her eyes aglow with hopeful expectation. "It would be the thrill of a lifetime to know he'd heard the name Edna Plumptree."

"I promise to tell him all about it the very next time I see him," Beryl said.

CHAPTER 4

"While I do appreciate how much your tendency towards mendacity has assisted us in the past, I cannot approve of you promising to mention that poor woman to the king," Edwina said as soon as the boarding-house landlady was out of earshot. "It was most unkind of you to raise her hopes."

"I cannot agree with you, Ed," Beryl said. "I will mention her eagerness to lend a hand to those around her the very next time I see him. It hardly seemed worth tarnishing her hopes by telling her I have no idea, however, when that will be."

"You are simply splitting hairs. You cannot deny you told her you would do it the next time, which clearly implies there has already been at least one occasion upon which you have met with His Majesty." Edwina felt a flush of indignation burning at the back of her neck. In her opinion one did not make light of the royal family.

"But I have met your George. Nice fellow. He once bent my ear for over an hour talking about his stamp collection," Beryl said without a trace of amusement in her voice. Really, Edwina thought, one never knew what to believe and what not to when it came to her famous friend. It was far too well-known that George V collected stamps for Edwina to give real credence to Beryl's claim. She decided rather than to press the matter she would be far better off in directing the conversation to more useful aspects of their investigation.

"Where do you think we should turn our attention next?" Edwina asked.

"You mean other than the pastimes of the monarchy?" Beryl said. Edwina bit her tongue and nodded. "I suggest we head to whichever colliery employed Mr. Cunningham."

"That would be the Hambley mine. It's just outside of Walmsley Parva." Edwina knew that Beryl would be thrilled to hear their destination was not within easy walking distance. Beryl liked nothing better than to take her shiny red motorcar out for a rattling ride through the countryside. Edwina had yet to adapt to it herself. The jouncing up and down on the hard seat and the grinding noises all left her feeling thoroughly worn out whenever they arrived at their destination. But she could already see Beryl's eyes sparkling with enthusiasm.

"I think we should drive over there immediately. I haven't taken the old bus out for a spin in ages. It will do that magnificent machine a world of good," Beryl said, tucking her hand through Edwina's arm and hurrying the two of them along towards the Beeches.

A harrowing half hour later Edwina found herself being looked up and down by a slim blond woman dressed from head to toe in a conservative blue frock. Edwina did not pay much mind to the latest fashions but she found herself looking approvingly at the modern, businesslike line of the younger woman's ensemble. While Edwina generally considered herself to be a traditionalist, she had learned to appreciate the loosening of fashion constraints upon women brought about by the Great War.

Her work with the Women's Land Army had taught her how very practical trading long skirts for a pair of trousers could be. While the woman before her was not dressed in any manner that would provoke criticism, she was wearing a garment that could be considered simultaneously flattering and utilitarian. Edwina wished she were in the financial position to have a similar frock made up for herself immediately. Perhaps, she thought in a moment of unbridled hopefulness, if the enquiry agency became a going concern she could go ahead and do so.

"Good afternoon," Beryl said. "We would like to speak with the owner and anyone else who might have worked with Mr. Lionel Cunningham." Beryl towered over the desk as if she had every right to expect her request would be granted. That was the thing about Beryl; almost all of her requests were granted. And quite willingly. Edwina did not attribute it simply to Beryl's fame but rather to her overall expectation that life would turn out exactly as she wished it to. Sometimes it was most exasperating. If she were to be entirely honest with herself, she would admit that sometimes she entertained the notion of someone flatly refusing to do as Beryl asked. Surely that was not the imaginings of her best self but it amused her nonetheless.

"Do you have an appointment with Mr. Ecclestone-Smythe?" the woman asked.

"Certainly not," Beryl said, drawing herself up to her full height and peering down at the young secretary. "I am not a great believer in appointments. They never seem necessary in the least."

"And you are?" the severe-looking young woman asked. Could it really be that there was one person in all the world who had not heard of celebrated adventuress Beryl Helliwell? Edwina wondered.

"Please let the owner know that Misses Edwina Davenport and Beryl Helliwell would like a moment of his time," Beryl said with her usual unflappable demeanor. After delivering a second withering head-to-toe survey of Beryl, the woman pushed back her chair and slowly made her way around the side of the desk. She approached a paneled wood door on the far side of the room and rapped firmly upon it before letting herself in and closing it behind her. After a moment she returned with a chilly look on her face. A tall, florid man who put Edwina very much in mind of the ringmaster of a traveling circus she had attended as a young girl followed in her frosty wake.

"Miss Chilvers, why don't you put the kettle on and fix us all a cup of tea. I'm sure a bit of refreshment would be most welcome," the ringmaster said as he beamed a showman's smile at Beryl. He caught sight of Edwina and turned to include her half-heartedly. "Ladies, if you will just follow me we can make ourselves comfortable in here." He held open the door to the room he had just exited and stood in attendance as the two women took seats on the visitors' side of a massive mahogany desk. Edwina was feeling a spot of déjà vu. Although this man was nothing like the vicar. Rather than pacing the floor and looking agitated, he immediately eased into his desk chair and gave them his complete attention.

"Now it's not that I'm not happy to receive a visit from such a celebrated woman as yourself, Miss Helliwell, but I can't imagine you're here simply to have a chat. Are you here to drum up sponsorship for one of your outrageous schemes? If so, I'm afraid you are out of luck," he said. Edwina detected a steely tone beneath his jocular words.

"For the record, sponsors of my adventures have always sought me out, not the other way round. In actuality, we are here looking for one of your employees," Beryl said. "We have business with a Mr. Lionel Cunningham. We understood from his landlady that he is employed here and that this would be where to find him at this time of day." Mr. Ecclestone-Smythe shook his head slowly.

"I'm sorry to say he never arrived for work this morning. Most irregular," he said. "I can't understand it. The man has been utterly reliable during the course of his employ." Edwina kept her eyes trained on his expression, looking for signs of dishonesty. Edwina prided herself in her ability to recognize fibs and untruths of all sorts. Her time spent volunteering on committees, working for the Women's Land Army, and a long-standing relationship with her gardener, Simpkins, had prepared her to recognize lies whenever she encountered them. She was surprised to realize she could not tell whether or not Mr. Ecclestone-Smythe was baffled by Lionel Cunningham's failure to appear at work that day.

"Do you have any idea where he may have gone?" Edwina asked. "Any family members he may have suddenly needed to visit due to illness or some other personal difficulty?"

"You mean has he toddled off to Brighton to tend out on an elderly spinster aunt or some such thing?" he said, turning to address Edwina for the first time. She nodded, hoping her face did not reflect her thoughts on his tone at the mention of spinsters. "Lionel never mentioned family other than to say his parents had both died and that he was an only child. I very much doubt familial obligations would have caused him to miss work, especially without a word of warning."

"So you have no suggestion as to where we might locate him?" Beryl asked.

"None whatsoever. It is dashed unpleasant to have unreliable staff, I don't mind telling you," Mr. Ecclestone-Smythe said, throwing his hands up in the air. "I wish I could help you but I am at a complete loss myself."

Miss Chilvers entered the room carrying a silver tray. She placed it upon a side table and set about pouring out cups of tea for each of them. Edwina noted the secretary knew exactly how her employer took his tea. "Milk? Sugar?" she asked Edwina and then Beryl. Edwina took the opportunity to include the secretary in the questioning. In her experience, from her visits to the local solicitor's office as well as the doctor's surgery, the secretary was the person who really knew all that went on.

"We are here asking about Mr. Lionel Cunningham. I suppose you knew him, too," Edwina said. She observed the secretary's steady hand holding the teacup as she responded to the question.

"I most certainly did. We have worked together for quite some time. We also each have lodgings at Shady Rest Boardinghouse. Which makes us neighbors in a way, I suppose," she said. Edwina noticed the muscles along Mr. Ecclestone-Smythe's jawline tightening at the mention of his secretary's living arrangements, and as he placed a broad hand over his paunch as if his stomach had begun clamoring for his attention. She wondered if he felt that it was not quite nice for the two of them to be living under the same roof.

"What did you think of him?" Beryl asked.

"I'm sure it's not for me to say," the secretary said.

"But surely you had an opinion of some sort," Beryl said. Edwina caught a quick glance between the secretary and her employer. He gave the slightest of shakes to his head.

"Mr. Cunningham is a most valuable employee and a pleasant gentleman. Our interactions are cordial but in no way personal. I respect the work he does here and I should like to think he holds my work in similar esteem," she said. "If there's nothing further, Mr. Ecclestone-Smythe, there are some letters I need to type up." Rather than waiting for an answer she turned sharply on her sensible low heel and left the room.

"You never said how Mr. Cunningham's disappearance came to your attention," Mr.

Ecclestone-Smythe said. Beryl placed her teacup on the edge of his desk and rose. Edwina followed suit.

"No, we did not. We'll see ourselves out," Beryl said.

CHAPTER 5

Beryl reminded herself to slow down as she rounded the corner and turned into the driveway that led to the Beeches. After all, while she did prefer high rates of speed, she had already had one mishap with the pillars flanking the end of the drive. While it had only been a few months since she had swerved to avoid hitting Crumpet, Edwina's beloved terrier, and had crumpled the hood of her automobile in the process, it seemed like far longer. Beryl had never felt quite so at home anywhere before. Really, she felt unwaveringly at peace for the first time in her life.

Edwina, on the other hand, seemed decidedly ill at ease. Beryl was certain her friend's mood could not be attributed to her driving. Surely Edwina understood she was in the hands of an expert. It must be their lack of progress at the colliery that was disquieting her friend. She took one hand off the wheel and patted Edwina's arm with it. Edwina clutched at the door handle with even more determination. Perhaps the right words would best put her mind at ease.

"We can't let our lack of progress at the colliery discourage us, Ed," she said. "We've only just begun poking around. I'm sure something will turn up any moment now." She pulled to a screeching stop directly in front of the Beeches. Edwina flung herself from the automobile and headed for the front door without a backward glance. Beryl told herself her friend was only hurrying as there was a visitor standing on the front step. Beryl eased herself from behind the wheel and followed the other two women into the house.

"You remember Mrs. Lowethorpe, I'm sure," Edwina said. Beryl knew how to take the hint. The middle-aged woman dressed in a shapeless frock the color of porridge seemed slightly familiar. But if Beryl had had to recall her name she would not have been able to do so. Nor would she have been able to recollect where in the world she had encountered a woman who was so obviously dedicated to the concept of re-spectability.

"The vicar's wife," Beryl said. "How could I possibly forget?" She followed Edwina and

59

their guest to the parlor.

"What brings you by for a visit, Muriel?" Edwina asked.

"I understand the two of you have agreed to assist Wilfred with his ill-advised pigeon club entanglements," Muriel said. She paused, looking from Beryl to Edwina. When they nodded, she continued. "I had intended to be there when you called but the work of a vicar's wife is never done. I was unfortunately attending to one of the many duties I shoulder in the community."

"I don't know how the village would function without you," Edwina said. Beryl snuck a glance at her friend's face.

"That's very gratifying to hear. Not that I expect praise or thanks from anyone. It's my job to provide service without thought to the toll it takes upon me," Muriel said.

"I'm sure I don't know how you manage it all," Edwina said. Edwina made soothing noises, a skill Beryl had never acquired.

"Still, one's activities make it difficult to attend to things on the home front as readily as one might like." Muriel sniffed loudly and squinted into a corner of the parlor whose housekeeping Beryl was certain would not hold up to her close scrutiny.

"You don't sound as though you entirely approved of your husband's involvement with the pigeon racing club," Beryl said.

"Well, it isn't quite nice, is it, a vicar spending time he could be working on his sermons or ministering to his flock associating with degenerate gamblers and brawlers." Muriel plucked one of Crumpet's buff colored hairs from the arm of her chair and flicked it to the floor. "I would never have permitted his involvement in any capacity, let alone in a leadership position if he hadn't convinced me that by participating he would provide a much-needed stabilizing and elevating influence on the existing members."

Beryl couldn't agree with Muriel's scathing assessment of the merits of racing and the people who participated in the sport whatever the capacity. If it weren't for gambling Beryl knew for certain her alimony checks would never have covered her living expenses. She could think of far less moral ways to make a shilling stretch but she didn't think mentioning them to Mrs. Lowethorpe would endear her to their only client's wife. If they were to earn their pay she would need to keep her thoughts to herself on that score.

"I'm sure the vicar provides a very reliable moral compass to any group in which he finds himself. It was most broad-minded of you to approve of his participation," Edwina said. Beryl gave Edwina a disapproving look before steering the conversation elsewhere. Smoothing and soothing was one thing. Nauseating displays of flattery were a different matter entirely.

"Was there some reason you wished to be in attendance at our meeting with your husband?" Beryl asked. "I can hardly imagine a woman with as many commitments as you would drop by simply for chat."

"There certainly was. Wilfred has a shocking memory. He never seems to remember a thing I say," Muriel said. Beryl thought perhaps the vicar had simply learned how best to survive living with a force such as his wife. She would have done the same herself. Beryl had always found those earnest women who engaged long-sufferingly in good works to be the most difficult individuals to bear with good humor and attentiveness. She attributed Edwina's ability to do so to her friend's unwavering sense of duty and to years of practice while caring for her hypochondriac mother. "I told him to be sure to mention the ill will brewing in the club but he claims he cannot remember if he brought it up or not. I rather expect he didn't." Muriel clucked her tongue.

"I'm sure we should have remembered any

mention of any unpleasantness within the pigeon racing club," Edwina said. "Wouldn't we, Beryl?"

"Edwina makes a practice of taking notes during all of our interviews and is very conscientious about such things," Beryl said. Edwina took the hint and pulled her notebook and pencil from her pocket once more. "We would be very eager to hear whatever information you can contribute to the investigation."

"Just as I thought. Wilfred is utterly hopeless in all practical matters," Muriel clucked again. "I knew he wouldn't tell you about the trouble with Mr. Scott."

"The greengrocer?" Edwina asked, her pencil at the ready.

"The very one." Muriel leaned forward in her chair. "I hate to go carrying tales but I feel I would not be doing my duty if I didn't tell you there was no love lost between Mr. Scott and Mr. Cunningham." Edwina paused in her scribbling and looked at their visitor.

"Are you quite sure about that?" Edwina asked.

"Indeed I am. The two came to blows in the front parlor of the vicarage not a week ago. I saw it with my own two eyes." Muriel nodded swiftly enough to set her second

63

chin swinging softly back and forth.

"Do you know what it was that they were arguing about?" Beryl asked.

"It would have been difficult not to know with the way the pair of them were carrying on. Shouting and waving their arms about. I actually had to remind them not to take the Lord's name in vain. In the vicarage no less," Muriel said. "I cannot for the life of me see how anyone could be so competitive about pigeon racing."

"Were Mr. Scott and Mr. Cunningham rivals? I thought they are both members of the same club," Edwina said. Beryl had noticed a decided lack of competitiveness on Edwina's part but had not realized how incomplete was her education concerning the world of sport. Beryl decided they would have to make a point of correcting that as soon as possible. Perhaps they could attend a cricket match or even a three-legged race at the upcoming village May Day fete.

"Belonging to the same club does not eliminate competitiveness between the racers, Edwina. If anything, such close quarters fan the flames of any rivalries that might lie lurking below the surface," Beryl said.

"Just so." Muriel nodded. "Mr. Cunningham and Mr. Scott took turns coming in first or second, at least in club standing. The rivalry between them could not be described as friendly."

"You mentioned brawling and gambling earlier," Beryl said. "Was Mr. Cunningham ever involved in any such thing?"

"I am sorry to say that at the last meeting he and Mr. Scott indulged in a shocking display of fisticuffs right there in my own parlor. They managed to shatter my best crystal vase. Not that I held it against them, mind you. A vicar's wife is above such petty grudges." Beryl wondered if there was a special risk to the soul of vicars' wives who told bald-faced lies. From the way she pursed her lips it was clear Mrs. Lowethorpe most certainly had not forgotten or forgiven the destruction of her ornament.

"It must have been very shocking for such a scene to take place in your own home. Do you know the cause of it?" Edwina asked.

"What didn't the two of them argue over? They berated each other over their choice in pigeon feed or in training schedules. They almost resorted to violence on the subject of breeding stock and fledging chicks. Most recently they disagreed about how to run the club," Muriel said. "Mr. Scott is the vice president of the club and he told Mr. Cunningham in no uncertain terms what he thought of his bookkeeping at the last meeting."

"When did the last meeting take place?" Beryl asked. A stir of excitement moved her chest.

"The night before Mr. Cunningham went missing. In fact, Wilfred thought it was rather big of Mr. Cunningham to offer to run the birds up for the race the next day considering how abusive had been Mr. Scott's manner," Muriel said. "Wilfred did not want me to mention the divisiveness to you but I told him it might have important bearing on your investigation."

"Indeed it might, Mrs. Lowethorpe. You were very right to bring this to our attention," Beryl said. Edwina made a last note and then snapped her notebook shut with finality.

The vicar's wife shot to her feet, startling Crumpet who lay quietly in his basket near the cold hearth. "My business is done then. I shall take my leave of you and trust you know how best to use this information." She nodded at each of them in turn and then swept from the room banging the front door behind her before Beryl could cross the room.

"What a lot of energy that woman has," said Edwina. Beryl winced at the tone of admiration in her friend's voice.

"That is one way of looking at it," Beryl said. "I should think the vicar's wife gives Prudence Rathbone a run for her money in the race to be Walmsley Parva's biggest gossip." Edwina looked satisfyingly shocked.

"How can you say such a thing? She is practically a member of the clergy," Edwina said. "And what's more, she's given us our only lead in the case."

"You think Mr. Scott, our mild-mannered greengrocer, might have done away with the missing man?" Beryl asked. She had not taken Mrs. Lowethorpe's concerns all that seriously. After all, in her experience men had a habit of getting worked up over sports. She had often used that fact to her advantage when it came to placing a wager or proposing a dare.

"You forget, Beryl, I may not be one to spread gossip, but that does not mean I never hear any of it. It so happens Gareth Scott has been locked up overnight on several occasions for getting into drunken altercations with other men down at the Dove and Duck. More times than I would like to mention his wife had to open the shop in his stead. The poor woman. What a thing it must be to be married to such a self-centered sort of a man." Edwina bent to give Crumpet a pat on his small head. "You are a much nicer sort of fellow to have around the place, I daresay."

"I suppose there is one other thing that could count against him," Beryl said.

"What is that?" Edwina straightened and turned her full attention to her friend.

"A man who sells vegetables would know a lot of market gardeners and farmers, wouldn't he?"

"Of course. It is a part of the trade."

"Then he would know where any number of patches of turned-up earth could be found. And should he wish to dispose of Mr. Cunningham he would know several places where it would be easy to do so," Beryl said.

CHAPTER 6

Edwina had demurred Beryl's offer to drive her into the village. She did not enjoy rides in Beryl's motorcar under the best of circumstances. She was quite sure she would not feel properly prepared for her interrogation of Gareth Scott if her heart was lodged in her throat as it so often was after going for what Beryl breezily referred to as a jaunt. In her mind Edwina always thought of it as more of a jounce but she never mentioned the fact. Far be it from her to spoil someone else's pleasures.

Edwina had armed herself with her third best hat and second best pair of shoes for her mission. Striking the right tone between what one would consider professional and what would make one appear to be flagrantly involving oneself in the grubby world of commerce was more difficult than she would have imagined it would be. She would not want it to be said about the vil-

lage that she esteemed a visit to a tradesman sufficiently to wear her best hat or
shoes.

She arrived in front of the greengrocer to
find the shop empty save Mr. Scott himself.
He was replenishing a basket filled with
spring onions as she entered. He turned and
wiped some smudges of soil from his fingers
against his striped apron. Edwina shuddered
to herself at the thought of poor Mrs. Scott
being confronted with a heap of her husband's washing.

"What brings you in this afternoon, Miss
Davenport?" Edwina could not help but
notice Mr. Scott's eyes sliding sideways to
the counter beneath which the ledger was
kept. Given the state of her household
finances, she was in no position to discuss
settling her account. Fortunately he had
given her just the opening she needed to
steer the conversation in a more comfortable direction.

"I am here with some questions about
your pigeon racing club," she said.

"What about it?" he asked. "You don't
seem the sort to take an interest in any manner of racing. Now your friend Miss Helliwell looks like the type of woman to enjoy a
flutter from time to time but I am surprised
to hear you are interested."

"I am here at the request of Vicar Lowethorpe. He has asked Miss Helliwell and myself to look into the disappearance of Mr. Cunningham." Edwina watched his face closely as she mentioned the missing man's name. A look of disgust flickered across it as though he were physically pained by the mention of the other club member.

"I can't see how Cunningham's disappearance is worth looking into. You'd be far better off looking into locating the club's missing birds. And our missing money," he said.

"We are looking into that too, of course. Which is why I am here speaking with you. I understood from something mentioned by Mrs. Lowethorpe that you disagreed with the way Mr. Cunningham kept the club books. I wanted to verify that with you," Edwina said. She pulled her investigation notebook from her pocket along with her tiny pencil and hoped it lent her an air of professionalism.

"I did indeed. Cunningham may know about the way a big outfit like the Hambley mine keeps books, but it isn't the way to organize a small concern like the racing club," Mr. Scott said. He crossed his arms over his chest and leaned against a wooden crate heaped with lettuces. He inclined his head towards his ledger once more. "The small businessman such as myself knows a sight more than any sort of rich man's lackey ever will."

"How different can the sorts of bookkeeping the two of you are engaged in be?" Edwina asked. "After all, isn't bookkeeping simply bookkeeping?"

"My bookkeeping is meant to make things plain." Mr. Scott crossed the small shop and pulled the ledger out from underneath the counter. "Take your account for example. For the longest time it was woefully overdue and I marked that fact with a red pencil every week when I tallied the accounts. Once the account was finally paid I marked it down in black. I do the same with all my accounts. At the end of every week it's easy for me to see what is paid and what is still owing." He gave Edwina a significant look and she felt her cheeks grow warm. It would never do to allow a suspect to put her on the defensive. She looked him boldly in the eye before proceeding with her questions. She stepped up next to him and ran her finger along the column of figures marking the page.

"I see you have a similar system for the accounts you owe to others and the accounts you have settled," Edwina said. "You must know at the end of the week how much you owe as well?" Mr. Scott cleared his throat and hastily closed the book. He quickly tucked it back underneath the counter.

"Just so. At the end of every week I have a clear picture of the state of my financial affairs. And that's how the club books should be kept as well, in my opinion."

"And they weren't kept that way?" Edwina asked. Mr. Scott shook his head vigorously.

"As far as I could see, Cunningham kept the books in such a way as to muddy the facts more than to reveal them. If I didn't know better I would have said that he was doing it on purpose in order to make sure none of the rest of us had any real sense of what we had in the coffers."

"Was that the nature of your argument with Mr. Cunningham the night before he disappeared?" Edwina asked.

"That amongst other things," Mr. Scott said. His voice took on a guarded tone as he looked for the first time at Edwina's notebook. In order to encourage him, she closed it and slipped it back into her pocket. Perhaps she would be better in future to make a note of things after she had concluded her interviews. The idea of being quoted exactly did not seem to put all interviewees at ease.

"We were given to understand the two of you were also rivals concerning your birds' prowess on the race course," Edwina said. "Could your argument have had something to do with that as well?"

"As a matter of fact it did. After I called his bookkeeping practices into question, he began spouting balderdash about my winning streak. But I am sure the man was not simply a sore loser. He was trying to turn attention away from whatever shenanigans he was trying to pull with the monies," Mr. Scott said. "I resented the way he cast aspersions not only on my character but on the capabilities of my birds. Imagine if they'd heard him? I don't know what it would have done to their confidence."

Edwina could see that he was truly offended by the insult to his racers. She had not thought much about the idea of honor amongst pigeons. While she did enjoy watching the birds that made their homes in her garden, she had not noticed any inclination on their part to acknowledge insults from humans. For the most part they seem to take very little notice of the comings and goings of the people strolling up and down between the garden beds and in the woods at the Beeches. Even Simpkins, for all his thrashing about the place, was someone to whom they paid very little mind.

"What exactly did he say about your birds?" Edwina said.

"He said he had no confidence that they could actually be as fast as they are," Mr. Scott said. "Not with their pedigrees at least, according to him." While pigeon racing was not an area in which Edwina would claim expertise, she did happen to know a little something about pedigree. Her mother had been deeply interested in the subject, especially as it pertained to the local families. She could understand with ease how Mr. Cunningham's words would have stung.

"You wouldn't have any idea where Mr. Cunningham could have gone off to, would you?" Edwina asked.

"Why would you think I'd have any idea where he'd be?" Mr. Scott said. "It isn't as if we were mates."

"I had understood from your comments, and that of others, that you were anything but friends. You weren't even friendly. But as a bird fancier yourself I thought it possible you would know where someone with a basket full of prized birds might successfully hide himself away for several days without detection," Edwina said.

"I see. Well, not being a criminal myself I

75

am sure I can't speak for Cunningham," he said.

"I had assumed if there was something Mr. Cunningham would know about caring for birds in any situation then you would as well," Edwina said. "But I suppose even the most enthusiastic hobbyist cannot be expected to have an encyclopedic knowledge of his pursuits." Edwina hoped to appeal to the delight so many gentlemen seemed to take in being experts at obscure bits of knowledge. She turned slightly away as if she planned to take her leave of him.

"Perhaps I spoke a touch hastily," he said. "I'm sure now that I'm putting my mind to it I can give you a few ideas where to have a look for him. He'd need to water and feed them of course, but in order to keep them from returning to their loft he would need to keep them secured."

"Would the basket he used to transport them to the race serve the purpose?" Edwina asked. Mr. Scott shook his head vigorously.

"No pigeon fancier worthy of the name would keep his prized birds, or any birds come to mention it, in such close quarters. Even if it didn't suffocate them, they would likely go mad from the experience." Mr. Scott shuddered and his sad, basset hound eyes bulged out of his head slightly. Edwina imagined how she would feel if Crumpet were closed in somewhere confining for several days in a row. She was startled to find the sting of tears pricking at the back of her eyes. "No, he would need to have prepared a loft for them in some manner or other wherever he took them."

"It sounds as though he would have needed to plan his disappearance," Edwina said.

"You know, you must be right. The scallywag would have known for some time what he was about. Considering his stance on feeding his birds, I knew I was right not to trust that man an inch."

"It sounds very complicated. I can't help but feel that it would do the investigation a great deal of good if I had a better sense of the world of pigeon racing," Edwina said.

"That it would, I'm sure," Mr. Scott said. "Why don't you and your friend Miss Helliwell plan to attend the next race?"

"Are you going to have one considering the missing birds and the lack of funds?" Edwina asked.

"It would take a lot more than that to keep our club from putting on a good performance at this week's competition. I never race all my best birds the same week so I have a few waiting in the wings, so to speak." Mr. Scott chuckled at his own joke. "I know the others have said the same. It would be a right treat to have the pair of you in attendance."

"I shall have to consult with Miss Helliwell and with my diary. When is the race to be held?" Edwina said, rather hoping the date was already engaged.

"Tomorrow, in fact. You are just in time. We start the race from the village of Pershing Magna. It should be a festive occasion as it is one of the best attended races of the season," Mr. Scott said. "There is sure to be coverage by the local press and maybe even the national papers, too."

"Is it possible to arrive by train?" Edwina asked, thinking of the terrors riding all that way with Beryl would surely mean. Her mind cast back to a harrowing trip she and Beryl had taken to London in the autumn. It was an experience she did not wish to repeat.

"It certainly is. As a matter of fact many of the railway lines offer special train fares to racers and those attending the races. Pigeon racing is practically a national pastime these days. You really ought to see it for yourself."

Fortunately for Edwina, before she could answer, Minnie Mumford, the owner of the local tearoom, entered the shop with a large wicker basket slipped over her arm. Minnie was almost as much of a gossip as her close friend Prudence Rathbone. If there were any hope of keeping the investigation a secret, at least for the time being, she would need to keep news of her questions, or her possible attendance at the race, from Minnie and Prudence. She quickly thanked Mr. Scott for his time and hurried out the door before Minnie could wonder why she had not made any purchases.

CHAPTER 7

"See, Ed, I told you we needed to see a race for ourselves. There is no substitute for firsthand experience in any number of things," Beryl said, looking out at the throng streaming past them on their way to the release point. "Races are no exception."

"I am still not convinced we could not have done just as well by consulting a book on the subject," Edwina said as she dodged out of the way of a passing cyclist whose sight line was obscured by a stack of crates strapped to a rack on the front of his conveyance.

"We need to get a feel for the milieu, Ed. We must get a sense of what makes these people tick if we are to imagine where Mr. Cunningham might have gone and what he might have done with the birds." Beryl felt her spirits soar as the crowd around them swelled. She felt caught up in the excitement of the crowd in a way she had not been in some months. Surely the time she had spent in Walmsley Parva with Edwina had done her real good. She actually felt herself looking forward to the excitement of the race. She just wished Ed were also inclined to enjoy herself.

Men carrying tightly woven baskets filled with the sound of gentle cooing shouldered their way past the onlookers and approached the starting line. Edwina stood erect and alert, her left hand holding her second best hat firmly in place while her right clutched tightly at Beryl's arm. If she didn't know better, Beryl would have said that Edwina was not enamored of crowds. She also doubted her old school chum had ever attended a sporting event the likes of a long-distance pigeon race in her life. Her heart went out to Edwina for all the moments of excitement she must have missed out on over the years. Not that Beryl thought a late start was the same thing as a failure to succeed. She was a great admirer of those women who kept trying new things throughout their lives and Edwina was turning out to be just such a woman.

Beryl would have expected nothing less from her girlhood friend. Even during their school days Edwina had exhibited a steely spine that surprised those who dismissed

81

her as a rule-abiding good girl inevitably headed down a predictable path. Those who had not been paying close attention would have expected Edwina to marry a respectable and conservative gentleman with good, though not ostentatious, prospects in life. They would have anticipated two or three children from such a marriage; any more would be vulgar. Her casual acquaintances and teachers would have guessed she would spend her spare time reading improving literature, and volunteering for worthy causes. Certainly none of them would have expected her to remain unmarried and to be a partner in a successful private enquiry agency. It was, however, exactly the sort of thing Beryl would have expected of her friend.

When it came down to it, Edwina had always been a person who knew her own mind. She might not kick up a lot of fuss about it, but she always managed to make her point, to stick to her principles, and to generally get her own way. Which is where Beryl thought she added the most value to their friendship. Beryl rarely allowed Edwina to cling to the familiar when she thought her friend would benefit from trying something new. Beryl was quite sure she knew Edwina even better than Edwina knew herself. Now if she could just convince her to enjoy the sporting life.

"Look over there, Ed," Beryl said. "We are making progress already in our investigation. Isn't that Mr. Ecclestone-Smythe from the Hambley mine?" Beryl waved to a portly gentleman standing near the release point. He spotted Beryl and lifted his hat in greeting. Beryl took Edwina by the arm and steered her through the crowd.

"Miss Helliwell and Miss Davenport, what a pleasure it is to see you here. Please allow me to introduce my wife, Lucretia," Mr. Ecclestone-Smythe said with a slight incline of his head towards a trim, well-dressed woman several years his junior who stood at his side. "You remember, my dear, me mentioning that these two ladies had visited me at the colliery just yesterday." Beryl couldn't say for certain, having just met Mrs. Ecclestone-Smythe, but it looked to her as though the other woman had spent a great deal of time in the last few hours sobbing her eyes out. She couldn't help but wonder at the cause.

"I've read all about you in the papers. I can't tell you how much I admire the way you take off for parts unknown." Mrs. Ecclestone-Smythe gave Beryl a half-hearted smile. She turned to address Edwina. "And of course I've heard of you too, Miss Davenport. Your investigation into the murder that took place last autumn left me in awe of your achievements."

"It is a pleasure to meet you too," Edwina said. Beryl could have sworn she noticed a bit of color creeping up the back of Edwina's neck. Beryl had become so accustomed to compliments herself that she took them as her due. Not that she felt arrogant about them in the least. They neither thrilled nor embarrassed her. They simply existed. For Edwina, on the other hand, such things were a novelty. Compliments for things other than her efficiency, commitment to the common good, and her gardens at the Beeches, that is. It was lovely to see Edwina having her chance at the spotlight.

"These two fine ladies were there looking for that no-good Mr. Cunningham. You haven't located him yet, have you?" Mr. Ecclestone-Smythe said. Mrs. Ecclestone-Smythe let out a small choking noise. Beryl decided the colliery owner's wife most definitely had something to hide. She let her gaze drift sideways to include Edwina who appeared to have noticed Mrs. Ecclestone-Smythe's reaction as well. Beryl could see her slipping her hand into her pocket where she kept her trusty notebook.

"I'm afraid we haven't. In fact, it is in the pursuit of him that we have decided to attend the race here today," Beryl said. "I assume from your question you have still not heard from him either."

"I most certainly have not. It's a dashed nuisance the way that man has disappeared on me. I would have thought him a far more decent fellow than that." Mr. Ecclestone-Smythe jammed his beefy fists into his trouser pockets. "You never did say why it was that you were looking for him. I can't imagine what business someone like you would have with a common clark."

Beryl decided it was time to poke at the hornet's nest. She hoped Edwina would not be too put out with her for revealing information they had not agreed to disclose. But nothing ventured, nothing gained.

"Yesterday we were not in the position to share such information. However, in light of his continuing absence, we feel it best to be forthcoming with those who knew him well. We have been hired to investigate his disappearance by a concerned member of the community who has an interest in his whereabouts," Beryl said.

"You've been hired to investigate?" Mr. Ecclestone-Smythe said, his eyes bulging from his florid face. "It's utterly outrageous to consider ladies such as yourselves should be involved in such an unsavory sort of thing." Edwina took a half step forward.

"I'm quite sure you did not mean to be offensive. However, we take our work seriously and would appreciate you doing the same," Edwina said. "As your wife mentioned only a moment ago we are experienced in matters of investigation and expect to be respected in our pursuit of justice."

"I meant no offense, ladies. It is just an extraordinary thing to think of women entering into such an unsavory field of endeavor. I hope I can rely on you to let me know if you do locate him," Mr. Ecclestone-Smythe said.

"We certainly can make no such promise as the wishes of our client supersede all other requests," Beryl said.

"Who is your client?" Mrs. Ecclestone-Smythe asked.

"I'm afraid we cannot divulge such sensitive information," Edwina said. "I'm sure you understand."

"I believe we are being hailed by our friends the Fosters, my dear," Mr. Ecclestone-Smythe said. He took his wife by the arm, lifted his hat, and sketched a slight bow. "I hope you will suspend your investigating long enough to enjoy the race." Beryl watched as the pair of them wandered in the direction of another couple whose fine clothing marked them as members of the same class as the Ecclestone-Smythes.

"Well, Ed, what do you think?" Beryl asked as Edwina pulled her notebook from her pocket.

"I think I'm glad that Mr. Ecclestone-Smythe is not our client. Not that it's likely that he would be considering his opinion of lady detectives," Edwina said. Beryl noticed Edwina was pressing her pencil down on her notebook quite heavily. She hoped Edwina had a pocketknife in her pocket as well in case she managed to break off the tip of the lead in her fit of pique.

"I spent most of my life dealing with men like him. The trick is to simply ignore them and go about your business as you see fit. What I meant was, do you think he knows more than he's letting on?" Beryl asked.

"I'm not sure the man knows as much as he's letting on. He seems an utter buffoon to me," Edwina said. "His wife on the other hand seems like quite an astute individual. She also appeared troubled by something. She looked surprised to hear Mr. Cunning-ham's name mentioned." Edwina chewed on the end of her pencil. It was a habit held over from their schoolgirl days. Beryl found it endearing. Or perhaps Edwina was simply hungry. She did have a tendency to forget to eat.

"I noticed that, too. I think we should make a point of speaking with her again," Beryl said.

"Here at the race?" Edwina asked.

"If we get the chance," Beryl said. "But for now let's see if we can find out a little bit more about Mr. Cunningham and pigeon racing. After all, I'm sure there will be plenty of opportunities to call on Mrs. Ecclestone-Smythe. But pigeon races are not held every day." Edwina nodded and followed her friend across the green. Up ahead was what appeared to be a staging area for the pigeon carrying baskets. There were large ones and small ones. Most were made of wicker but some of the containers were wooden slatted crates.

Young boys ran up and down the aisles between the rows of baskets calling to each other excitedly. A small boy, much younger than the others, tripped and fell to the ground. Edwina and a younger woman both rushed to his side to inspect for damage. Beryl kept watch from a safe distance. With rare exceptions, like Jack, the Walmsley Parva newsboy, children made her feel slightly queasy and light-headed. Part of her contentedness in life stemmed from the fact that she had avoided ever producing any children of her own. From the way Edwina crouched next to the small boy and wiped at his scraped knees with her handkerchief, Beryl felt certain her friend did not feel the same sense of elation at her own childless state.

The war had been cruel on many fronts and the lack of men to go round was not the least of them. She and Edwina had not spoken of such things, but Beryl had noticed, and mentioned, how Charles Jarvis, the solicitor in Walmsley Parva, had shown more than a passing interest in her old friend. Maybe, if fate were very kind and inclined to miracles, it would not prove too late for Ed to experience the joys of motherhood for herself. Although Beryl would find life at the Beeches far less pleasant with a small person in residence, she would not want to ever stand in the way of Edwina's happiness.

The other woman assisting with the boy appeared to be in her twenties, but then one never knew anymore. So often the young were old beyond their years. Another small suffering to be laid at the feet of the war. The young woman grasped the boy's chubby little hand firmly and raised him to his feet. In a flash he scampered away as if the incident had never occurred, shouting for the older boys to wait for him. Beryl, content that the coast was clear, approached the other women.

"I wish I were as resilient as that," the younger woman said as she watched him run off.

"He was lucky not to have been badly injured. If he had fallen a few feet to the right he could have needed looking at by a doctor." Edwina nodded to a bale of barbed wire coiled up nearby. "I should not have liked to have seen such a thing at all."

"I know just what you mean. I saw enough needless injuries during the war years," the woman said.

"Were you a nurse?" Edwina asked.

"I was. In France. It was an experience I would not like to repeat but at least I met my husband out there." The younger woman smiled. "I'm Alice Morley. Are you here for the race?"

"Edwina Davenport. And allow me to introduce my friend Beryl Helliwell." Edwina turned to include Beryl in the conversation. She stepped closer.

"We are here for the race. It seems like quite the to-do." Beryl swept her hand about her at the crowd and the eager vendors filling the green. "Are you here as a spectator, too?"

"My husband, Dennis, is one of the racers. In fact, he participates in both long- and short-distance racing," Alice said. Her thin face broke into a wide smile as she mentioned her husband's accomplishments.

"Isn't that quite unusual?" Beryl asked. "I thought most racers picked one distance or the other to commit to."

"They do generally but my Dennis is an unusual case. He was in charge of a mobile pigeon loft during the war and he never lost his love of the birds. When he was demobbed he was lucky enough to find work at the Hambley mine. Naturally he started racing with the other miners as soon as he managed to purchase his first bird. In fact, he went to the owner and asked if the miners could set up an area dedicated to lofts in the mining village. Fortunately he agreed."

"So how did he get involved in long-distance racing?" Edwina asked.

"When the head clark at the mine, Mr. Cunningham, heard about my Dennis' expertise with the birds, he asked him to become a member of his own long-distance racing club. Dennis wasn't sure he wanted to look as though he were getting above himself by joining, but some of the miners encouraged him to give it a try. He's been participating in both types of races ever since."

"He must spend a great deal of time engaged in his hobby. Not all wives would understand that kind of commitment," Edwina said.

Alice shrugged. "It keeps him happy and anything that does that is fine by me. So many of our boys are still feeling the distressing effects of the war. Any bit of happiness we can manage to cling to is worth whatever it costs as far as I'm concerned."

Beryl had heard the same sentiment more often than she cared to remember. So many young, and not so young, men of her acquaintance were maimed in body, spirit, or both. If all it took for some of them to find happiness were a few stolen hours and a flock of birds, there were few who would begrudge them that.

"Did you know Mr. Cunningham too then?" Edwina asked. Beryl was so lost in thoughts of the past she had forgotten entirely about their investigation. It was one more reason she was certain she and Edwina would make a success of their joint venture. One of them would be sure to be attentive to their cases at all times.

"I knew him from the club and also from the mine. I live in the mining village with my husband but I am also employed as the village nurse," Alice said. "Mr. Cunningham was in charge of handing out the pay packets."

"Were you aware that he has gone missing?" Edwina asked.

"My Dennis told me all about it. One of his birds was amongst those that went missing," Alice said. "Dennis is still distraught about it. He does worry so about his birds."

"It seems so odd to think a grown man and a basket of birds could simply vanish in broad daylight," Edwina said.

"Dennis says it wouldn't be so hard to do if someone wanted to. He said Mr. Cunningham could have taken a train and sold off the birds to fanciers anywhere in the country," Alice shielded her eyes with her hand and looked out over the crowd. "It seems as if my husband has vanished himself. I don't know where he could have gotten to."

"Does your husband believe that Mr. Cunningham deliberately made off with the pigeons?" Beryl asked.

"Too right he does. Those birds were all worth a pretty penny and there isn't any other explanation for him disappearing without a trace, now is there?" Alice said. "There's my husband. It has been very nice chatting with you ladies but I need to catch up with him." Alice gave them a small wave then picked up her skirts and hurried away across the green.

"I do hope that Mrs. Morley is right about that," Edwina said, turning her head to watch the younger woman disappear into the crowd.

"About our missing man setting off to sell the birds somewhere in the hinterlands?" Beryl asked.

"No. About that being the only explanation for why Mr. Cunningham vanished," Edwina said.

"I think we are right to be concerned that his disappearance may not have been his idea," Beryl said. "If it turns out he has come to harm I think we need to add Mr. Morley to our growing list of suspects."

CHAPTER 8

A horn sounded and pigeons filled the sky and flew off in all directions. The sound of their beating wings almost drowned out the sound of the crowd of spectators. Beryl felt her heart soar at the sight of them. It had been many months since her own last flight and she suddenly felt earthbound. With a light heart she tucked her arm through Edwina's and joined in the cheering along with the rest of the crowd.

From behind she felt someone lightly touch her shoulder. She turned her head and found herself staring directly into a familiar pair of dark blue eyes. A cry of surprised glee escaped her lips. She dropped Edwina's arm and reeled to envelop Archie Harrison in a firm embrace.

"Archie, what are you doing here?" Beryl asked. "I thought you made it a point of honor to rarely leave Australia." Beryl released him and looked his lanky frame up and down approvingly. With his bush-whacker ensemble and his straw fedora he looked every bit the man of action she knew him to be.

"I'm here covering the pigeon racing. I'm just as surprised to see you as you are to see me," Archie said with a broad smile. "Last I heard, you had crash-landed somewhere in Africa."

Beryl had been keeping a very low profile for months. During her last escapade, a hot-air ballooning expedition over the Sahara Desert, she had realized her penchant for adventure was fading fast. When her balloon collapsed near a desert oasis she threw herself upon the mercy of the handsome Bedouin who helped secret her away from the crash site without a trace. She had taken a circuitous route from Africa to England using a combination of disguises and aliases. She spent many weeks living as a variety of different women. One of them was a Russian countess, another was a minor member of the Swedish royal family, and a third was a midwestern farmer's daughter who had left the North American continent for the first time during the Great War.

The subterfuge had provided just the sort of break from her own high-profile identity that she had desperately needed. It wasn't until she had spotted Edwina's advertisement for a lodger in a newspaper that she had admitted who she really was to anyone in months. Not that she could have possibly fooled Edwina with any sort of false identity. The two had been friends for far too long for that kind of thing to work. She wasn't, however, surprised that someone like Archie would have had no word of her. As much as she enjoyed his company he was not on her very short list of people with whom she corresponded even somewhat regularly.

"I haven't been in Africa for months. But let's not talk about all that. Allow me to introduce my dearest friend, Miss Edwina Davenport." Beryl shifted her stance to better include Edwina in the conversation. "Ed, this is Archie Harrison, celebrated sports reporter and my favorite Australian," Beryl said. Edwina stepped forward and extended her gloved hand.

"A pleasure to meet you, Mr. Harrison. Welcome to England," Edwina said.

"Thank you very much, ma'am," Archie said. "I've always wanted to visit and when my newspaper suggested a trip to cover current sporting enthusiasms in the old country I couldn't think of a valid excuse to stay at home. My editor booked me on the first boat out of Sydney so here I am." Archie

97

looked around as if still a bit bemused to find himself in such an entirely different landscape than that of his homeland.

"When was the last time we saw each other?" Beryl asked.

"I believe it was during your divorce proceedings. I seem to remember being named in the complaint brought by your husband," Archie said. Beryl was pleased to note his freckled face crinkled into a crooked grin.

Beryl heard Edwina stifling a sort of recriminating gasp with a gloved hand pressed firmly over her mouth. "I hope you're not still holding that against me," Beryl said.

"The only thing I ever held against you about any of it was the fact that I was not the only one named in the proceedings," Archie said. This time even Edwina's best efforts could not disguise her surprise. A decided squeak made its way past her pursed lips. Archie turned to her, his broad grin still fixed firmly on his face. "If you're an old friend of Beryl's I'm sure none of this comes as a surprise to you." Beryl knew she should step in. Edwina was simply not prepared to have that sort of conversation. In fact, there was every possibility she had never had a conversation with a reporter before in her life, and certainly not one who worked for the sporting pages.

"Tell me the truth, Archie, are you really here because your editor sent you, or have you lost your job again? Have you run out of newspapers in all of Australia that will hire you?" Beryl said. Archie was the sort of man who lurched from one newspaper to another just barely ahead of the wrath of a managing editor. He took far too many chances and had absolutely no sense of self-preservation. Most of his stories involved infuriating wealthy and powerful people, especially those people who spent a large number of advertising dollars supporting his publication. The only reason he was still employable was that he was so very good at sniffing out newsworthy stories.

"Guilty as charged, Beryl," Archie said. "I knew I shouldn't have tried to sneak anything past you."

"It's only because we're such kindred spirits, Archie, that I'm able to look straight through you. Are you here working for a newspaper or is this a freelance job?" Beryl asked. Archie shrugged.

"A little of both, I suppose. I've been hired on a trial basis by an outfit out of Dover. If they like my writing they'll take me on full-time. It's quite a comedown from the papers in Sydney but beggars can't be choosers, now can they?" Archie said. "And jobs aren't exactly easy to come by in England right now. I'm lucky to have this shot at a job in journalism."

Beryl's heart went out to her old friend. What he really needed was a story far juicier than that of local pigeon race. Perhaps she could do them both a good turn.

"Would a really surprising human interest story impress your new overlords?" Beryl asked. Next to her Edwina cleared her throat. Beryl felt a warning glance scalding the side of her face. Sometimes Edwina was positively psychic.

"It might. What did you have in mind?" Archie asked. He reached into his pocket and pulled out a notebook remarkably similar to the one Edwina had started to carry. He licked the end of his pencil and held it poised above a blank sheet of paper. Edwina cleared her throat again.

"I'm not quite sure we are ready for all that, Beryl," Edwina said. "You shouldn't like to make a liar out of this nice young man, now would you?"

"I have no intention of making a liar out of anyone, Ed. Besides, if anyone can take care of himself as well as I can, it's Archie Harrison," Beryl said. She batted her long eyelashes in Archie's direction. "What would you say to an exclusive interview with Edwina and me about our new business venture?"

Archie began scribbling furiously. "What sort of a business venture? You've not suddenly gone into pigeon racing, have you?"

"Not even close," Beryl said. "See if you can guess." Beside her Edwina let out a disapproving sigh.

Archie turned his attention to Edwina. "Knowing Beryl, it would have to be something extraordinary. A mountaineering expedition company for ladies?" Archie asked. Beryl shook her head. "A cooking school for women who cannot open tins unassisted?" Beryl decided to take no notice of Edwina's ill-concealed guffaws.

"Be serious, Archie," Beryl said.

"I am being serious. You would have expertise in either of those arenas of endeavour. How about a school for avid markswomen?" he asked. Beryl shook her head once more. "I know. A gambling den for high-society ladies?" Edwina chortled disloyally.

"Not even close. Although I will say it is distinctly possible that my skill with the pistol will be required at some point," Beryl said, arching an eyebrow at Edwina.

"I certainly hope not," Edwina said. Perhaps Beryl had allowed Archie to get just the slightest bit under her skin. There was no call to ruffle Edwina's feathers.

"Not to worry, Ed. I only say that to provide drama for Archie's story. Do you give up?" Beryl said.

"Well, if you aren't about to start your own hangar and some sort of aviation school for young ladies, I suppose I do give up Archie said. "Do tell."

"Edwina and I have started a private enquiry agency." Beryl had the satisfaction of watching Archie's eyes bulge out of his head. For a moment it appeared they might leave his face entirely and go walk about. She had to give him credit though; he recovered quickly and resumed his furious note-taking.

"You set yourself up as gumshoes?" he asked. "No, I never would've guessed that if I'd kept at it all year. How long have you been in business?" Edwina started to answer but Beryl cut her off with a glance.

"I'll tell you what. Why don't you come to the Beeches the day after tomorrow? We'll give you the entire scoop then," Beryl said. "We haven't any engagements that morning, do we, Edwina?" Edwina shook her head.

"We would be delighted for you to pay us a call then, Mr. Harrison," Edwina said as she handed him a calling card with their address printed upon it.

"It's a date," Archie said. "This is just the sort of thing my editor would love to hear. I am absolutely certain the world is eagerly awaiting another story about the latest adventure of the celebrated Beryl Helliwell."

"I expect they'll be equally delighted at their first glimpse of Miss Edwina Davenport, too," Beryl said generously. It was a joint venture and one she did not wish to appear to be taking all the credit for. She turned to look at Edwina. Not surprisingly, two spots of color dotted her dear friend's cheeks. Edwina had always been far too modest. "After all, she's the one with the real detective skills." Archie flipped the page in his notebook and continued writing. At this rate he would need a new notebook for the interview.

"We look forward to seeing you then," Edwina said. "Beryl, as we are here on a case, I suggest we get back to work. Besides, I'm sure Mr. Harrison has other things to do besides chat to us. He was here on a story before we caught up with him." Beryl nodded and Archie slipped his notebook back into his pocket and stuck his pencil behind his ear.

"Until then, ladies," he said. He lifted his hat in salute and strode off through the crowd. Edwina turned to Beryl and put both hands on her hips.

"What in the world were you thinking? We aren't ready to give an interview for a newspaper. We've just barely taken on our first case," Edwina said.

"On the contrary, Ed. I've just secured for us the sort of publicity that any fledgling business would be overjoyed to have. Besides, Archie's an old friend. He won't put anything in the article that would do us anything but good," Beryl said.

"How can you be sure of that?" Edwina asked. "He sounds like a man desperate to carve out a new career for himself. A scathing exposé on Beryl Helliwell well might be just the sort of opportunity a man in his position is looking for."

"Archie would never do a thing like that. Not only has he always been more than a little in love with me, there are things about him he'd rather I didn't go around telling to any other newspapers. I am quite certain he will not be eager to do us harm," Beryl said. "Besides, if there's one thing I've learned over the years, it's that any publicity is good publicity."

CHAPTER 9

With the exception of a few hours spent pottering about her garden there was nothing Edwina found more soothing than a trip to the Walmsley Parva reading room. As the garden was unpleasantly sullied by the sound of Simpkins loudly singing sea shanties, Edwina decided the reading room was exactly the remedy her jangled nerves needed. Yesterday's trip to the pigeon race had proven nerve-racking on several levels. She had not anticipated spending a moment of her life at any form of race more sporting than a sack race at the church fete.

Beryl's decision to recruit Mr. Harrison to interview them well before she had any reasonable expectation of their success as detectives had made the outing all the more harrowing. She had slept poorly on account of recurring dreams that she and Beryl were the laughingstock of the nation. And other dreams in which they had been forced to open a cookery school at the Beeches. Just the idea of Beryl having anything to do with the kitchen was Edwina's idea of a terrifying nightmare.

It was far too early for Beryl to be out of bed as her tendencies were that of the night owl rather than the lark. For once, Edwina was glad to be on her own. She decided to forgo breakfast and hurriedly consumed nothing more than a cup of Darjeeling. Crumpet capered around her heels and insisted on accompanying her. She snapped on his lead, retrieved the books she needed to return to the reading room from her desk in the library, and slipped out the door as quietly as she could.

The walk did her good. A fresh breeze carrying the spring scents of lilac and mock orange brushed her cheeks and filled her nostrils. As she walked along the narrow lane leading from the Beeches to a more traveled road, she felt her troubles fall behind her. By the time she reached the door of the reading room she felt more like herself than she had since Simpkins announced the vicar wished to hire them. She looped Crumpet's lead around the iron railing in front of the modest stone building and admonished him to behave himself while he awaited her return.

Edwina replaced her borrowed books in the stacks and turned her attention to the section wholly devoted to American Western novels. While Edwina found the idea of Beryl wielding a pistol quite unsettling, she was more than enthusiastic about the use of firearms when it was confined to the pages of a Zane Grey novel. She added *Desert Gold* to the towering stack of books she planned to take with her. Behind her she heard the door to the reading room open and then a shaft of sunlight ran along the floorboards.

"Good morning, Edwina," Charles Jarvis said. Charles, the local solicitor, was a long-term friend of Edwina's. Although it could not be said she felt easy in his company of late, a state of affairs she attributed entirely to Beryl's unsolicited observations. It was Beryl's opinion that Charles took more than a friendly interest in Edwina, a possibility she had never considered. She found herself scrutinizing his every word whenever the two of them met. Still, despite her discomfort, she could not possibly make her concerns felt by Charles. It simply would not do to compromise their acquaintance with such foolishness. "What brings you out so early? Have you run out of things to read in your library at home?"

"I found that I was eager for something

different than what I have at home. Mother did not approve of books like these." Edwina held up the copy of *Desert Gold.*

"I think a rollicking Western adventure would have done your mother a world of good," Charles said. "I happen to love those myself." Charles always did say the nicest things. He had been the junior partner at her father's firm for years before the older gentleman had passed away.

"That's very kind of you to say. And what brings you here? Some scholarly tomes for a client?" Edwina asked.

"In fact, I was hoping to find some books on the art of cookery. I am without domestic help at present and I find I am ill-equipped to fend for myself," Charles said. Edwina looked at him more closely. He did look just the slightest bit gaunt. She felt guilty that she had not noticed before and that she had not thought to ask after him several months earlier when he had suddenly, and dramatically, lost his household help. As his friend, she should have thought to inquire if he had needed anything.

"Is there no one in all of Walmsley Parva you could hire to replace Polly?" Edwina asked.

"I'm afraid the domestic help crisis is at a pinnacle in the village. You should count yourself exceedingly lucky to still find Simp-kins willing to oblige you with your gardens," Charles said. "I'm lucky to get a charwoman in to beat the rugs twice a year."

"I understand there are many newfangled gadgets available to help with all sorts of domestic chores. Perhaps it would be best to invest in something of that sort," Edwina said. "So many women have turned into career women at this point that those sorts of devices have become extremely popular."

"I heard you have become just such a career woman yourself, Edwina," Charles said. "Are the rumors true?" He took a step towards her.

"Is the news all over the village?" Edwina asked.

"Simpkins was boasting about you to everyone within earshot. He seems to think that you and Miss Helliwell are about to change the course of modern history with your new business."

"Well, it may not be as important as all that, but we are quite looking forward to our venture," Edwina said, feeling a warm flush creeping up the back of her neck. What would her mother have said about it all? she wondered. Once again she was glad she could not ask her such a thing.

"I wish I were as willing to take risks as

you are, Edwina. I've always quite admired your verve. I wonder if I might be able to assist you in your search for Mr. Cunningham," Charles said. He looked so eager that she hated to disappoint him. "As it happens, I actually saw him the day before he went missing." Perhaps, Edwina thought, she would not need disappoint him after all.

"You did? Where was he? What was he doing?"

"I was painting, down by the river, and I saw him having a rather heated conversation with another man," Charles said. "At least it looked heated from a distance."

Edwina felt a surge of excitement. "You don't happen to know the name of the other man, do you?" Edwina asked.

"In fact I think I do. The wind carried their voices a bit and I heard Mr. Cunningham shouting at the end. I believe he said the other man's name," Charles said. "Not that I would be willing to say so in court. I just cannot be entirely certain enough for something like that."

"But you could make an off-the-record statement to me, couldn't you?" Edwina asked. Really, Charles could be quite maddening sometimes. "I won't hold you to it in any way."

"Of course. Mr. Cunningham said something like 'I don't want anything to do with this, Martin,' " Charles said.

"Do you have any idea what the *something* he was speaking of involved?"

"No, I do not. But I can tell you that the other man shoved an envelope into Mr. Cunningham's hands before he stomped away," Charles said. "It did not appear to be a friendly conversation. Not in the least."

"What did Mr. Cunningham do next?" Edwina asked, wishing she had not left her trusty notebook on her bedside table. She must develop the habit of keeping her notebook with her at all times if she wished to succeed in her new profession. Just the thought of embarking on something so deliciously forbidden as a profession sent shivers of pleasure up and down her spine. As much as she thoroughly disliked the idea of giving credit to Simpkins for anything besides mud upon her kitchen floor, she had to admit, at least in the privacy of her own mind, that he had really done her a service by urging Beryl and herself to open their own business.

Not that she would tell him so. He was far too inclined to get above himself without any encouragement whatsoever. If she gave him the slightest compliment she was certain he would move right into one of the

111

spare rooms without so much as a by-your-leave, hobnail boots and all. No, Edwina would keep her appreciation to herself, but perhaps as an acknowledgment of his help, she would allow him his head as far as the autumn cleanup of the gardens was concerned. That is if things were still going well by then.

She felt it best to leave the dying foliage as a sort of a natural cover for the crowns of the plants slumbering beneath them. A sort of counterpane of their own making to see them safely through the winter. Simpkins, quite wrongly, supported the notion that any such leavings harbored fungal diseases and did more damage than good. Perhaps by the autumn she would be too busy with a steady stream of intriguing cases to concern herself with such matters, one way or the other.

Charles said, "He waited until Mr. Haynes was well out of sight and then headed in the opposite direction. I wondered at the time if he had wished to avoid encountering him anew."

"What did he do with the envelope?" Edwina asked.

"I seem to remember him tucking it into his jacket pocket. Well, he must have done so unless he chucked it away because he took out a cigarette and began smoking. He couldn't have done that with his hands still filled." Charles cocked his head to one side as he always did when concentrating. Edwina felt a slight shock as she noticed how much grey had slipped in amongst the brown hair at his temples. "He didn't have it in his hands when he passed me either."

"Did he pass quite near to you?" Edwina asked.

"Yes. We spoke briefly. He looked a little embarrassed to see me but I gave no indication I had noticed anything other than the play of the light upon the river as I painted. It was easy enough to pretend I had just noticed his arrival."

"He didn't happen to mention any plans to leave town, did he?" Edwina asked without any real expectation that Mr. Cunningham's whereabouts would be so easily discovered.

"We spoke very briefly and only about our respective hobbies. He complimented me on my painting. When I asked if he was an artist too he laughed and said his only pastime involved his devotion to rearing and raising pigeons. I asked if he might be amenable to me sketching his birds sometime and he encouraged me to do so whenever I wished."

"Did he mention the race the next day?" Edwina asked. "Any suggestion he and his birds might not be around for you to sketch in the near future?"

"None whatsoever," Charles said. "I was very surprised to hear he had gone missing. From the way he spoke of his hobby I can't see him leaving the birds still left in his loft locked in to fend for themselves."

"Maybe he believed a fellow member of his club would tend to them once they discovered his absence," Edwina said.

"Perhaps, but I shouldn't have thought he would be willing to leave any of his birds' well-being to chance," Charles said. "Even from our brief conversation I'd say he seemed far too concerned with their welfare for that."

"Did he seem agitated in any way? Upset or flustered?" Edwina asked.

"I can't say that he did. But then, I hardly know the man," Charles said.

"I wish there was more information than a possible given name for the other man. He might have a better idea of Mr. Cunningham's state of mind or his upcoming plans," Edwina said.

"I made a quick sketch of the two of them as it happens. They were so animated and it gave me a wonderful opportunity to try my hand at sketching unguarded anger. I tucked it out of sight when Mr. Cunningham headed my way." Charles glowed with the memory of his artistic endeavor. Edwina knew he was an avid watercolorist and he had once mentioned he spent many of his happiest hours far from his chambers and out in the fresh air pottering about with his paint pans and brushes. "Besides, it is not every day that one is able to observe a miner away from the pits."

"How did you know he was a miner?" Edwina asked.

"He was shouting something or other about the colliery. Besides, I pride myself on having an observant nature. The man in question was decidedly encrusted with coal dust."

"Do you still have the sketch that you made of him?" Edwina asked.

"I keep all my sketches," Charles said. "Do you think it would be possible to identify the man with Mr. Cunningham from it?" Edwina asked.

"I flatter myself that the likeness was quite a good one, if that is what you are asking," Charles said. Edwina hurried to smooth any ruffled feathers.

"I am quite sure it is. I simply meant to ask if the subject was represented with his face showing in the image or even if the figure was drawn at close enough quarters in your sketch to make his identity known," Edwina said with what she hoped was a soothing tone.

"I see, of course. I believe it could aid you in your enquiries. If you would like, I would be more than happy to stop in at the Beeches to give you the sketch. You could use it as you see fit in your investigation." Charles leaned forward eagerly.

"I would be most grateful for the loan of your sketch if it is not too much trouble. When do you think it would be possible for you to make it available?" she asked.

"I would be delighted to bring it by this very morning. In fact, I'll take my leave of you and return home to look for it amongst my stack of drawings. I'll plan to meet you at the Beeches within an hour if you will be at home by then."

"I shall make a point to be there," Edwina said. Charles hurriedly selected two books from the shelves lining the reading room and headed out the door.

Edwina added another book to her own towering stack before thinking better of it. She realized with a surge of excitement that there was every possibility she would have

little time for reading until Mr. Cunningham
was found.

CHAPTER 10

Ever the faithful retainer, Charles Jarvis dutifully arrived at the Beeches with a sketch of a man who might be a miner. Beryl found interactions with Charles most refreshing. It was a rare treat to be in the company of a gentleman who seemed to value Edwina so highly. In fact, he reminded her of Crumpet in that way. So eager to caper round Edwina's heels awaiting her decisions. So much did the image ring true and delight her as it bubbled to the surface of her imagination that she had to stifle a giggle as she watched him take his leave of the Beeches after Edwina assured him she and Beryl were perfectly capable of visiting the mining village without an escort. He gave her exactly the same look Crumpet did moments later when Edwina told him he must stay home while she and Beryl at-tended to business elsewhere.

"I do hope you will manage to act more

seriously when we arrive at the mining village, Beryl," Edwina said, pulling the front door closed behind her a little more firmly than strictly necessary. "It is hard enough for women to be taken seriously in this business without one of us giggling like a schoolgirl every time we stand within five feet of an eligible man."

"I was simply laughing to myself at the way you completely ignore poor Mr. Jarvis' dogged devotion," Beryl said, setting herself into another fit of giggles. She managed to get herself firmly in hand before climbing into her shiny red automobile and backing down the driveway. By the time they reached the mining village of Hambley, only a few miles away, Beryl felt she had been forgiven. She had resolved to drive sedately by way of apology and was gratified, and a little surprised, to see her passenger relaxing into the seat and allowing her hands to remain in her lap rather than in her customary motoring position of clutching the door handle with one hand and her hat with the other.

In fact, Edwina seemed to actually enjoy the ride. She kept pointing out passing bits of scenery and remarking on the weather. Beryl wondered if her friend might like to learn to drive herself. She resolved that when the moment seemed right to do so she would suggest it.

Beryl slowed down even more as she turned off into the entrance to Hambley. Kentish coal may have given rise to hopes in the region, but she had no desire to end up in the bottom of the pit for lack of local knowledge. Besides, there were miners everywhere about and her rather vast, even if she said so herself, experience of men of every class, informed her that the men in Hambley would not be able to resist a look at her automobile. There would be plenty of locals to ask for directions. She rolled to a stop in front of a building with a sign hanging in front declaring it to be the grocer. Before she and Edwina could exit the vehicle, five men and seven boys had clustered about the automobile.

Whereas Edwina looked as though they had been descended upon by an unwelcome flock of seagulls whilst picnicking at the beach, Beryl saw an opportunity. She put on her brightest smile and pushed open the driver's door.

"Good morning, gentlemen. I see you have an eye for beauty," Beryl said, pointing at the automobile. "What do you think of her?"

"You're Beryl Helliwell," one of the men

said as he peeled his gaze from the vehicle's reflective scarlet finish and gave her an equally appraising look.

"That's right. I am," Beryl said, sticking out her hand. "And you are?"

"Jim Noyes," he said, stepping forward and gripping her hand firmly and pumping her arm up and down with enthusiasm. "I'm a devoted admirer, Miss Helliwell. I've followed all of your exploits in the newspapers. I was down in the dumps for I don't know how long when it looked like you had turned up your toes in the African desert. Chewed up by lions I thought probably. But here you are right as rain."

"It's a pleasure to meet you, Jim. And I'll let you in on a little secret." Beryl leaned in close to his soot-streaked ear but pitched her voice at a stage whisper to include the others. "Although there are lions in the desert I had more trouble with some of the two-legged wildlife."

"Hostile desert bandits, ma'am?" Jim asked, reaching a hand to his throat.

"Not exactly. The trouble came from the natives being entirely too friendly. The head of the group that found my balloon crash site got it into his head that I ought to stay and live out my days as one of his many wives. When I declined, things became a bit heated."

"How did you manage to escape?" A small boy tugged on her sleeve.

"I showed him this and then helped myself to one of his camels." Beryl pulled her pistol from the pocket of her long duster coat and held it above the child's head. "Despite a bit of trouble in the language department he understood my meaning immediately." A gasp went up from the assembled boys and nods of silent approval circulated amongst the miners.

"A camel, you say?" one of the other boys said. "What's it like to ride on one of them?"

"Surprisingly soothing once you get the hang of it. It undulates beneath you in a way that almost puts one to sleep." Beryl noticed Edwina had stepped out of the automobile and was raising an eyebrow in her general direction. Perhaps it was best to leave the crowd wanting more. "As much as I would love to stay and chat about it all with you fellows for the rest of the day, my associate and I are actually here on a mission. I wonder if you might help us with it?" she asked. The boys and Jim all bobbed their heads up and down eagerly. The other men shifted a bit from one foot to the other in uncertainty. "We are looking for one of your fellow miners. We understood from an artist friend that he was down near the river a few days ago and we were hoping he could help with our search for something," Beryl said. Edwina stepped forward and handed her the drawing. One of the boys piped up immediately.

"That's Martin Haynes," he said, pointing a grubby finger at the sketch. "Your friend is a dab hand at drawing. It looks just like him." Edwina came round the side of the automobile and stood next to Beryl.

"Thanks so much for your assistance, young man," Beryl said. "Now I don't suppose any of you could tell us where we might find this Mr. Haynes?"

"The shift is about to change so he should be coming up out of the pit in the next few minutes or so. You should see him if you wait at the entrance to the mine," Jim said. "If you want I can show you the way to the pit. My shift starts just as the current one ends." Beryl noticed that the other men nodded in agreement. They each held a tin lunch bucket in their hand and all wore clothing so encrusted with black dust that it was impossible to guess with any certainty the garments' original colors.

"We would be very grateful," Edwina said. The tone of her voice indicated she meant it. If she had to guess, Beryl would have said Edwina felt out of her depths in such a working-class environment. She closed the distance between them with a few long strides and took her friend by the arm.

"On all my journeys I make it a practice to rely on local guides, Jim. In this case that guide is you," Beryl said. Jim nodded and gestured that they should follow him round the back of the store and along a hard-packed dirt path. Everywhere Beryl turned her gaze there were signs of poverty, industry, and desperation. The farther they left the mining village behind them, the dirtier and noisier the atmosphere became. When Jim stopped and pointed to the place where they should wait, Beryl continued to grip Edwina's arm.

"If you ladies will wait right here I expect you'll see Martin Haynes emerge from the pit before long. I expect you'll be all right, won't you?" Jim asked.

"Of course we shall," Beryl said. "Thanks ever so much for your help." Jim nodded and stepped away, swinging his lunch bucket and whistling. Beryl watched his retreating back and hoped that he would have a safe shift far beneath the surface. She turned to Edwina.

"Is something troubling you?" Edwina asked.

"Why do you ask?" Beryl said.

"Your hand is serving as an admirable tourniquet. My lower arm has gone completely numb," Edwina said.

Beryl quickly dropped her hand from Edwina's arm. "I'm sorry about that. I have been making time for some hand strengthening exercises lately and must have progressed more quickly than I realized."

"Whyever should you need to strengthen your grip, Beryl?" Edwina asked. Beryl was once again grateful for her ability to make up convincing stories on the spot.

"One never knows when being physically fit will be useful, Ed. Especially in our line of work. Perhaps you would like to take up a practice of calisthenics yourself," Beryl said.

"You mean capering about the back lawn and then attempting to touch one's toes whilst standing straight-legged?" Edwina asked. "Certainly not. I have no intention of flitting about in such a manner. Just imagine the tales Simpkins would carry to the pub." Beryl felt the waves of indignation rolling satisfactorily from Edwina and was certain there would be no need to explain her discomfort concerning the mine. She was free to speak closer to the truth once more.

"I simply cannot imagine how these men

can stand it down there," Beryl said. Edwina's glance followed the miners as they staggered up out of the mine and into the open air. Many of them squinted at the sunlight and shielded their eyes with a filthy hand. Most of them looked thoroughly exhausted.

"It's certainly not a job for someone with claustrophobia," Edwina said. "Or anyone with a fear of drowning."

"Drowning?" Beryl asked. She had been quite uncomfortable enough without that piece of information.

"Yes, drowning. When I was a small child, one of the mines suffered a horrific flood and nearly two dozen men were drowned underground," Edwina said. "The men returned to the mine just as soon as they stopped the water rushing in and recovered the bodies. I could not believe they had the nerve to do it."

"I don't suppose they had any more choice than these men do today," Beryl said. "It's not the sort of job you would take on a whim. These men need to feed their families."

"I suppose that could make someone do what otherwise would seem impossible," Edwina said. She pulled out the sketch of Martin Haynes. "Let's take another glance at the man we are looking for. Not that I'm certain we will be able to recognize him straight from the mine. His face may be too covered in dust to identify him with ease."

The two women stood watching as miner after miner came up out of the hole in the ground. Beryl thought they must have missed him when finally a few last stragglers exited the pit. A man looking just like the one in the sketch was amongst them. In deference to Edwina's fear of falling down the mine shaft, Beryl waited for him to get well away from the mine entrance before she approached.

"Excuse me, but are you Mr. Martin Haynes?" she asked. The man she believed to be Mr. Haynes stopped and looked her up and down unabashedly. It was not the first time someone had so boldly attempted to take her measure. But it was the first time it had been attempted by someone covered in coal dust from head to toe.

"You're that woman from the papers," he said. He snapped his fingers. "Beryl Helliwell. That's it, isn't it?" He smiled, the white of his teeth standing out all the more starkly against the soot clinging to his lips.

"I am if you are Martin Haynes," Beryl said with a smile of her own. He crossed his arms across his chest and widened his stance.

"Why do you want to know? Are you here to offer me a job that will take me away from all this?" he said.

"We are looking for Lionel Cunningham," Beryl said. "Are you aware that he's missing?"

"There have been rumors around the pit that he'd simply vanished. I can't say too many of us were too upset by it. Including me. That still doesn't explain why you have come out looking for me. Shouldn't you be talking to the bosses?" he said.

"We are speaking with everyone who's had any contact with him in the last week or so," Beryl said.

"And what makes you think that I've had anything to do with Cunningham besides waiting in line for him to dole out my measly pay packet?"

"We have it on good authority that you were seen speaking with him near the river the day before he went missing," Beryl said.

"What if I say that your authority is mistaken?" he asked.

Edwina stepped forward and held out the sketch. "We identified you from this sketch, which was made that morning by the river. As you can see, you were seen by someone who took careful notice," Edwina said. Mr. Haynes bent over the sketch then looked back at Beryl.

"Even if it was me, what makes you ladies think you ought to come around asking these sorts of questions?" Mr. Haynes said.

"We are private enquiry agents hired to ask just such questions," Edwina said. Beryl was surprised at the ring of authority in Edwina's voice. Surprised, but delighted nonetheless. "Not only were you seen with Mr. Cunningham, you were seen arguing with him."

"All right, I admit it. I was talking with Cunningham near the river. I suppose our conversation could have been interpreted as an argument by someone who was observing from a distance," Mr. Haynes said.

"What were you talking about that would give such an impression?" Edwina asked.

Mr. Haynes turned around and gestured at the pit opening behind him. "Do you know what it's like down there? Do you have any idea what it is like in the pit?" Beryl felt Edwina stiffen. Both women shook their heads. "I didn't think so. Anyone who hasn't been down there can't possibly imagine just how difficult it is. Especially after so many of us spent so much of the war down in other sorts of pits and holes."

"Memories of the trenches must make things difficult for many of you. Were you arguing with Mr. Cunningham about his understanding of working in the pit?" Beryl said.

"Every year there are accidents which lead to injuries and to deaths. Did you know that conditions in the mines in Kent are the worst in all the British Isles?" he asked. Beryl shook her head and Edwina nodded. "It's the water, you see. It makes the shafts unstable. Cunningham has the boss's ear. I wanted him to speak to Ecclestone-Smythe about worker safety. I gave him a pamphlet about ways to improve the working conditions but he didn't want to take it."

"I've been reading about that sort of thing in the local papers ever since coal was first discovered in the region," Edwina said. "Why didn't Mr. Cunningham want to take the information to his superior?"

"Cunningham didn't want to have anything to do with something as unpopular with the boss as worker safety. Too expensive, too likely to give workingmen ideas," Mr. Haynes said. He hacked up a glob of dust and spat it on the ground. He looked at both the women as if to dare them to criticize him for his poor manners. Beryl was relieved that rather than comment on his ungraciousness, Edwina simply ignored him and continued with her questions.

"But in the end you simply shoved an envelope at him. Was the pamphlet inside?" Edwina asked.

"It was. I told him I had to get back to the mining village. I had better things to do than to spend what little free time I had chewing the fat with him," Mr. Haynes said.

"Did he agree to give the pamphlet to Mr. Ecclestone-Smythe?" Beryl asked.

"He said he would consider it. I don't know if he did or if he didn't and he hasn't been around to ask since. I guess I'll just have to give it to the boss myself no matter what comes of it," he said.

"What do you mean 'what comes of it'?" Edwina asked.

"Mr. Ecclestone-Smythe doesn't prefer to mix with the men who do his dirty work. If you come to his attention in any way, you run the risk of being tossed out on your ear," Mr. Haynes said. "But sometimes you just have to take a stand. And maybe the situation's gotten dire enough that he can't afford to lose any more workers and I'll be able to say my piece and keep my job, too."

"The situation at the mine is dire?" Beryl asked. "It looks quite busy." She indicated the steady stream of men heading down into the mine.

"Like I said, the conditions in Kent are the worst in the nation. Nobody wants to work here and they won't unless they have to. But the economic situation in the country is miserable too and some people don't have a lot of choice. Mr. Ecclestone-Smythe has found himself in the position of needing us almost as much as we need him."

"It sounds like maybe you'll be able to change his opinion," Beryl said. "If the owner really needs you, maybe he'll be more open to your requests."

"For someone who is so well traveled you sure are naive," he said to Beryl. "Even the villagers in Walmsley Parva look down on us and don't want anything to do with us. Can you imagine that someone as wealthy and powerful as a colliery owner would want to lower himself long enough to imagine what life is like for the likes of us? Or to take any responsibility for his part in creating those conditions?"

"I should like to think people are capable of change," Edwina said. "Otherwise, what is the point of things like the pamphlets you mentioned?"

"Very likely there is no point at all. Now, if there isn't anything else that you ladies need enough to keep me from getting cleaned up and tucking into a ploughman's, I'll take my leave of you. My next shift will come all too soon," Mr. Haynes said. Without waiting for an answer he turned his back on them and walked away.

"Do you believe him?" Beryl asked.

"About the conditions at the mine? About the desperate need for workers? About the need for jobs? Or about his conversation with Mr. Cunningham?" Edwina asked.

"About all of it, I suppose," Beryl said. "But mostly about the argument with our missing man."

Edwina kept staring at the entrance to the pit in front of them. She gave a deep sigh.

"I wish I didn't believe him about the conditions or the desperation on all sides. I want to believe him about the nature of his conversation with Mr. Cunningham," Edwina said.

"I feel exactly the same. Mr. Haynes gave a strong argument for worker safety. It's hard to believe in the middle of the English countryside something as ugly as all this exists. Somehow I never would have imagined anything so industrial could be found so close to idyllic Walmsley Parva," Beryl said.

"It came as quite a shock to all of us, I assure you. Even though the first mine started up when I was a very small child, I still

133

remember the brouhaha it caused," Edwina said. "When there were difficulties in many of the mines, I am sorry to say that some people in the village were happy to hear about them."

"I can imagine it must have been worrisome to many, but didn't any of the shopkeepers have hopes that their businesses might grow with an influx of outsiders to shop at them? I should think they would be glad of the additional business," Beryl said.

"There may have been some that felt that way privately but Mr. Haynes is right about the lack of a welcome from the villagers in Walmsley Parva. A number of folks were outspoken about their relief when the mining village was built and the miners could live and shop out of sight of those people who had always lived here," Edwina said.

"That sounds rather harsh. What would have caused such bad feelings?" Beryl asked.

"A lot of people weren't happy when coal was found in Kent. I remember my parents were very distressed by it. They said that it would change the character of the area and that it would not be for the better," Edwina said. "Others said we shouldn't resist the march of industry in progress. The community has been somewhat divided on the subject ever since it first came up."

"What do you think about it?" Beryl asked.

"I think there has been too much needless suffering over the last several years and it behooves each of us to do what we can to make the path of life smoother for our fellow travelers. Besides, from a practical sense, the country runs on coal. Mining strikes arise from unhappy workers who feel poorly treated. I don't wish to see another rash of unrest occur because the good people of Walmsley Parva think they are above needing to see where their source of fuel comes from." Edwina carefully tucked Charles' sketch back into its folder.

"I'm not sure we've made any more progress than we had before we got here," Beryl said.

"But we're no further behind than we were either. Who would have thought we would make this much progress?" Edwina said. "I think we have done all we can for now here in the mining village and should head back to the Beeches."

CHAPTER 11

The conversation with Mr. Haynes left Edwina feeling disquieted. She knew there had always been an order to things amongst the classes. Goodness knew she felt it every time she interacted with Simpkins. But the war had wrought so many changes and had created so many rifts in society that more and more often she found herself questioning the way things had always been. She was a bit embarrassed to acknowledge it, even to herself, but before the war she would not have given the slightest thought to whether or not the miners should expect better working conditions. She would have simply felt it their duty to know their place and to pitch in to help keep the nation strong by hewing coal out of the ground.

But the working class lost as many limbs and lives as the social classes above them. As far as Edwina was concerned, there was a leveling out on that fact alone. It simply would no longer do to expect those who sacrificed so much to continue to have so little. After years in a trench, could a man be asked to go back into a dangerous hole in the ground? He certainly could not without expecting society to do its best to ensure his safety.

She followed Beryl wordlessly back along the path they had taken from the mining village and soon they arrived in sight of Beryl's motorcar. She was startled from her thoughts by a woman's voice.

"Hello there," said Alice Morley, the young woman she and Beryl had met at the pigeon race. "What brings the two of you here?" Alice stood with a wicker laundry basket perched on one of her hips.

"Hello, Mrs. Morley. We are still searching for Mr. Cunningham and our investigation brought us here. What a happy coincidence that we should run into you," Edwina said. She suddenly had a stroke of inspiration.

"Why is that? Are you feeling a desperate urge to hang out some washing?" Alice asked, inclining her head to her basket. "If so, I can help with that straightaway."

"Actually, I wanted to ask if you would encourage your friends and neighbors here in Hambley to attend the upcoming May Day festivities in Walmsley Parva. I serve on the committee planning the day and I would be delighted to have the residents of Hambley participate in the celebration," Edwina said.

"Why would you ask me?" Alice asked, shifting her basket to the other hip. Edwina wondered why she didn't just put it down, and then realized it would become simply filthy as soon as it touched the ground. Come to mention it, the clothes in the basket and the basket itself were greyish with coal dust just from exposure to the breeze.

"As the colliery nurse I'm sure you have a lot of influence in the community. And your husband sounds like a man others would be inclined to listen to as well," Edwina said.

"I'll have to talk it over with Dennis. I'm not sure he'd like to hear I had agreed to something like you're suggesting without speaking with him first," Alice said, casting a glance over her shoulder. Edwina had thought Dennis Morley sounded like a pleasant young man, but seeing the hesitation Alice exhibited, she began to have doubts concerning his character.

"We have a committee meeting coming up in three days' time. I'd like to tell the committee I have secured the help of a woman in Hambley in bringing our two villages closer," Edwina said. "I noticed a post box on my way into the village. Do you think you would be able to send me a note letting me know before the meeting if you are able to help spread the word?" Edwina asked. "You can reach me at The Beeches, Walmsley Parva. She took a calling card from her handbag and passed it to Alice.

Alice looked back once more. "I'll write to you as soon as I know if I am able to assist you," Alice said. Edwina noticed a furrow had appeared between the younger woman's brows.

"I look forward to receiving your note," Edwina said before nodding her good-bye and leaving Alice to tend to her washing. She wondered if Alice would actually broach the subject with her husband or if she would simply send along her regrets without ever mentioning a word to him. She looked over at Beryl and noticed her friend looking in the same direction that Alice had cast her worried glances.

Together they watched as Alice walked away and disappeared behind a cluster of small cottages.

"It's been quite a day so far. I'd say we deserve lunch. How about I make you my famous camp side stew?" Beryl asked.

"I've had your cooking, Beryl. I don't

think I've ever done anything to deserve something like that," Edwina said. "But I appreciate the sentiment. Fortunately we have a leftover roast chicken just waiting to be turned into sandwiches."

CHAPTER 12

Beryl spent the better part of the next morning secreted away in the guest room at the Beeches. While she would not have cared to admit it and certainly would not have wanted anyone to observe what she was up to, Beryl was busy primping and preening. She didn't tend to think of herself as a vain woman, but she did know how large a role her appearance played in her success. It was one thing to be known as an adventurous woman. It was quite another to be perceived as glamorous, too. She knew in her heart of hearts that much of her fame was derived from her uncanny ability to combine her dual reputations.

But such reputations required mainte-nance. She had learned, much to her cha-grin, that such maintenance took longer and longer with each passing year. Seated at the vanity table near the window, she noticed a quantity of fine lines around her eyes and at the corners of her lips stood out starkly in the abundant natural light. She carefully inspected the skin on her neck and lavished a quantity of beauty cream up and down its length. She selected a tube of lipstick from a vanity table drawer and rolled it up to consider the color.

It was a daring shade of red, one that only women with no concern whatsoever for their reputations would have donned when Beryl was a young girl. It wasn't entirely smiled upon even for modern women in 1921. Certainly Edwina would never be caught wearing something so flashy. Beryl touched it to her lips and with a practiced hand created a perfect Cupid's bow on the top lip and a voluptuous pouch on the bottom. She deftly applied a spot of rouge to each of her cheeks and smudged her eyes with just a hint of kohl.

A little voice in the back of her head reminded her of how much fun she had had with Archie Harrison when she had known him in Australia. Perhaps that was the reason she had selected such a flattering silk coat and wide leg trouser ensemble from the wardrobe. She wound a black and red scarf around her head like a turban and fastened a large pair of ruby ear drops to her earlobes. She spritzed some perfume at her wrists and at the back of her neck before giving herself a final inspection in front of the long mirror positioned at the end of the room.

She did not look like the woman she had been ten years earlier. But then, she told herself, almost no one did. It wasn't just the years, it was the way she had lived them. Careening across the globe under the beating sun or the howling Arctic winds left its mark. Outliving so many friends and companions claimed by the war had taken even more of a toll. Beryl considered herself most fortunate indeed to still look ten years younger than her actual age.

Whenever anyone asked her secret, she was more than happy to share it. Generous applications of quality gin and a steadfast refusal to bear children to any of her former husbands was how she accounted for her youthful appearance. Most women scoffed at her response, but now and again she found herself in the company of a kindred spirit who nodded as if Beryl's words were a lifeline in a turbulent sea.

Beryl slipped her feet into a pair of satin slippers completely devoid of a heel. While many women preferred shoes that added to their height, Beryl was not one of them. She was as tall as most men already and found that she preferred footwear that allowed her to make a hasty escape should the need arise. After all, she had often found that it did.

She took a deep breath and left the safety of her boudoir sanctuary for whatever the meeting with Archie Harrison might bring. It was true she had extolled the value to their fledgling business of newspaper coverage to Edwina, but that did not mean she felt no butterflies at the thought of Archie's scrutiny. At one time he had meant a great deal to her, and while she didn't like to think of herself as the sort of woman who cared about other people's opinions, the fact remained that she wished for him to be impressed by her latest venture.

Edwina was in the kitchen stirring something at the stove. Archie Harrison had made himself at home at the kitchen table. Beryl had not expected to find him there before she had a chance to settle herself. Both Archie and Edwina looked up as she entered the room. On the table in front of him Archie had laid one of his reporter's notebooks and had made good use of it from the words that Beryl could see scrawled across the surface of the paper.

"It's high time you joined us," Edwina said. "I told Mr. Harrison I couldn't imagine what was taking you so long as you knew he was expected." Beryl hoped Edwina would make no mention of her clothing, and to her relief her friend contented herself with pointedly looking her up and down.

"I'm glad you took your time, Beryl. That way I've had the chance to have Miss Edwina all to myself," Archie said, giving Edwina a broad wink. Edwina's cheeks flushed becomingly and she batted her eyelashes like a coquettish young girl. Archie did tend to bring out the romantic in most women, Beryl thought. Even she had not been immune to his charms.

"I'm glad the two of you are getting along so well. What have I missed?" Beryl said. She headed for the stove where Edwina had thoughtfully left a percolator on one of the burners. Beryl fetched a cup and poured herself a full measure of a thick, dark brew. She lifted the percolator and waggled it at Archie who indicated he would like a cup of his own. She poured one for him then joined him at the table.

"The morning post has brought a note from Alice Morley saying she will help to encourage the residents of Hambley to attend the May Day festivities," Edwina said.

"And Miss Edwina has told me all about the adventure the two of you had last autumn," Archie said. "And she filled me in on your current case, at least as much as she could, considering client confidentiality." Archie blew across the steaming cup and took a tentative sip. He grimaced and arched an eyebrow at Beryl. She raised a finger to her lips. While she hated to be disloyal to Edwina, the fact remained that her dear friend had simply not gotten the hang of brewing a pot of coffee. It either came out looking like tea that had been cut in half by water or was so strong you could feel your teeth protesting as it slipped past them on the way down the throat. There was simply no in-between. That was just like Edwina. Most things in her orbit seemed to be black or white. Very little middle ground existed.

"So what sort of an article are you planning to write?" Beryl asked.

"I rather thought it would turn out to be an exposé," Archie said with a wink. "Two ladies with very little experience conning the local gentry out of wads of cash or some such a thing." Beryl noticed Edwina stiffen and drop the spatula she was using to stir the contents of the skillet.

"Don't worry, Ed," Beryl said. "Archie has always been the most horrific tease." Beryl gave Archie a look that she hoped he would interpret as a notification that he would miss out on a good thing if he continued to pester. Edwina had been hard enough to convince to begin the endeavor of running their own enquiry agency. Any whiff of scandal from the newspapers was certainly going to set back the enterprise more than Beryl wished to consider.

Archie shrugged and gave Beryl one of his almost irresistible grins. "Of course I don't believe the two of you are intent on duping your neighbors. But I would like for the article to be more than just an interview. I really want to be able to show the readers a sense of what it's like to be out in the field, following leads and questioning suspects. What have you got on the docket today?" Archie asked.

Beryl looked over the top of Archie's head, hoping to catch Edwina's eye. Edwina had retrieved her spatula and turned to the table. She slid a perfectly fried egg onto the plate in front of Archie.

"After we've all eaten Beryl and I had planned to head out to the missing man's pigeon loft. We intend to do a thorough inspection, which we hope will turn up new avenues of enquiry," Edwina said. Beryl let a silent slow sigh escape her lungs. Edwina really was an excellent partner. She helped herself to a slice of bread from the basket in front of her and proceeded to slather it with butter and some of Edwina's outstanding black currant preserves. Archie jotted a few lines in his notebook before turning his attention to the plate before him.

Within three quarters of an hour the three of them were within sight of the Walmsley Parva allotments. The allotments were popular with many of the villagers, especially those without sufficient space in their own gardens to grow vegetables, flowers or to keep small animals like chickens or rabbits. It was more than that though. The allotments provided a chance to socialize with others who enjoyed such pursuits and it also gave villagers an opportunity to indulge in a spot of good-natured competitiveness. It was easy to see which of the residents of Walmsley Parva had green thumbs and which certainly did not.

Edwina headed straight for an elderly gentleman seated on top of an overturned bucket in front of a tidy row of lettuces. After a moment's conversation and some animated gesticulation on the part of the gentleman, Edwina returned with a satisfied look on her face. "According to Mr. Wilkes, Lionel Cunningham's allotment is six spots down on the right," she said. Edwina lifted the edge of her skirts above the damp ground and determinedly led the way. Beryl followed and Archie brought up the rear. Even over the sound of the birds chirping and the whistling of the wind through the vegetable plants Beryl could hear Archie's pencil scratching against his notebook. She hoped he was busy adding notes of local color to his report and that they were of a flattering nature. Even if his article cast a positive light on their venture, Edwina would not be pleased if he made Walmsley Parva appear to be a backward and ridiculous out-of-the-way spot.

CHAPTER 13

Beryl carefully picked her way along the dirt path. It was strewn with all manner of vegetable matter and muddy ruts. Ordinarily she would have concerned herself with choosing appropriate footwear for an outdoor expedition. Had she and Edwina consulted about their plans for the day, she would have chosen an outfit far more suited to the great outdoors. But when she had dressed that morning, she had only considered impressing their guest. There had been no time to change before Edwina hurried them out the door. It wasn't the sad effect the conditions had upon her shoes that worried her but rather the possible deleterious effects on her ankles. One of the first lessons she had learned early on in her career was to respect one's feet above most other things. As her right foot caught on a partially submerged rock she could not help but feel it would be good advice for a detective as well.

"This should be it," Edwina said, pointing to a surprisingly tidy wooden structure. Neat, raw wood siding cladded the outside of the small building. A sheet of corrugated metal spanned the roof. As they approached, Beryl noticed a door fitted into the front, the bottom of which was set at approximately knee height. Windows, covered in screening, were built into either end. Lattice skirting trimmed the underpinnings and gave the building a finished look.

Unlike the allotments of most of its neighbors, Mr. Cunningham's plot was devoid of any deliberate plantings. Tufts of grass and patches of weeds covered the bare earth and here and there a clump of violets peered out from amongst their less attractive neighbors. It would appear Mr. Cunningham was no gardener. It also seemed that pigeons made for odiferous neighbors. Beryl wrinkled her nose as the wind shifted and brought the smell of them to her. Being the good countrywoman that she was, Edwina took the lead with the actual pigeon loft. She approached the gable end of the loft and stretched up on tiptoe and looked through the screening into the small building.

"There are quite a number of birds roosting inside here. All of them look fed and watered and quite tranquil." She beckoned for Beryl to join her at the window. Beryl stepped up to the screening and peered inside. There was nothing to see but feathers and straw and dark-eyed birds resting on perches. Of Mr. Cunningham there was no trace.

"Someone must have stopped in to feed and water them, don't you think?" Beryl asked. "Otherwise they would have shown some sign of distress by now."

"I expect you're right. But I do wonder who he could have gotten to help," Edwina said. "I don't know how Mr. Cunningham could stand the stench. It smells quite unlike any other coop I've ever been near." Edwina was right. Beryl thought it was enough to make her wish she had not breakfasted quite so heartily. Edwina stopped in her tracks, and rather than covering her nose delicately with a handkerchief as Beryl would have expected her to do, Edwina drew in a fuller breath. Her friend shook her head, a perplexed look on her face.

"I'm very much afraid that what you are smelling has nothing to do with the wholesome animal smell one would associate with poultry," Beryl said. She could almost see

Archie's ears lengthening. She and Edwina each took a step back from the pigeon loft. Beryl glanced at Archie and a look of comprehension passed between them. Both had spent time on or near the battlefield and the memories created by the odor chilled Beryl to the core.

"What is it then?" Edwina asked. She looked around, searching for the source of the smell. Beryl bent over and wrapped her fingers around the lattice skirting the bottom of the pigeon loft. She gave a tremendous tug and heard nails wrenching free of the loft's wooden underpinnings. Covered by the debris from the birds and cloaked in the shadows cast by the loft, she could barely discern the outline of a man's shoe. Given the angle at which it sat, she was absolutely certain there was a foot still inside it.

"I'm rather afraid we have discovered the whereabouts of our missing Mr. Cunningham," Beryl said. Entirely forgetting about the unfortunate effect it would have upon her silk outfit, she ducked her head and crawled beneath the pigeon loft. "Archie, have you a book of matches on you?" she asked. She heard hurried footsteps behind her and then Archie wedged himself into the tight space on the other side of the body.

153

She heard a scratching noise, and felt the sting of sulfur fill her nostrils. Even in the quavering light of a single match the waxen face of a man fitting the description of Mr. Cunningham stood out clearly.

Beryl leaned closer and felt her breath catch in her throat. A dark stain saturated the bits of straw and the bare ground around the body. She told herself quite firmly not to be sick. Edwina's voice reached her from behind.

"What do you see?" Edwina asked.

"I believe I was right about our missing man," Beryl said. "There is a body here that fits the description we were given."

"Oh my." Beryl heard Edwina's voice quite near to her ear. Her friend had crouched down and was leaning towards her. "Are you quite sure he's dead?" Edwina asked. Archie lit a second match as the first had burnt down to his fingertips. As he moved it farther down the body, Beryl lifted the man's jacket away from his chest and the flickering light illuminated a dark patch on the man's shirt.

"It looks like a knife wound, doesn't it, Archie?" Beryl said. She heard Edwina let out a startled cry. Archie nodded slowly and she reached out a hand and placed it on his arm. She happened to know from firsthand experience that Archie cried out about such things in his sleep.

"He's definitely been stabbed by something," Archie said.

"How can you be sure, Mr. Harrison?" Edwina asked. Beryl wished she hadn't. Archie winced before answering.

"Suffice it to say I am familiar with the look of damage caused by bayonets," he said. Beryl turned around to look at him as he wriggled out from beneath the loft. "If you don't mind, I shall yield my spot to you." Beryl watched as he pressed his book of matches into Edwina's hand and retreated a step or two before sitting upon the ground to observe from a bit of a distance.

Edwina rose to the occasion and squirmed into the spot he had vacated. She struck a match and slowly inspected the corpse before her. "I don't expect this is quite what the vicar had in mind when he asked us to locate his missing treasurer," Edwina said. "I suppose this is the end of our investigation."

"Nonsense. If anything, the scope of the case has increased," Beryl said. "I say we go on full speed ahead."

"We must fetch Constable Gibbs. There is nothing else for it," Edwina said in the warning tone Beryl had noticed she tended to use when she felt things were about to stray too far from the straight and narrow.

"There is no question that we will alert her. However, I see no reason not to do a little poking around before we do." Beryl reached for the dead man's jacket once more. She felt it would be a breach of professional conduct not to at least riffle his pockets. Edwina nodded then looked back over her shoulder. From Beryl's angle beneath the loft she noticed a pair of men's work boots and the accompanying legs had appeared beside Archie.

"Mr. Wilkes," Edwina said softly. "We were lucky he waited so long to join us. His rheumatism must be playing up. With his bad knees it will take him a moment to crouch down." Edwina made a fluttering motion with her hand that Beryl interpreted to mean she should get on with whatever poking about she wished to accomplish.

"I'll be quick," Beryl said. "Who is Mr. Wilkes, anyway?"

"He was the constable here in Walmsley Parva before Doris Gibbs took over the job. The two are on very good terms. He spends at least one day a week in the station chatting with her about cases, old and new," Edwina said as she scooched back out from under the pigeon loft. Beryl could hear her friend doing her best to buy a little time by trying to engage the elderly man in conversation whilst screening Beryl from view by a clever use of her long skirt. Beryl slipped her hand into the right inside pocket of the dead man's jacket and felt around. Her fingers closed over a folded-up sheet of paper. She just managed to place it in her own pocket before Mr. Wilkes' pasty face loomed into the opening behind her.

"What are you doing mucking about under there, missy?" he said as he peered into the gloom. "That's Lionel Cunningham. What's he doing lying there on the ground?" He went so far as to put a gnarled hand on her ankle and he proceeded to give it a firm tug. While it was never her first choice, Beryl knew when to accept defeat. She slid out from beneath the loft, stood, and brushed the pigeon droppings and straw from her silk trousers as best she could before turning to address the elderly man.

"It appears that he is dead," she said. She took a step towards Edwina and Archie who stood conferring a few feet away. She felt something grasp her arm and looked down. She wondered fleetingly if the man had some sort of a mania about her limbs. She tried to pull away but his grip held fast. If his strength was diminished by rheumatism, Beryl would have been loath to have suffered his grip during his prime.

"I always said he'd come to a bad end. Shameful it was the way he didn't put the rest of the land on his patch to use." Mr. Wilkes pointed at the weeds and brambles blanketing the parts of the allotment not covered by the pigeon loft. "I tried to tell him he should have used the entire space since he rented it all, but he told me to mind my own business."

"I doubt it was his lack of interest in gardening that did him in, sir," Beryl said. "Do you think you could summon the constable? I believe we are looking at a crime." She hoped to rid them of Mr. Wilkes long enough to make a more thorough search of the body.

"Indeed I will not. I plan to keep a close eye on the pair of you." Mr. Wilkes pointed a knobby-knuckled finger first at Beryl and then at Edwina. "I shouldn't be surprised if you had something to do with what happened to him. Doris Gibbs said you two had set yourself up as some sort of sleuthing spinsters and that it was impossible to predict what sort of trouble such nonsense would cause."

"For a police officer, Doris Gibbs is

remarkably ill informed," Archie said.

"So they aren't those women who think they're detectives?" Mr. Wilkes asked, taking stock of Beryl's figure with a frankness that was as unwelcome as it was impolite.

"They are detectives, but no one would categorize them as sleuthing spinsters," Archie said. "Not with the number of husbands Beryl has had." Beryl wasn't quite sure it was wise to encourage Mr. Wilkes to give any additional thought to her experience with men. Especially not given the way he had made free with her ankle.

"No matter what you call yourselves, you need to stay put. Doris will sort out your stories when she arrives," Mr. Wilkes said. He turned his attention on Archie. "You're the one to go fetch Doris. You look spry enough to run all the way to the police station and back." Beryl sent a pleading look at Edwina who seemed to take the hint.

"Isn't he a suspect, too?" Edwina asked. "After all, he was under the loft with Miss Helliwell and the remains of the unfortunate Mr. Cunningham."

"He looks like a trustworthy feller to me. I'm starting to think there is some reason you all don't want the police to be informed of this," Mr. Wilkes said. Beryl noticed Edwina shaking her head in warning. She would have to endure the unwanted attentions of an unpleasant old man as well as foregoing the opportunity to inspect the crime scene and the body more thoroughly. Still, it was better than giving Mr. Wilkes reason to encourage Doris to place either Edwina or herself at the top of her suspect list. She was altogether too inclined to distrust them without encouragement.

"Of course we wish to alert the authorities. Archie, the station is right off the high street. You can't miss it," Beryl said. "Edwina and I will eagerly await your return."

CHAPTER 14

It was just like Constable Doris Gibbs not to show the slightest bit of appreciation for the help she and Beryl had provided. Constable Gibbs would not have the good manners to say thank you should God himself descend from on high to pass her a glass of iced water should she find herself thirsting in the desert. That's just the sort of person she was. When it came to her profession she was far more likely to feel irritation than appreciation for any assistance others might give.

To some extent Edwina understood. Constable Gibbs had achieved the position of sole law enforcement agent in Walmsley Parva during the Great War. She never would have been hired when Mr. Wilkes had retired if most available men weren't off at the front. She had managed to keep the position when those same men returned, through hard work and remarkable tenacity.

It did not hurt that no one else seemed inclined to take an interest in the job. Which is likely why Doris Gibbs was so defensive whenever Beryl or Edwina made any contribution whatsoever to the curtailing of local criminal activities. Edwina supposed that Constable Gibbs perceived them as a threat to her position.

Edwina was quite certain it would do no good to assure the officer that she took no interest in the day-to-day workings of the local constabulary. And she was quite sure the rules and regulations such a post would require would reduce Beryl to tears of frustration. Constable Gibbs was exactly the sort of person who took no end of delight in codes and regulations of any ilk. In fact, she began reciting a number of infractions to Beryl and Edwina the moment she appeared within shouting range.

"Trespassing, impeding a police investigation, impersonating a police officer, and interfering with a corpse. I don't suppose there's anything else you've done so far today that you ought to confess to, is there?" Constable Gibbs asked, turning from Beryl to Edwina.

"As you and I both know, this is a public space so trespassing is an impossibility," Edwina said. "And from what is said around the village there was no police investigation of Mr. Cunningham's disappearance. According to our sources you declared that a grown man is free to take leave of the village without anyone's permission." Edwina ran her finger across some writing in her notebook. No one had in fact made any such accusation but knowing Constable Gibbs as she did, it was likely those were her exact sentiments. The bright red splotches, which sprang immediately to the constable's face and neck, confirmed Edwina's theory. Before Constable Gibbs could sputter out any objections Beryl added her own two pence.

"I, for one, would never consider impersonating a police officer. For one thing I don't believe the uniform would suit me," Beryl said, looking Constable Gibbs up and down. It may not have been kind but it was true. It was hard to imagine Beryl swaddled in dark blue serge devoid of all embellishment. It was equally difficult to imagine her supporting the sort of scowl that was permanently etched on Constable Gibbs' visage. "And as to the charge of interfering with the corpse, I must protest. If we had not found him when we did, there would have been less corpse to find. Between the heat and the pigeon droppings it was a good job we discovered him when we did."

Edwina felt a twinge of guilty satisfaction as the red blotches on Constable Gibbs' face were replaced with a far greener hue. But Edwina had to give the constable credit. She recovered her nerve quickly and with little more than a grunt clambered beneath the pigeon loft.

By the time the unfortunate Mr. Cunningham's body had been extracted from its unsavory resting place, wrapped in a shroud, and placed in the back of the waiting ambulance, the sun was high in the sky. Unladylike noises emanated from Edwina's digestive tract despite having consumed two eggs, a slice of toast, and a rasher of bacon. Considering her friend's prodigious appetite she hardly dared think how Beryl was feeling. Archie seemed oblivious to any such concerns despite the reputation of gentlemen as being most interested in getting their three square meals a day.

He moved around the edges of the crowd that had gathered asking a question here, taking a note there, and through it all watching everything Constable Gibbs did. Edwina found she wished he had not tagged along as Constable Gibbs once again turned her eagle eye on Beryl and herself. Despite Beryl's utter confidence in him, Edwina still felt a nagging trepidation about the scrutiny of a reporter.

"Why is it the two of you have such a knack for discovering dead bodies?" Constable Gibbs said.

"Such a thing is to be expected in our line of work," Beryl said. "After all, private agents never know what sort of dangers will crop up from day to day." She turned to Edwina who nodded her head sedately in a manner she hoped appeared to be both credible and astute.

"The pertinent point is that you are private agents and have no authority to investigate crimes that are the purview of the local constabulary. I absolutely forbid you to continue to pursue any investigation connected to this man's death."

"I'm not sure you have the authority to do that," Beryl said.

"I do, and now that I come to think of it I'm inclined to credit the theory suggested by my predecessor, former Constable Wilkes, that you may have murdered this poor man yourself."

"Mr. Wilkes may be well intentioned, but he is mistaken," Beryl said. "As I am sure you are well aware, we were hired to discover where Mr. Cunningham had scarpered off to."

"What better way to drum up clients for your fledgling business than to create a crime yourself?" Constable Gibbs said.

"That's ludicrous, Doris," Edwina said. "Even you cannot imagine we would be involved in something like that." Edwina was so outraged she felt her throat constricting and her hands clenching and unclenching involuntarily. At that moment she could think of nothing she would like more than to make Constable Gibbs mysteriously disappear. She doubted very much anyone would hire them to investigate that case however. In fact, she would be surprised if even the constable's own husband would be willing to hire them for that.

"You're right. I can't actually imagine the two of you having the foresight to plan something as complex as all that," Constable Gibbs said with a scowl upon her face. "Still, I'm going to have to ask you both to remain in the vicinity until I discover what happened to Mr. Cunningham. So don't get any ideas about floating off in any hot-air balloons or other such nonsense. Although perhaps that shouldn't be such a concern now, should it? After all, I seem to remember your last venture of that nature ending in a crash landing somewhere far off course." Constable Gibbs turned her back on Edwina, Beryl, and the small crowd of people who had assembled to watch the goings-on. She climbed into the passenger side of the ambulance and hurried off.

"I hope you didn't take Doris' comment to heart, Beryl," Edwina said, laying a hand on Beryl's arm.

"If there's one thing that's never bothered me, Edwina, it's a critic. If I had ever listened to any of them I should not be where I am today. But I will say that should I ever wish to take flight again, we had better stick to our investigation. If we need to stay in the vicinity of Walmsley Parva until Constable Gibbs manages to discover the murderer, I fear we shall be too old to attempt to leave."

"Do you have any idea where we should start?" Edwina asked.

"As a matter of fact I do," Beryl said. She patted the pocket of her filthy silk jacket and smiled.

CHAPTER 15

Edwina reached for the piece of paper Beryl had extracted from her pocket and smoothed it flat on her lap. Even though it was typewritten she still found it difficult to read. She supposed it was because Beryl took each turn in the winding road at sufficient speed to roll the motorcar up on two wheels. Edwina found she felt all wobbly in her stomach trying to read whilst the motorcar was in motion. From what little she could focus upon, it was clear that the sheet contained a list of names.

"What does it say?" Beryl asked, taking another turn like they were fleeing for their lives from a gang of highwaymen.

"I'd be delighted to tell you if only you'd slow down enough for me to read it. My stomach is lurching about so badly, I keep needing to close my eyes," Edwina said.

"Sorry about that. I tend to overdo it a bit when I am excited." Beryl let up on the accelerator and Edwina took a deep breath before glancing at the paper in her lap once more. "So what is it?"

"It is a letter addressed to Mr. Ecclestone-Smythe. Apparently it is a blacklist of miners who have been dismissed from more established mines in other parts of the country and it requests that Mr. Ecclestone-Smythe help to keep the list up to date should he have any outbreaks of labor agitators at Hambley," Edwina said.

"Do you recognize any of the names on the list?" Beryl asked. Edwina read over it as quickly as she could.

"No. Not a one."

"I wonder how that letter came to be in Mr. Cunningham's pocket," Beryl said, pushing down firmly on the accelerator once more. Edwina's heart lurched in her chest and she braced herself against the dashboard with her hand.

"I don't suppose we can just come out and ask anyone about it since you really shouldn't have taken it in the first place," Edwina said.

"Then we shall have to take the scenic approach. We can start out by asking that frosty secretary of Mr. Ecclestone-Smythe about office efficiency. We can tell her we are looking to set up with a secretary of our

169

own and would appreciate her advice. It should be a simple enough thing to turn the conversation to the topic of managing correspondence," Beryl said as she reached for some sort of a lever and moved it about.

"I suppose we could also ask around about the possibility of labor organizers at Hambley. Maybe Mr. Cunningham was keeping an eye on such things for his employer," Edwina said.

"See, I knew I was right to pocket that paper."

"Whatever possessed you?"

"I always make a point to follow my instincts when on any sort of an expedition. Searching for Mr. Cunningham was very much like trekking through the jungle in search of lost cities or exotic plant species. My first thought was to pick the dead man's pockets, so I did. And it was a good thing, too."

"I'm not so certain you can say that," Edwina said. "Looking for a missing person is one thing. Solving a murder is really quite another. I think you may be letting our success last autumn go to your head." Edwina had never felt as confident as Beryl had seemed to do that their help with a murder case a few months previously had been anything other than an extraordinary and exceptional success with little chance of being repeated.

"After our encounter with Constable Gibbs I feel entitled to getting a bit of our own back. Besides, you know what she's like far better than I do. Wouldn't you agree that poor Mr. Cunningham stands a better chance of receiving justice with us seeking it for him?" Beryl asked. Edwina felt the gravitational pull of Beryl's mischievous grin. As usual, there was no resisting such a force of nature.

"Perhaps you are right. I suppose we can at least give it a try since we now have little else to investigate. That is, if we manage to make it home in one piece."

Edwina looked shattered by the time they reached the Beeches. Beryl chose to believe it was the harrowing conversation with Constable Gibbs and a delayed reaction to the discovery of Mr. Cunningham's body rather than the way she put her beloved automobile smartly through its paces on the way back home. She did not like to admit it but she had found the whole affair to be a bit nerve-racking herself. Upon arriving back home she steered Edwina into the sitting room and proceeded to apply herself to her only real culinary skill, the concocting

171

of cocktails.

But before the first gin was fizzed Crumpet raced out of the room and down the corridor barking with every step. Edwina followed him quickly and returned escorting Lucretia Ecclestone-Smythe into the room. The lady looked even more miserable than she had the day of the pigeon race. Her eyes were rimmed with red and her hat sat askew upon her untidy hair. Edwina directed her into the most comfortable chair in the sitting room and Beryl immediately handed her a cup filled with restorative libations.

Mrs. Ecclestone-Smythe drained the glass before speaking. "Is it true that you found Lionel's body?" she asked in a low voice.

"Yes, I'm afraid that it is. I suppose the news has traveled all over Walmsley Parva and beyond if you've heard of it," Edwina said.

"Naturally, as Lionel was one of my husband's trusted employees, that officious policewoman telephoned him at home straightaway," Mrs. Ecclestone-Smythe said. "Will you be continuing to pursue the case on behalf of your client now that Lionel is no longer a missing person?"

"That, naturally, will be something for us to discuss with our client. However, as we did in fact find him there is not much left for us to do," Edwina said. As the vicar had wished to keep the missing birds and money a secret Edwina saw no need to mention them to their guest.

"You aren't going to simply leave the investigation to that policewoman, are you?" Fresh tears appeared in Mrs. Ecclestone-Smythe's eyes and threatened to spill down her pale cheeks.

"Surely you are not here on behalf of your husband's mining interests?" Beryl said. She kept her gaze fixed on Mrs. Ecclestone-Smythe. The other woman tipped her head to the side and shrugged ever so gently.

"You really are a detective. No, I am not here on my husband's behalf. In fact I'm here concerning my own interests and will be most grateful if my husband were not to find out I came to speak with you," the visitor said. Beryl sensed a confession was on its way. She reached for Mrs. Ecclestone-Smythe's empty glass and took it to the drinks tray to refill it. In her experience very little loosened the tongue more quickly than well-applied quantities of quality liquor. After handing their guest her cocktail, Beryl set about completing the gin fizzes she had intended to make before Mrs. Ecclestone-Smythe had appeared unexpectedly at the door. She pressed one into Edwina's reluctant hand and settled back into her own chair with the other.

"You can be absolutely assured of our discretion," Edwina said. "Isn't that right, Beryl?"

"As ladies of a certain standing ourselves, we understand that not everything is everyone else's business," Beryl said. "Having had quite a number of husbands of my own I can assure you I completely understand the place in any marriage for privacy. I never considered a marriage vow to negate my right to keep what I wished to myself." Mrs. Ecclestone-Smythe took a long sip of her drink then cleared her throat.

"I could not agree more," Mrs. Ecclestone-Smythe said. "I confess, I am here on a far more sordid business than any mining concern."

"Are you here to ask us to discover if your husband has been unfaithful to you?" Edwina asked.

"Sadly, I have no need of private enquiry agents to help me to discover that. I am quite certain Ambrose has been behaving as expected with his latest secretary. Helen Chilvers, I think her name is. Blond, just the sort my husband fancies." Mrs. Ecclestone-Smythe lifted a hand and patted her dark brown hair. "Ambrose has spent the entirety of our marriage chasing, and I daresay, catching, other women."

"I am very sorry to hear that," Edwina said. Beryl could tell her friend meant it. Like so many women who had never married Edwina was a desperate romantic underneath her reasonable exterior. It was the reason, Beryl believed, that Edwina had not ever married. Real life could never live up to her fanciful imaginings of what love should be. Hearing that a woman with as much in her favor as Mrs. Ecclestone-Smythe had made an unfortunate match would be a sore trial to Edwina's tender sensibilities.

"The fact of the matter is my marriage has not been one based on romance but rather on practicalities. In truth, it was one of which my parents strongly approved. Not to put too fine a point on things, from the way he has treated me, I think it is fair to say my groom approved of the money my parents agreed to settle upon me far more than he ever approved of me." Mrs. Ecclestone-Smythe let out a long sigh. It rattled her slight frame and Beryl felt quite sorry for her.

"It's a story with which we are quite familiar. Is that not so, Edwina?" Beryl asked. Edwina nodded vigorously.

"Beryl and I were at Miss DuPont's Finishing School for Young Ladies together many years ago. I think it would be true to say that at least half of the other girls attending with us entered into similar sorts of marriages," Edwina said.

"Do you wish us to provide you with incontrovertible proof of his conduct?" Beryl asked. She felt herself more than qualified to pursue that particular sort of an investigation having been on both sides of the divorce proceedings based on those very grounds. Twice.

"No. I have no need of proof. Perhaps I might have done if Lionel had not been murdered," Mrs. Ecclestone-Smythe said. "I hope you will not feel too much loathing for me when I share with you what brings me here today."

"It is not our place to judge our clients," Edwina said.

"Certainly not," Beryl said, rattling the ice in her glass. "Besides, I have often found myself in a position where it would not do to be judgmental towards anyone else." Mrs. Ecclestone-Smythe gave a ghost of a smile and placed her empty glass on the table beside her chair.

"As you may have guessed from my reaction and my appearance here today Lionel and I did not only know each other through my husband's business. Of course that's how we met, but it was not long before we meant more to each other than employee and employer's wife." Mrs. Ecclestone-Smythe twisted her ornate, gold wedding ring round and round on her finger.

"The two of you were conducting an affair?" Beryl asked. She always found it best to get such things out in the open early on in a conversation. In her opinion, beating around bushes was only the least bit useful when one was out hunting. In all other circumstances it simply slowed down progress. She stole a glance at Edwina who was rising remarkably to the occasion. If Beryl did not know her friend so well she would never have guessed such conversations made Edwina deeply uncomfortable. In fact, if she had not been able to see the side of Edwina's neck, which had taken on a color remarkably like strawberry jam, she would've had no idea her friend did not speak of such things with shocking regularity. She made a mental note to ply Edwina with gin fizzes whenever a new client appeared.

"Yes, that's it exactly. It's such a relief to be able to say it to someone. Lionel and I were very much in love. In fact, we had planned to run away together. We had arranged to meet after Lionel had delivered the birds to the pigeon race," Mrs. Ecclestone-Smythe said.

"Did you accompany him out of Walmsley Parva?" Edwina asked.

"No, I did not. We had arranged for him to go in one direction to the race and for me to head to London. We were supposed to meet up there that evening but he never arrived. I simply do not understand how he came to be found dead here in Walmsley Parva," Mrs. Ecclestone-Smythe said.

"What is it that you think we can do for you?" Beryl asked. "Did you want us to look into his murder? Or was it something else that was troubling you?"

"I hate to sound as though Lionel's death is not uppermost in my mind. I hope you will understand if I have practical matters to consider as well," Mrs. Ecclestone-Smythe said. "Which is how I pray that you can help me." She leaned slightly forward in her seat.

"Do you mind if I take notes?" Edwina said. Mrs. Ecclestone-Smythe shook her head. Edwina took out her notebook and retrieved a pen from a nearby table before settling back in her chair once more.

"While I longed for a relationship that provided me with a greater emotional attachment, I am accustomed to a certain lifestyle. It is fair to say it is not one that can be supported by an absconding clark. In order to make a new life for ourselves that was the sort I would enjoy, it was clear to me we would require a source of funds. My husband has had sole charge of our money throughout the duration of our marriage. Ambrose has provided me with a generous allowance every week since we married. However, the only items of value I own outright are my pieces of jewelry," Mrs. Ecclestone-Smythe said.

"I don't suppose you expected the allowance to continue after you left your husband for his employee?" Beryl asked.

"That's it exactly. However, my jewelry is quite valuable. In fact, to say it's worth a fortune would not be overstating things," Mrs. Ecclestone-Smythe said. "And that's where the two of you come in. When I last saw Lionel the night before the pigeon race, I entrusted him with all of it except for the pieces you see me wearing today." She held up her left hand and fluttered her ring finger, sending a shower of sparkles from a large diamond around the room. She turned her head from one side to the other, displaying a pair of emerald earrings dangling from her earlobes.

"Do you think Mr. Cunningham was murdered for your jewelry?" Edwina asked.

"I hate to consider that that was a possibility but I can't think of any other reason anyone would want to harm him," Mrs. Ecclestone-Smythe said. "I can't help but feel his death is somehow my fault." She retrieved a lace-trimmed handkerchief from her small handbag and dabbed discreetly at her eyes.

"Besides the two of you, who would have known he had your jewelry?" Beryl asked.

"I haven't any idea. I certainly didn't tell anyone. And I can't imagine that Lionel did either. We had promised each other to keep this entirely between the two of us. My husband is a powerful man and one of the largest employers in the area. If anyone had gotten the slightest hint of what we were up to, they might have been very happy to carry tales to him in order to ingratiate themselves with him," Mrs. Ecclestone-Smythe said. "It was one of the reasons we did not wish to even be seen leaving Walmsley Parva on the same train."

"So you wish for us to recover your missing jewelry?" Edwina asked.

"Exactly. And I need you to do so before

my husband discovers that it is missing. While I have not been happy with Ambrose, I have no wish for him to discover my unfaithfulness. I'm rather afraid he would make my life a misery. One of the things that concerns me the most is that my jewelry will come up in the course of the police investigation. That would be most unfortunate indeed," Mrs. Ecclestone-Smythe said.

"We would be happy to be of assistance," Beryl said.

"We will of course require a retainer," Edwina said, letting out the tiniest hiccup to punctuate her assertion. Beryl hid a smile behind her hand.

"I had assumed as much." Mrs. Ecclestone-Smythe withdrew a tidy stack of bills from her handbag. "Shall we say this much to start?" She fanned out the money on the table in front of her. Beryl stole a glance at Edwina and noticed her friend experiencing far less discomfort with the conversation concerning fees than she had at the vicarage. Beryl had long suspected there was a steely businesswoman lurking under Edwina's prim exterior. Even if much of her change of heart could be attributed to strong drink, Beryl felt a swell of pride at her part in bringing that side of Edwina to the surface.

"I'm sure that that is enough to get us started. We will provide you with an itemized account of our expenses and our hours. Should we need to send you a bill, how would you prefer for us to contact you?" Edwina asked.

"I'll check in with you in a few days. I'm afraid my husband may have some suspicions. It was very difficult for me to hide my reaction to the discovery of Lionel's body. I would not put it past him to begin opening my post."

"We will await a message from you then," Beryl said. Mrs. Ecclestone-Smythe drew on her gloves and quickly took her leave of them. Edwina walked her to the door and when she returned sank back into her chair.

"I don't know quite what has gotten into me. I've never been so forthright concerning money in my life. Although now that I come to think of it, I'm not quite sure how I feel about aiding one spouse in keeping secrets from the other," Edwina said. Beryl noticed Edwina sneaking glances at the bills laid out across the table. She scooped them up and handed them to Edwina to count. She watched her friend's face as she did so. Beryl very much doubted Edwina had ever held anywhere near so much money in her hand all at one time. Beryl toyed with the notion of introducing Edwina to the game of poker then thought better of it. Perhaps it would be best not to introduce too many new experiences all at once. Edwina might make a hasty retreat back into her far more respectable way of life and then where would they be?

"As fledgling business owners acquiring new clients should be first and foremost on our minds, Ed," Beryl said. "We didn't even have to go looking for this one. And the fee will come in rather handy too, don't you think?"

"I can't help but feel that it amounts to ill-gotten gains," Edwina said.

"You felt much the same way about my poker winnings, but the money still took care of the accounts outstanding at the butcher and the greengrocer," Beryl said. "Besides, it's not all that much money."

"How can you say that?" Edwina said, fanning herself with the stack of bills.

"It looks like a moderately good evening at the cards to me," Beryl said. "We've already agreed to take her on so I can't see leaving her to her fate with the likes of Mr. Ecclestone-Smythe. Can you?"

"She does remind me rather of Cynthia Billingham," Edwina said. A vague memory tickled at the back of Beryl's mind.

"Wasn't she the one rumored to have committed suicide shortly after her wedding?" Beryl said.

"Within weeks, if my memory serves me correctly. She had also been persuaded to marry by her well-intentioned but misguided parents," Edwina said.

"We will feel terrible if we allow such despair to befall Mrs. Ecclestone-Smythe," Beryl said.

"I suppose there's no harm in looking into it for a few days," Edwina said, crossing the room and placing the wad of bills in a milk glass vase on the bookshelf. "Where do you suggest we begin?"

"As much as I hate to say it, we are going to have to make inquiries of Constable Gibbs."

"But Mrs. Ecclestone-Smythe is anxious that no one know about the investigation into her missing jewels. We certainly would not want to involve the police in that," Edwina said.

"We shan't say anything about the jewels, but we do need to be sure that they were not on Mr. Cunningham's body when it went off in the ambulance. I can't think of anyone else to ask besides Constable Gibbs, can you?" Beryl said.

Edwina slowly shook her head. "Unfortunately, I'm afraid you're right. I'm just not sure I'm up to two conversations with Doris Gibbs in one day."

Beryl returned to the drinks cart once more. This time she concocted a drink made of more gin than fizz and handed it to Edwina. "Get this into you and I think you'll understand why it's called liquid courage."

CHAPTER 16

Given the quantity of both gin and fizz, Edwina made the remarkably sound decision that the pair of them should approach the police station on foot. Beryl had asserted that she was never in finer form behind the wheel than when she had indulged in a cocktail or two, but Edwina insisted the fresh air would do them both good. Once again she disappointed Crumpet by leaving him at home, but she did not feel entirely up to the responsibility of his care considering how rosy and wavy the world around her looked.

By the time they had reached the police station she felt far more clearheaded. But Beryl was right; she did feel rather brave. Constable Gibbs's churlish glance hardly seemed to reach her when they pushed open the door of the police station and approached the front desk.

"I don't suppose I'm lucky enough that

the two of you are here to confess to Mr. Cunningham's murder?" Constable Gibbs said, scraping back her wooden chair and getting to her feet.

"I'm afraid that would simply make an excess of unnecessary paperwork for you," Beryl said, "as we are still not the ones to have committed the crime. However, we are here in the course of our own investigation."

"I told you not to meddle any further in this matter or I would consider you to be interfering with the police investigation. I don't think I was unclear about that in the least," Constable Gibbs said. She crossed her arms over her chest and did her best to appear menacing despite the fact that Beryl towered over her.

"We simply wish to conclude our business with our client. Mr. Cunningham was, as I'm sure you know, an important member of the local pigeon racing club. He had on his person at the time of his disappearance two or three valuable books on the subject of pigeon racing. The club would be very grateful to have them back and wished to know if he had them upon his person at the time of his death," Edwina said.

"What makes you think he would have had them with him?" Constable Gibbs said.

"When we first began our investigation

into his disappearance Edwina and I searched his room at his boardinghouse," Beryl said.

"So I should just add unlawful entry to your list of criminal activities?" Constable Gibbs said, reaching for what Edwina was certain amounted to an official form of some sort. Doris Gibbs loved nothing better than official forms.

"We were there in the company of the landlady, Mrs. Plumptree," Edwina said. "I doubt very much that could be considered any form of illegal entry. All we want to know is if we can return those valuable books to the pigeon racing club. I'm sure the vicar would be most grateful." Edwina had seen in the past how eager Constable Gibbs was to associate with the vicar. Edwina couldn't help but wonder if there was something weighing on the constable's conscience. Perhaps if there were a lull between clients she and Beryl should investigate that little mystery. She stifled a hiccup and wondered what had gotten into her.

"I'm sorry, but I don't believe the vicar would like to have the books back. They were in his vest pocket and were completely ruined," Constable Gibbs said. "I doubt very much the vicar would even like to view them let alone to handle them."

"Ruined how?" Edwina asked.

"Both of them were completely saturated with the victim's blood. I expect they are completely illegible. Now if there's nothing else, unlike the two of you, I have important work to get back to," Constable Gibbs said.

"You're sure there were only two books in his pocket? I could have sworn Mrs. Plumptree reported three missing from his room." Edwina turned to Beryl. "Although I'm not sure why I'm asking. Doris has never been known for her attention to detail."

While Edwina had said it hoping the constable would rise to the bait, it also happened to be true. Doris Gibbs on more than one occasion had left the house in mismatched shoes. More often than seemed possible she had forgotten her own husband in town and had headed home without him. One day she walked out of her house with her favorite budgie perched on her shoulder. It flew off never to be seen again.

"I'll have you know the contents of Mr. Cunningham's pockets were thoroughly inventoried as per regulation as soon I reached the body," Constable Gibbs said. She whipped out a folder and dangled a piece of paper right in front of Edwina's nose before commencing to read what was written upon it. "One pocket handkerchief,

189

two pounds and three shillings, a book of matches, two blood-soaked books on the subject of pigeon racing, and a wrapper from a boiled sweet." Constable Gibbs smacked the paper back down on her desk and slapped the folder shut.

"Edwina, it sounds as though we shall have to report this sad loss to the vicar," Beryl said. "Thank you so much for your assistance. It's always a pleasure to stop by to see you."

"Flattery will get you nowhere with me, as well you know. And if I find out the pair of you are still meddling in this case after you've been expressly instructed not to do so, I will arrest you," Constable Gibbs said. It occurred to Edwina that Constable Gibbs seemed to have conveniently forgotten whom it was who had solved the murder that had occurred only a few months before. She was surprised to discover she had entirely lost patience with the constable's posturing. There really was something quite magical about Beryl's libations. The constable's face was suffused with color and an unladylike quantity of perspiration was making its way down her low forehead. Edwina reached her small, square hand across the counter and drummed her fingers upon its surface.

"I urge you to reconsider, Constable. Perhaps you have not heard about the investigative services we have been privileged to render to His Majesty from time to time. I assure you it would be most ill-advised to impede this investigation, or any other we decide to undertake, if you value your own position in law enforcement," Edwina said. "I bid you good day."

Edwina turned on her heel and strode out of the police station with her head held high, not even waiting for Beryl to follow her. Which, as it turned out, she did, directly on Edwina's heels.

"That was marvelous, Ed," Beryl said, grabbing hold of Edwina's arm. Edwina felt as though she had somehow floated up and out of her own body and that she was looking down on an entirely new version of herself. "Although I must give you a bit of a ribbing about claiming a connection with royalty after all the trouble you have given me for doing so."

"I'm thoroughly stunned by all that just took place. The only thing I can say in my defense is that you have had a shocking influence upon my character," Edwina said.

"I'm pleased as punch but am not really surprised." Beryl beamed at her. That was the only word for it. Beryl beamed with enough wattage to light the high street on a midwinter's night.

"Of course you weren't. You were the one who recommended your liquid courage in the first place. You must have known the effect it would have on my temperament."

"I wasn't referring to the power of gin fizzes. They aren't magical, after all," Beryl said. "I firmly believe that within reason, of course, imbibing in strong drink only encourages what is already lurking under the surface. You are a sleeping tiger on the inside, Edwina Davenport, and all it took was the right sort of pointy stick to wake it up."

Edwina was not sure if she was proud to be compared with such a ferocious creature or horrified to know that she might put someone in mind of a wild beast. As the comment had come from Beryl she decided it was most likely a compliment and determined to treat it as such.

"Thank you. But now, if you don't mind, this tiger would like to head back home for a nap. There has been altogether too much excitement for one day." Beryl tipped her head to one side, a pose Edwina knew meant she was concocting something else for them to do. She felt the promise of her cozy armchair, a Zane Grey novel, and a few moments in Crumpet's calming company slipping away.

"We have a client to consider, remember. As the police station did not turn up Mrs. Ecclestone-Smythe's missing jewelry, we shall have to continue the search," Beryl said, steering Edwina down the steps away from the police station and towards the street. "We can stop in at the Beeches but only to pick up my automobile. I for one do not relish the idea of walking to the village of Hambley this afternoon."

"What business do we have at the Hambley mine? I should think in order to keep Mrs. Ecclestone-Smythe's business a secret we ought to steer clear of her husband's place of work," Edwina said.

"We know that her jewels are not in his room at the boardinghouse. We also know they were not found upon his person when his body was discovered. The next logical place to search is in his desk at the Hambley mining office," Beryl said.

"But we have no business doing so if we do not indicate that we are there on behalf of Mrs. Ecclestone-Smythe," Edwina said.

"I'm afraid we're going to have to stoop to stretching the truth for a second time today," Beryl said.

"Are you sure it's only been stretched

twice?" Edwina asked. By her count they had told enough porky pies between them to cast serious doubt upon the likelihood that either of them could be considered upstanding citizens.

"Who's counting?" Beryl said. "The point is we are going to have to employ a bit of deception if we wish to serve our client. That is the nature of the business we are in and the sooner you reconcile yourself to the necessity of the odd little white lie, the happier we both will be."

CHAPTER 17

Beryl bundled Edwina into the automobile as soon as it came into view. She slid behind the wheel and tore off down the drive with her customary gusto. Edwina felt the courage she had enjoyed back at the police station entirely evaporate. Beryl's driving had that effect on her. She doubted she would ever be enough of a tiger to enjoy outings in Beryl's motorcar. She remained bolt upright with her hands braced against the dashboard until the vehicle screeched to a stop directly in front of the mining office.

She was not the least bit happy with the story Beryl had concocted to explain their visit. She was even less pleased with the role Beryl had assigned to her in the deception.

"Remember what I said, with or without the emboldening effects of gin you are, in your heart of hearts, a tiger. I am relying on you to bear that in mind," Beryl said, giving Edwina's hand a reassuring squeeze before sliding out the driver's side door. Edwina exited the vehicle with as much enthusiasm as a small boy heading for a bath. She reminded herself of their outstanding debts at the local shops, squared her shoulders, and followed Beryl into the colliery office.

Miss Chilvers sat just as she had before behind her tidy wooden desk. She glanced up when they entered, and from the stony expression fixed on her face she seemed no more pleased to see them on this occasion than she had on the last.

"And how may I help you ladies today?" Miss Chilvers asked. "I'm quite certain you do not have an appointment." The secretary ran a well-groomed, elegant finger across an appointment diary that even from several steps away Edwina could see was entirely blank.

"As Mr. Ecclestone-Smythe is one of the leading citizens of Kent, we were quite certain he would wish to make a donation to the tombola stall for the May Day celebration which will be held on the green in Walmsley Parva," Edwina said. "I am on the committee which organizes the event and felt sure he would not wish to be overlooked when so many other prominent people are being included." Miss Chilvers pushed back her chair and held up a hand like a traffic warden.

"Please wait here while I ask Mr. Ecclestone-Smythe if he is willing to see you," Miss Chilvers said. The secretary crossed the room, rapped upon the door to her employer's office, and stepped inside, closing it firmly behind her. Faster than Edwina would've thought possible, Beryl crossed the room and opened a door centered on the wall behind Miss Chilvers' desk.

"Quick, there is just enough room for you to hide in here," Beryl said, pointing into the small, dark space. "I'll tell her you needed the powder room and I will ask her loudly for tea. When you hear her leave the room to fix it, come on out and look through Mr. Cunningham's desk."

Edwina squeezed herself between a stack of cartons and a filing cabinet. Beryl shut the door and blotted out all of the light. For a moment Edwina felt a wave of claustrophobia. She took herself firmly in hand by replaying in her mind the conversation that she had had with Constable Gibbs. Surely tigers were not afraid of the dark. After a moment her eyesight adjusted to the gloom and she noticed the outline of a keyhole. Silently she bent over and peered through it, thankful that her back had not decided to play up that day.

From her crouched position she managed to get a surprisingly decent view of the door to Mr. Ecclestone-Smythe's office. She watched as Miss Chilvers beckoned Beryl inside with ill grace. Beryl's voice boomed out across the room and into the closet.

"I don't suppose you have any tea on the go? I shouldn't like to ask for myself but Miss Davenport just can't seem to get enough of the stuff," Beryl said. Edwina could not make out what was said by the secretary or her employer, but within a second or two Miss Chilvers had headed down a narrow corridor and out of sight. Edwina turned the doorknob as silently as she was able and crept out of the closet.

As there were only two desks in the room, she made straight for the one Miss Chilvers did not make a habit of occupying. She tugged on the kneehole drawer and found it slid open with ease. A quick perusal of its contents revealed nothing more sinister than a fountain pen missing its nib and a pencil sharpener with a rusty blade. She tried the top drawer to the left of the kneehole and found it locked tight.

Although she considered Beryl to be the one more likely in possession of dubious skills, the fact was she had some experience at picking locks. Her mother had been a forgetful creature and more often than not locked drawers to desks, doors to cabinets, and even lids of trunks before promptly forgetting where she had placed the keys. Since Mrs. Davenport was not a woman known for her patience Edwina had found it in her best interest to learn how to open a wide variety of locks using improvised tools. It always took a bit of doing but, generally, she managed in the end.

She opened the pencil drawer once more and rummaged about. In the back, under a packet of throat pastilles, she found a paper clip. She unbent it and knelt down before the drawer. She worked the end of the paper clip into the lock and began to twist it this way and that. Just as she felt the tumbler click, she heard footsteps behind her.

"I assure you, Miss Davenport, the powder room cannot be found in there," Miss Chilvers said, banging a tea tray down on the top of Mr. Cunningham's desk. "But I don't suppose that's what you're looking for, is it?" Edwina tried to call upon the tiger within but found herself feeling disappointingly domesticated as she got to her feet and faced the self-righteous secretary. She knew telling lies would eventually get them in trouble. She would have to try the truth and trust that Miss Chilvers would be swayed by the real story.

"May I speak frankly with you as one career woman to another?" Edwina asked.

Something in Miss Chilvers' demeanor softened ever so slightly. Perhaps it was the set of her jaw or maybe the slope of her shoulders. Whatever it was, Edwina felt a flutter of hope.

"If you feel you must," Miss Chilvers said.

"Miss Helliwell and I are not here exclusively to solicit a donation for the May Day celebration. We would, of course, be delighted for your employer to contribute to such a worthy cause. However, we are also here on behalf of a client who wished for us to investigate Mr. Cunningham's disappearance," Edwina said.

"I had understood that you had already found Mr. Cunningham's body. It would seem that your business was concluded," Miss Chilvers said.

"It would be if we were only asked to locate Mr. Cunningham himself. I hope that I can trust your discretion and not bring dishonor down upon a man who can no longer speak for himself," Edwina said.

"I have always held Mr. Cunningham in high regard. I will not say anything to discredit him," Miss Chilvers said.

"We were hired not only to find Mr. Cunningham but also to discover the whereabouts of the funds entrusted to him in his capacity as the pigeon racing club treasurer. Unfortunately for our client, the funds went missing at the same time as Mr. Cunningham himself. I was checking to see if he had placed them for safekeeping here at his place of employment," Edwina said.

"And have you found them?" Miss Chilvers said.

"I was about to unlock this drawer when you came upon me. I have not had the chance to look inside," Edwina said, pointing at the paper clip still wedged into the lock. "Shall I continue? If the funds are not in the drawer it may be that Mr. Cunningham was not the one who took them." Miss Chilvers looked at Edwina and then down at the drawer.

"If it will help to clear his name, go right ahead. Although I don't know how long your friend will be able to keep Mr. Ecclestone-Smythe's attention. He is sure to start shouting at me for something at any moment." Miss Chilvers darted a glance at the door to her employer's office. Beryl's muffled voice came through it.

"Beryl is more than capable of securing the attention of most any gentleman she chooses," Edwina said. "But perhaps it would be best if you stood shielding me from view should either of them decide to open his office door." Miss Chilvers nodded and shifted her stance slightly. Edwina directed her attention once more to the paper clip and within seconds had opened the lock. She slid the drawer open and looked inside.

The drawer was filled with ledgers and envelopes tied up with serviceable cording. She reached her hand all the way to the back of the drawer and felt her heart stutter in her chest as her fingers wrapped around a box tucked in the back. She pulled it forward and lifted off the lid. Inside lay nothing more than some empty paper wrappers and a few smears of chocolate. It would seem the only thing Mr. Cunningham was hiding in his desk was a predilection for sweets.

Miss Chilvers smiled triumphantly. "Nothing more nefarious than an empty chocolates box, I see," she said. "I trust this will clear Mr. Cunningham's good name?"

"That depends on you," Edwina said. "Our client is very eager to keep this matter private. I would not have mentioned it to you had you not found me in a compromising position that required explanation. I certainly have no intention of spreading such tales to the public at large." Miss Chilvers nodded in agreement.

"If you'll just follow me into Mr. Ecclestone-Smythe's office, you can let your friend know you are done nosing about." Miss Chilvers retrieved the tea tray from the top of Mr. Cunningham's desk and led the way to her employer's office.

CHAPTER 18

"So she caught you red-handed, did she?" Beryl said, putting the automobile in reverse. Edwina had looked well and truly rattled when she entered the room in Miss Chilvers' wake. Not that the average person would have been able to tell, mind you, but with years of experience under her belt, Beryl knew the signs. As an accomplished card player, Beryl prided herself on her ability to pick up on those subtle facial twitches and mannerisms that betrayed emotion. She was quite certain it was a skill that would serve her in good stead as a private detective. There had been no doubt about it. Edwina's face had most definitely twitched.

"I don't know as I've ever been so embarrassed in all my life," Edwina said. "Assuredly it has been a most unsettling day. All I want to do is head home, kick off my shoes, and settle back with a hot drink and a good book."

"That we will do, just as soon as we take another look at Mr. Cunningham's pigeon loft," Beryl said. Out of the corner of her eye Beryl saw Edwina's usually upright posture slump in defeat. "It has to be done, Ed. I wouldn't insist if it wasn't absolutely necessary." She could not stand to see her friend looking so crushed. Honestly it was quite disturbing. Beryl firmly applied her foot to the gas pedal and felt a sense of relief as Edwina's posture regained its customary rigidity.

"I'm sorry you were caught but I'd have to say our visit to the Hambley mining office was quite the success nevertheless. Don't you agree?" Beryl said as the country-side whipped past them in a blur.

"I was completely humiliated and we still did not turn up Mrs. Ecclestone-Smythe's jewelry. I don't see how you can count it as any sort of success at all," Edwina said.

"I counted a success in two ways." Beryl took one hand off the wheel and raised her index finger. "Firstly, we know one more place where the jewels are not. Secondly, we secured a large donation of coal as a tombola prize. Time well spent in my opinion."

"Don't forget we managed to press Miss Chilvers into duty at the tombola booth for the fete," Edwina said. Beryl felt certain Edwina was not irreparably damaged if she was already turning her attention to her civic responsibilities.

They bumped along the rutted lanes and roads that wound between the village of Hambley and the allotments in Walmsley Parva. Beryl pulled the automobile onto a grassy verge just before the entrance to the allotments and took a deep breath of the fresh spring air. Edwina turned to her and fixed her with a piercing look.

"This is absolutely the last bit of detecting for today. I will look over the pigeon loft with you but not one thing more," Edwina said. Beryl nodded.

"I promise. Even if we discover another body in there we will simply walk away and head back to the Beeches without a word to anyone," Beryl said. "Are you sure you are up for the company of the birds?"

Beryl recalled her friend's reaction to Mrs. Plumptree's parrot, Cyril. She wondered if Edwina's affection for birds only extended to the non-domesticated sort. She was inclined to go on to an irritating degree about the unfeeling manner Simpkins displayed when rooting out any appropriate spots for sparrows, thrushes, and wrens to find shelter. But perhaps she had no love of birds that found their way under a roof.

"You know I love birds. Why would you ask me that?" Edwina said, turning on the bench seat to face Beryl.

"After the way you acted with Mrs. Plumptree's parrot I thought perhaps you preferred birds of the non-domesticated variety."

"I have no problem with domesticated birds. It's just that Cyril's vocabulary can be quite shocking," Edwina said.

"You make him sound like quite the character," Beryl said. "I should have paid him more attention while we were at Shady Rest."

"It's a good job you didn't. He would have been encouraged to make even more outrageous comments."

"So you aren't afraid of birds in general?" Beryl asked. "Just Cyril?"

"Of course I am not afraid of birds. What sort of countrywoman would I be if I were?" Edwina said.

"I'm glad to hear it. There are far too many birds involved in this case for one of us to have a horror of them." Beryl snuck a peek at Edwina from the corner of her eye. She wasn't entirely certain her friend was not putting up a brave front. Just in case that was the situation, she tucked her arm reassuringly through Edwina's as they approached Mr. Cunningham's pigeon loft.

Beryl felt the comforting heft of her pistol in her pocket. Not that she would have said as much to Edwina. There was no need to alarm her friend with any additional concerns as there was clearly enough already on her mind. Beryl couldn't help but notice Edwina hung a half step back as they approached the spot where they had discovered Mr. Cunningham's body only a few hours before. For someone not accustomed to encountering corpses, Beryl thought Edwina was doing a bang-up job of keeping her upper lip as determinedly stiff as it ever was.

"I'll just open the door and stick my head inside, shall I?" Beryl said. She reached for the latch on the pigeon loft door.

"I suppose that depends on your affinity for birds soaring about your head," Edwina said. "I have no idea what they'll do should a strange woman appear in their domicile."

"I'm afraid there's nothing for it but to give it a go. What's the worst that can happen?" Beryl said. "After all, someone has already stashed their keeper's body here. I don't suppose I'm about to do anything more disturbing." She pulled on the latch and cautiously stuck her head through the opening, taking care not to allow the birds to fly away. She wasn't sure why that worried her. After all, these were birds that specialized in knowing how to return home, even from vast distances. But somehow it seemed wrong to simply fling open the door when there was no one left to be sure they made it home again.

Beryl did not know much about birds. Animals in general were not something that interested her in particular beyond those she encountered on safari or whilst trekking to one of the poles. Exotic animals captured the imagination in a way that commonplace creatures from her own neighborhood did not. She would pause and take note of a passing giraffe, a galloping zebra, or a waddling penguin. But even though she had no real expertise with poultry keeping, she still could easily see there had been a disturbance in Mr. Cunningham's pigeon loft and one she suspected was not of the birds' doing.

"It would seem that we are not the first ones to think about looking here for something," Beryl said.

Despite her earlier hesitation Edwina joined her at the door and peered inside. "Someone has assuredly been searching through the nesting boxes. Look at the way the straw has been carelessly strewn about," Edwina said, pointing at the signs of disorder inside the pigeon loft. The birds seemed flustered. Their heads darted back and forth and some of them flew about the inside of the loft from perch to perch, unable to settle down.

"They were none too careful with what they found in the boxes either, were they?" Beryl said, pointing at the remains of several broken eggs spattering the ground.

"Do you think someone else knew about the missing jewelry?" Edwina said.

"I suppose it's possible. Just because Mrs. Ecclestone-Smythe was in love with Mr. Cunningham did not necessarily mean that he felt the same way about her. Perhaps he wooed her to con her out of her jewelry and had no intention of running off with her in the first place," Beryl said.

"Do you think he had an accomplice who came looking for the jewels? Or perhaps someone he planned to sell them on to?" Edwina asked.

"I think that's a theory well worth exploring. It also could have been his killer. Maybe the murderer only had enough time to hide his body but not enough time to search the loft," Beryl said. She turned to Edwina as she felt her friend shrink away from the pigeon loft.

"Do you think we are in any danger by being here?" Edwina asked.

"I shouldn't think so. Whoever did this is gone and they either found what they were looking for or they did not," Beryl said. She looked around the allotments. Most of them had no one standing within view. Far down at the other end a solitary man with a hoe stood with his back to them. She supposed someone could be hiding behind one of the many small potting sheds or hothouses, but she did not think it would help matters to mention that to Edwina.

"Do you think it's safe to say our business here is complete or do you wish to make a search ourselves of the loft?" Edwina asked.

"As much as I hate to say so, I believe it's necessary to be thorough. I'm afraid we shall have to investigate it for ourselves or we won't have done our duty by Mrs. Ecclestone-Smythe," Beryl said. She hoisted herself into the pigeon loft. Edwina followed and the two began a systematic search despite the protestations of Mr. Cunningham's collection of pigeons. They fluttered and flitted around their heads and swooped from perch to perch as Beryl and Edwina tucked their hands into each nesting box in turn and came up empty.

The women carefully peered into each of the corners and toed stray piles of straw out of the way in an effort to uncover anything secreted away. The air in the loft was stuffy and Beryl found herself instinctively breathing through her mouth. A coughing fit overtook her and she decided she had done her duty by Mrs. Ecclestone-Smythe. With a final glance round, the pair of them left the pigeon loft and Beryl shut the door firmly behind her, making sure the latch clicked back into place.

"I don't know much about bird keeping but I would venture to say there was absolutely nothing hidden in there one would not expect to find in a pigeon loft," Beryl said. "But now I won't spend the night tossing and turning, wondering if we should have checked inside."

Edwina reached up and plucked a bit of straw from Beryl's platinum blond hair. "I say we head directly back to the Beeches for an early supper and a quiet night sitting in front of the fire," Edwina said. "I'm so desperate to get there I shan't even complain about how fast you drive."

CHAPTER 19

It could not be said that Edwina passed a peaceful night. She tossed and turned and saw images of Mr. Cunningham's body, Constable Gibbs' angry face, and the look of surprise on Miss Chilvers' visage every time she closed her eyes. By the time the sun was peeking through her draperies she realized she had never spent a less restful night. She sat upright, pushed back the coverlet, and slipped her bony feet into her scuffed carpet slippers. Crumpet cocked a bleary-eyed look in her direction from his basket at the side of the bed. He looked as though he had not slept any better than she had. She reached for her dressing gown and slipped her arms into the sleeves before knotting it firmly around her trim waist.

Crumpet followed her as she quietly made her way along the hallway and down the stairs. She felt the strong urge for a bracing cup of tea to start what would surely prove to be a long day. Even when she was well rested she often felt exhausted by the mere thought of the diplomatic negotiations required for a successful May Day celebration committee meeting. Although to be honest it was not the May Day celebration that was the source of the trouble. Rather, it was any interaction between herself and local postmistress and sweetshop owner Prudence Rathbone.

Edwina opened the back door to the garden and Crumpet slipped out into the dewy grass. She filled the teakettle and put it on the hob. Within an hour she had breakfasted, dressed, and walked the half mile from the Beeches to the village hall where the meeting was to be held. She arrived a few moments early in order to settle herself before Prudence was likely to arrive. Edwina prided herself on her punctuality, especially when she felt a bit unsure of herself.

Edwina let herself in and took her preferred place at the table, near the head where there was a clear view of the door. As the vice-chairwoman of the committee she felt it her responsibility to give each person entering the building a friendly smile as they entered. And she wanted to keep an eye on Prudence from the very start of the meeting. She could not dismiss from her mind the impression that Prudence was eager to oust her from her position or even to have her removed from the committee entirely, or at least that's how it felt to Edwina. Before long the other members of the committee had gathered around the long wooden meeting table. Prudence sat opposite her and fixed her bright blue eyes firmly on Edwina.

Muriel Lowethorpe, the committee chairwoman, looked around and called the meeting to order. After approving the minutes of the last meeting she began taking reports on the progress of the committee members in their various tasks. After updates on the refreshments tent, the maypole dancers, and the volunteers for setting up and tearing down were delivered, Muriel turned to Edwina.

"How are you managing with the advertising and the tombola donations?" Muriel asked.

"I have wonderful news to report on that front. I have made the acquaintance of the nurse at the colliery and have asked her to stoke interest in the festivities within the mining village. The addition of the miners and their families should make the numbers swell beyond our usual attendance," Edwina said. Even from across the table she was sure she felt a draft caused by the sharpness of Prudence's indrawn breath.

"You invited the miners of Hambley to a Walmsley Parva event? I should have thought you would understand that the folks around here want no truck with the likes of them," Prudence said. Her eyes shone with indignation as murmurs moved through the assembled committee. "Surely it would have been best to consult with the committee before approaching anyone at the colliery."

"I can't see how it is a problem. Muriel herself is already acquainted with Mr. Morley from the Hambley mine, through the vicar's association with the pigeon racing club," Edwina said. "Isn't that right, Muriel?"

"You are referring to Mr. Dennis Morley, I presume?" Muriel asked. Edwina detected a faint bit of color rising to Muriel's cheeks. She wished it had not seemed necessary to discomfit the chairwoman, but Muriel was not one for change unless she was pressured into it.

"Yes. My friend Miss Helliwell and I met Mrs. Morley, who seems a very sensible woman, and as the colliery nurse is someone in just the sort of position to encourage the

216

miners to attend. I had no notion I had done anything that could be considered questionable." Edwina glanced around the table. Some of the members nodded encouragingly while others leaned back in their chairs with their hands folded in front of them. A few kept their gaze firmly fixed on the table in front of them.

"As I am quite certain you are aware, Edwina, it isn't the nurse that is of concern," Prudence said. "It is all the rest of the miners."

"May Day celebrations are a firm part of country life all across our fair land. Nowhere is this more true than in Walmsley Parva. As you all well know, the miners here in Kent have all come from far-flung places. They bring traditions and ideas that will only improve our festivities," Edwina said.

Prudence crossed her arms over her concave chest and scowled back at Edwina. Edwina never did understand how a woman who spent her day surrounded by sweets could have such a sour temperament.

"Our association with Hambley is already proving to be a positive one," Edwina said. "Miss Helliwell and I have secured a donation of a substantial quantity of coal for a prize at the tombola stall."

Muriel nodded slowly and looked at the

rest of the committee, many of whom expressed delight at the donation. "That is very generous of Mr. Ecclestone-Smythe. Still, I wonder if you have been a bit hasty in deliberately encouraging the miners to attend," Muriel said.

"If Beryl and I had not thought to engage the mining community we would not have such a valuable prize offered." Heads all around the table bobbed thoughtfully in agreement. All except Prudence Rathbone's.

"Remind me what took you to the village of Hambley in the first place." Prudence asked, "You were over there on account of some rather nasty business, weren't you?" All eyes turned on Edwina once more. She should have known, as the worst gossip in the village, Prudence would find a way to turn the conversation to Mr. Cunningham's murder.

"It is true that business rather than volunteerism originally put me in contact with the colliery at Hambley and its owner, Mr. Ecclestone-Smythe. But isn't that what we all do? Don't we all use the opportunities afforded to us to support our fundraising efforts on behalf of Walmsley Parva?" Edwina said.

"I'm not quite sure Walmsley Parva should be accepting such ill-gotten gains. It almost amounts to blood money, does it not?" Prudence said, smiling at Edwina and exposing her long pointy teeth.

"I don't follow your reasoning. The fact that I met the colliery owner while investigating the disappearance of one of his employees does not make his gift any less generous or less valuable for our purposes," Edwina said.

"I believe you make my point for me. The fact that you have debased yourself by engaging in such an unladylike pursuit as private detection has rendered you unable to recognize the finer sensibilities the rest of us would notice as a matter of course. I think it's likely the good citizens of Walmsley Parva would be reluctant to praise you for such an association. You have gotten yourself mixed up in a murder for a second time. I cannot be the only one who thinks it does not reflect well on you," Prudence said. "In fact, in light of what some might consider a character flaw, I suggest we take a vote as to whether or not you should continue to serve on this committee at all."

Gasps whipped around the table. All eyes swung from Edwina to Prudence and back again. The venom in Prudence's voice surprised Edwina. While she had long realized the other woman did not think kindly of her, she had not realized the extent of her dislike. She paused to consider whether or not she wished to remain on the committee. She was startled to realize she had more important things to do than to fill her days by volunteering for every organization that wanted her.

She felt a wave of indignation swelling in her chest and threatening to boil over. Still, it would not do to give Prudence more cause for recriminations. Despite her anger she would not give Prudence the satisfaction of provoking her into behaving intemperately. She cleared her throat and smiled at the rest of the committee members.

"When I look around this table I only see women. Women who are intelligent, productive, and hardworking. Some women around the table have turned their God-given gifts to raising families and caring for their homes. Others, like yourself, Prudence, have engaged in the world of commerce. I seem to remember that the postal service has suffered its own share of unpleasantness. Overdue bills, illicit love letters, even reading material that some others might find offensive make their way through post offices all across the land. Even the post office in Walmsley Parva. Based on your reasoning, Prudence, you are no more fit to serve on this committee than I am," Edwina said. "If Muriel wants my resignation she will ask for it. If she asks, I will tender it, but I will not do so because a fellow businesswoman feels herself above me." Edwina and all the rest of the committee turned their eyes towards Muriel.

"I have no intention of refusing help from anyone who is willing to give it. The May Day celebration requires a tremendous amount of work and it requires all hands if we are to pull off a successful event," Muriel said. "The meeting is adjourned."

CHAPTER 20

Beryl had skipped breakfast that morning as Edwina was already out the door before she awakened. Beryl's skills in the kitchen extended to pouring herself a cup of coffee and not a great deal further. Instead she had taken her automobile out for a run and on her way back had encountered Alice Morley heading towards Walmsley Parva. The younger woman was heading to the chemist shop and Beryl convinced her to accept a ride. Alice finished her errand in far less time than she had expected and Beryl invited her back to the Beeches for a visit.

Edwina seemed very pleased that they had a guest and had concocted an elaborate luncheon spread out of thin air the moment she arrived home from her meeting. Much to Beryl's astonishment the three of them were seated at the dining room table within a half hour of Edwina's return. Beryl was not sure what had happened at the committee meeting but whatever it was it had lit a fire under her friend.

"We were back at the mining village again yesterday," Edwina said to Alice. "Your Mr. Ecclestone-Smythe was very generous in his contribution to the May Day celebration festivities."

"He isn't generally known to be particularly generous. How did you manage to charm him out of a donation?" Alice asked.

"It was Beryl's doing, of course. She just has that effect on people, especially gentlemen," Edwina said, passing a relish tray to Alice.

"Is he a mean man, Mr. Ecclestone-Smythe?" Beryl asked. "The wealthy ones so often are I have found." Beryl reached for a cheese and pickle sandwich. She still was not in the least used to the sorts of fillings that were so favored on this side of the Atlantic. In fact, she wasn't even sure that what she was tasting was a pickle at all. It was more of a brown jam sort of substance both sweet and sour at the same time and filled with unidentifiable chopped vegetables. Or were they fruits? Beryl had made a habit throughout her life of adventure of not scrutinizing the comestibles too closely. When wandering the desert or a dense jungle it simply wasn't the done thing to offend a gracious host because one assumed she would not like the taste of camel or beetles.

"That's his reputation," Alice said. "He hasn't been willing to part with a shilling for safety gear or to replace broken equipment. In fact it's causing quite a stir amongst the miners, and if he isn't careful he may end up with a strike on his hands." Beryl placed her half-eaten sandwich on her plate and gave Alice her full attention.

"Are there signs of agitation amongst the workers?" Beryl asked. She met Edwina's searching gaze. Trouble at the mine could have something to do with Mr. Cunningham's murder.

"Someone has been leafleting the entire village. I hate to say it but the language and the images on the pamphlets are really very disturbing. I spoke to my Dennis about it. I said it wasn't the sort of thing that children should ever have to see," Alice said.

"Do you have any idea who is responsible for the leafleting?" Edwina asked.

"I don't. There are always rumors of course about who happens to be the most dissatisfied with the working conditions. But I have never seen anyone actually in the act of passing out the leaflets," Alice said.

"Why is the information so disturbing?" Beryl said.

"They're inciting violence. They call the workers to rise up and to do whatever it takes to make conditions fairer for those going down into the mines. They rail against the upper classes and the elevation of profit over people. There are line drawings showing someone who looks a good deal like Mr. Ecclestone-Smythe dangling from a rafter in a mine shaft by his necktie," Alice said.

"That does sound worrisome," Edwina said. "What's the reaction from the miners? Are they in agreement with the sentiment? Is Mr. Ecclestone-Smythe really so unpopular with his employees?"

"The men are glad of the work. Jobs are so hard to come by that they'd be foolish not to be. But they don't like working for a man who so blatantly does not care one whit about their safety. The mines here in Kent are notoriously unstable. They flood easily and the shafts are liable to collapse without warning. Mr. Ecclestone-Smythe could make things safer for the workers if he were of a mind to, but he shows no sign that he is," Alice said. She shook her head. "As a nurse at the village I can tell you some of the injuries are quite severe. We've had men crushed, others have lost limbs. Coughing and chest complaints are simply a way of life."

"It's the same as all over the country," Edwina said. "The unrest has been popping up from one region to the next ever since the men came back from the war. They were supposed to be coming back to a nation worthy of them, one filled with good jobs and opportunities for those who had done so much for their country. Instead, men who spent so long fighting the enemy are finding their own government is an enemy fighting them."

"Is there a sense that things really are going to turn violent at the mine?" Beryl asked. "Or do you think it's all talk, just a way to let off some steam?"

"At first I thought that's all it was, but now I don't know. The leafleting has gotten to be more frequent and the tone is more aggressive. I've even mentioned to Dennis that perhaps we should consider moving on to another mine if he can find the work. But Dennis says it's not likely there will be any openings anywhere else," Alice said.

Beryl heard the distinctive sound of Simpkins' hobnail boots coming along the hallway. The elderly gardener poked his head round the corner of the dining room door, his hat in his hands. In recent weeks Simpkins had developed the habit of stopping in with a question or a concern right around lunchtime. Somehow he always managed to join them for the rest of their meal. Beryl quite enjoyed his company but it had to be said that Edwina did not. She certainly would be unlikely to welcome Simpkins and his muddy boots into her dining room while they had a visitor.

"Yes, Simpkins?" Edwina said. Beryl was surprised at the pleasant tone of Edwina's voice. She would have expected her to be quite curt. "Is there something you require?"

"I wanted to ask if you had decided on the bedding flowers you'd like me to put out in the pond garden." Simpkins said. "I'll need to get a start on that soon if you're to have a decent display come summer." He took several steps into the dining room and turned his head to give Beryl a wink.

"We can discuss it after lunch," Edwina said. "Won't you join us?" Beryl fought back a gasp. Then she realized Edwina might not wish to appear class conscious in front of their guest. Or perhaps she was simply grateful to Simpkins for helping them to get started on their business. Either way she was delighted by this change in her friend's attitude. Edwina indicated the fourth chair at the table and Simpkins took a seat. She then hurried to the china cabinet and pulled out a plate and some cutlery and placed it before Simpkins.

Simpkins helped himself to several sandwiches and tucked in with gusto. He would certainly not have any trouble accepting hospitality in the desert or the jungle. Beryl very much doubted he would be concerned about the contents of his meal, even if he were to be served beetles.

"Mrs. Morley, please allow me to present Albert Simpkins, the gardener here at the Beeches. Simpkins, Mrs. Morley is employed at the Hambley colliery as a nurse in the infirmary and has agreed to help promote the May Day celebration to the rest of the mining village," Edwina said.

"Mrs. Morley and I are already acquainted through her husband and the pigeon races," Simpkins said. "How did the three of you happen to meet? I don't think of you ladies as spending a lot of time over in Hambley." He took a massive bite of one of his sandwiches. Beryl was relieved to see he remembered to chew with his mouth closed. Edwina might become accustomed to servants at her table but Beryl could not imagine her ever tolerating a complete lack of manners.

"We met at a pigeon race during the course of our investigation into Mr. Cunningham's disappearance," Beryl said. "The whole thing was rather exciting."

"Long-distance pigeon racing is bound to get even more exciting still now that Mr. Cunningham's out of the sport," Simpkins said after swallowing.

"Why is that?" Edwina asked.

"Well, now that Mr. Cunningham is dead, there's no real certainty as to who will be coming in second place," Simpkins said, taking another bite of his sandwich.

"Was there ever certainty as to who came in first, second, third, or whatever in the races?" Beryl asked.

Simpkins bobbed his head. "Sometimes Mr. Cunningham would beat Gareth Scott, the greengrocer, but not often. He generally came in second. Now that Cunningham's gone and gotten himself bumped off, there's no telling if second place will go to the vicar or to Dennis Morley. Isn't that so, Mrs. Morley?" Simpkins asked.

"That's what my Dennis says. He was remarking on it last night at tea. It's causing quite a stir amongst the club members, especially those who like to place a wager on the race results," Alice said.

"Why is it that Gareth Scott keeps coming in in first place so frequently?" Edwina asked.

"Dennis says Mr. Scott is convinced it's the diet of fruits and vegetables that he gives to his pigeons that accounts for his incredible results on the course," Alice said. "Would you agree, Mr. Simpkins?"

"I can't rightly say," Simpkins said. "Maybe it's just luck and maybe it's his technique. All I know is that Gareth Scott's pigeons have been pretty much a sure bet for either first or second place since I don't know when."

"You don't happen to know where I might be able to place just such a bet, do you, Simpkins?" Beryl asked. Simpkins shot a look at Edwina whose left eye twitched alarmingly.

"If you're looking to place a wager in Walmsley Parva you'll want to go down to the pub," Simpkins said. "That's where all the betting is done before race day. You can place wagers on the day of the race with people at the starting point too but my advice is to head down to the pub and get your wager in early."

Beryl looked over at Edwina who was doing her best not to appear shocked. "Then that is exactly what I shall do this very evening. I don't suppose you'd like to accompany me, Simpkins?" Beryl asked.

"It would be my pleasure," Simpkins said. "It would be even more so if you are buying."

"You can be sure of it, my dear man. I would consider it fair payment for a good tip," Beryl said. "Shall we say seven o'clock?"

CHAPTER 21

"I've been thinking, Ed, about Mr. Scott the greengrocer," Beryl said as she applied her usual slapdash methods to drying the lunch dishes after Alice and Simpkins had departed. Edwina sometimes wondered if Beryl had had any sort of maternal influence in her life whatsoever. She was aware, more from what Beryl had not said, rather than what she had, that Mr. and Mrs. Helliwell had displayed a notable lack of interest in their only child. In fact, Edwina was inclined to suspect Beryl's desire for celebrity grew from a deep desire for someone to notice her. Still, one would have thought a governess or housekeeper might have fostered some sort of domestic skill during Beryl's formative years. Her friend's complete lack of housekeeping knowledge or ability never ceased to amaze.

"And where have your thoughts taken you?" Edwina asked before realizing that

that sort of open-ended question was likely to take Beryl into places Edwina did not wish to travel.

"The greengrocer, shopping in any form really, is far more your purview than mine. I suggest we split up this afternoon. You could take your shopping basket to the high street and interrogate Mr. Scott on the subject of vegetables while I drive over to the mining village and make some enquiries about the dissatisfaction amongst the workers," Beryl said, clattering a plate down onto a stack in the cupboard. Edwina worriedly cast a glance at the crystal glasses. They had belonged to her grandmother and she had no intention of seeing them smashed to bits. She had started using them as everyday dishes rather than saving them for best as it seemed unlikely she would have a daughter of her own to pass them along to. Even so, that didn't mean she welcomed Beryl's rough treatment of one of her prized possessions. When her finances had gotten into a shocking state the previous autumn she had been humiliatingly forced to sell off many of the bits and bobs previous residents of the family home had collected over the years. Grandmother's goblets were amongst the few treasures she had not considered parting with.

"That seems a very fine idea which plays to each of our strengths. Since it's farther to Hambley than it is to the greengrocer, why don't you head out straightaway? I'll finish up here on my own and depart as soon as I have completed the washing up," Edwina said, relieving Beryl of her kitchen towel. "We can meet back here in time for tea."

Beryl seemed as pleased to be relieved of her kitchen duties as Edwina was for her to desist with them. She rushed down the corridor and Edwina heard the door banging behind her before she had slipped the last goblet into the soapy water.

Crumpet was delighted to finally be allowed to accompany her on the investigation. He pranced about Edwina's feet with such vigor, she had difficulty attaching his lead to his collar. He continued to display enthusiasm all along their walk by rushing ahead to sniff at clumps of flowers or to bark at frisking squirrels. Edwina felt a cheerful, positive glow as she made her way along the high street towards Gareth Scott's establishment, her wide wicker shopping basket dangling from her arm. As she waited for Crumpet to finish sniffing the peeling bark at the base of a river birch she noticed

Gareth Scott exiting his own shop and making straight for the local teashop owned by Minnie Mumford.

She gave Crumpet's lead a gentle tug and corrected course for the Silver Spoon Tearoom. She tied the dog's lead to a lamppost just outside Minnie's eatery and went inside. The heady scent of cinnamon filled the air. Edwina generally did not hold with snacking between meals, but as this was in service of the investigation she decided to make an exception. With a nod to Minnie she brazenly approached the table where Gareth Scott was seated.

"Do you mind if I join you, Mr. Scott?" Edwina said, laying a gloved hand on the back of the chair nearest her. "I do so hate to eat alone." Edwina noticed Minnie's ears lengthening with every word she uttered. While Prudence Rathbone was the biggest gossip in the village she did not outpace Minnie by a great distance. In fact, it was remarked about the village, that the two of them had a friendly rivalry as to who would be the first with any juicy bits of news.

"It would be a pleasure, Miss Davenport, to have some company," Mr. Scott said, scraping his chair back and standing to pull out a seat for her. Minnie approached the table, a wide smile fixed on her eager face.

"I'm surprised to see you here at this time of day, Edwina," she said. "Does anything special bring you into the village today?"

"It was such a lovely day I thought I would take Crumpet out for a stroll. We worked up such an appetite in all our ramblings that I thought I would stop in and enjoy some of your delicious refreshments," Edwina said, hoping to cut off any hope Minnie might have concerning choice tidbits of gossip.

"I'm surprised to see you out of the company of Miss Helliwell. The two of you aren't on the outs, are you? A new business venture can certainly put a strain on any relationship. I remember when I started the tearoom, Mr. Mumford was not always as supportive as he might have been," Minnie said, a small furrow appearing between her greying eyebrows.

"Beryl and I are always in complete accord," Edwina lied. "As a matter of fact, we have found our partnership makes our investigations all the more thorough and efficient. But even the best of friends need not spend every moment of every day together. Have you already ordered, Mr. Scott?" With that Edwina steered the conversation back to the business of the tearoom, placed her own order, and waited for Minnie to disappear into the kitchen before turning the conversation to Mr. Scott's success with his pigeons.

"Speaking of my business venture, it has come to my attention during the course of our investigation that you are extraordinarily successful at racing your pigeons. I had absolutely no idea you were so famous," Edwina said. She noticed Mr. Scott's posture improve under the glow of her praise.

"Well, it's very kind of you to say that, although I shouldn't like to brag. It's true that I've had quite a bit of luck over the last few months," Mr. Scott said.

"My gardener, Simpkins, says that it's rather difficult for anyone to beat you," Edwina said. "He said the amount of success you've had has been remarkable."

"There have been others who've acquitted themselves nicely on the course as well," Mr. Scott said. "The unfortunate Mr. Cunningham and Dennis Morley both managed to oust me from first place now and again."

"Mr. Cunningham won't be jockeying for position anymore though, will he?" Edwina said.

"I suppose not. Although we didn't see eye to eye in all matters, I shall miss the thrill of racing against him," Mr. Scott said, shaking his head.

"It's rumored that you attribute your enormous success to your feeding regime," Edwina said. "I've always believed that a healthy diet can work wonders on all manner of creatures." There was a pause in the conversation as Minnie approached the table with a tray laden with a teapot, cups, and an assortment of teacakes and scones. Edwina assumed Mr. Scott was no more eager for Minnie to eavesdrop upon their conversation than she was herself. Edwina poured tea for the two of them and noticed Mr. Scott waited until an elderly pair of women entered the shop, diverting Minnie's attention, before speaking again.

"What you say is entirely true. Access to a diet rich in fresh produce has made a world of difference in the performance of my birds. It's almost unfair really that I have such an abundance of fruits and veg because of my business, but I suppose one cannot make the field of combat entirely level for all the racers," Mr. Scott said, helping himself to a teacake. "Not that either Cunningham or Morley were all that interested in my technique, as it happened."

"They don't believe that diet makes all the difference?" Edwina said, selecting a currant bun from the pastry plate. All this talk of fruits and vegetables was making her feel even guiltier for her between-meal snacking. Still, she told herself, it was all for a good cause. In for a penny in for a pound, she thought as she reached for the jam pot and slathered her already-decadent treat with some of Minnie's deservedly renowned preserves.

"Cunningham seemed very resistant to the idea that diet could improve the performance of the birds. He felt it was all about the breeding." Mr. Scott took a noisy slurp of his tea before clattering his cup back into the saucer. Edwina noted the topic impassioned her dining companion. Her fingers itched to take out her notebook and jot down her thoughts but she resisted the urge, deciding any such formality might stem the flow of conversation. It would also draw the already bothersome Minnie back to the table like a wasp to a pitcher of lemon squash.

"That would explain his collection of books on the subject of pigeon breeding," Edwina said. "What does Mr. Morley think of your regime?"

"He has said nothing on the subject whatsoever. He has not agreed nor has he told me to my face he believed anything to the contrary. But what you have to understand about Morley is that he's really above his station in our club."

"Above his station?" Edwina asked.

"Indeed. The vicar was insistent that we invite him after hearing from Mr. Cunningham that Morley had a level of experience with the birds that the rest of us did not. If it weren't for that he never would have been allowed to join. The man's a short-distance pigeon racer, no doubt about it," Mr. Scott said. He helped himself to a bun of his own.

"Is that so? How does one know?" Edwina asked.

"He's a miner, isn't he?" Mr. Scott said. "A workingman, not a tradesman or a gentleman. Workingmen are invariably short-distance pigeon racers. They can't afford to do otherwise."

"So Mr. Morley is only a part of the club because of his experience as someone who ran a mobile pigeon loft during the war?" Edwina asked.

"Of course. We heard about Dennis through Cunningham, and the vicar was eager to include him. He thought that it would improve everyone's chances at the races. Considering I continued to win most of the time it hardly seemed useful to me to have him join the club. But I had no real objection, other than the fact that he wasn't quite one of our sort," Mr. Scott said.

Edwina was all the more glad she had been the one to speak with Mr. Scott. She could only imagine Beryl's reaction to his comments. His mention of class distinction would certainly have put her back up. No, it was altogether better for someone with a greater understanding of local sensibilities to handle a man like Mr. Scott.

"What about Mr. Cunningham? Was he the right sort even though he was involved in work at the mine as well?" Edwina asked.

"Cunningham was different because he had a job in the office at the colliery rather than working down in the pit. A bookkeeper is really a sort of professional and he managed to barely squeak by. Not that I thought he was much of a bookkeeper, as well you know," Mr. Scott said. He dabbed at the crumbs clinging to his bushy mustache with a dainty, chintz serviette. Edwina thought, not for the first time, that he put one in mind of a disgruntled walrus with his gleaming bald head and fleshy torso. It was no wonder the other members of his club gave little credence to his dietary recommendations for birds or otherwise.

"I'd hate for anyone to form the wrong impression concerning the nature of your disagreements with Mr. Cunningham," Edwina said pointedly, glancing over at

Minnie. Mr. Scott followed her gaze and nodded slowly. "Perhaps it would be in your best interest to make sure the story was known all about as to where you were when Mr. Cunningham died."

"While I appreciate you thinking of my reputation, as I have no idea when he was killed, how could I possibly say that?" Mr. Scott said.

"To be on the safe side perhaps you should tell me your movements for the day of the race," Edwina said. Mr. Scott nodded. "Would you mind terribly if I took notes? I feel it is important to be sure to get this absolutely right." She would have to risk reticence from Mr. Scott and unabashed curiosity from Minnie if she wished to keep the details straight. Edwina pulled out her trusty notebook and well-sharpened pencil without waiting for an answer. She placed them upon the table between them and gave him an encouraging look.

"The morning of the race I was at the shop receiving the day's quantity of fruits and veg from my suppliers. Then I attended to customers on my own until my boy came in to help," Mr. Scott said, pausing for Edwina to catch up with her scribbling. She nodded and he continued. "After that I took my van over to Blackburn's garage to be seen to. The engine has been playing up a bit lately and I wanted to be sure to have them look at it before something small turns into an expensive repair job."

"Very sensible, I'm sure. What did you do when you left the garage?" Edwina asked. Minnie spotted the notebook and was making a beeline for their table. Mr. Scott noticed her approach and lowered his voice.

"I returned to the shop and spent the rest of the business hours there. My boy can vouch for that. I had my tea at home with my wife and then headed out to the pub for a pint that evening. After that I headed home and went to bed." He snapped his jaw shut as Minnie sidled up to the table. Edwina closed her notebook and returned it to her pocket.

"Interviewing a suspect, are you?" Minnie asked. "Do you have a guilty secret, Mr. Scott?" Minnie turned her practiced gaze on the greengrocer and playfully waggled a finger at him most unbecomingly. Having been the frequent subject of idle gossip herself in the recent past Edwina felt a white lie was in order.

"Mr. Scott was simply giving me the benefit of his wisdom on the subject of animal husbandry. I was enquiring as to whether or not my dog might benefit from an addition of fruits or vegetables to his diet. As Mr. Scott has had so much success raising his pigeons I thought he might be the one to ask," Edwina said. Mr. Scott's eyes widened slightly before he caught himself and gave her a slight nod.

"That's right. I was very flattered that Miss Davenport would look to me for advice," Mr. Scott said. Edwina noticed he lied quite convincingly. She would have to take that into account when considering all he had shared.

"Are you considering racing your dog?" Minnie asked, her eyes widening with the possibility of a story to spread around the village.

"Certainly not," Edwina said. "It's his overall health that prompted me to solicit advice from Mr. Scott. The very idea of dog racing is quite preposterous."

"The idea of you opening a private enquiry agency would have seemed preposterous just a week ago, Edwina. I thought there was every possibility a decision to participate in dog racing was simply another fit of eccentricity on your part." Minnie placed the check on the table squarely in front of Mr. Scott before stomping off.

"I would say your reputation is in a great deal more danger than mine, Miss Davenport," Mr. Scott said.

"I daresay you may be right," Edwina said.

CHAPTER 22

Beryl felt the slightest bit disloyal as she whipped down the country lanes on her way to the village of Hambley. While she thoroughly enjoyed Edwina's company almost all of the time, it felt quite wonderful to open up her automobile full throttle and to really put it through its paces. She took each curve in the road with verve and arrived at the mining village in record time. Once again a gaggle of men and boys clustered around the vehicle and she came to a stop in the center of the village. By the time she had answered their questions and thanked them for their admiring comments, any time that she had saved on the road had been well and truly used up.

She finally managed to make enquiries as to the whereabouts of Dennis Morley. Luckily he had been on an earlier shift and she was told, if he were adhering to his usual routine, he could be found tending to his pigeons on the outskirts of the village. A grizzled old man pointed the way. She thanked him and headed straight for a grassy patch stretched out beyond the small living quarters.

There were quite a number of pigeon lofts clustered together but one seemed more professionally assembled than the others. She guessed it likely that a man with Mr. Morley's experience would be the one in charge of such a thing. It was large, far larger than the one Mr. Cunningham had assembled on his allotment. In fact, it was large enough to look more like a toolshed than a coop. It put Beryl in mind of the potting shed where she had often enjoyed a furtive tipple with Simpkins.

She rapped upon the door and waited for a voice from within to beckon her to enter. When one did so she pressed on the latch and stepped inside. There at the end of the small room sat a man in his twenties. Unlike so many others, he had all his limbs intact and no visible facial disfigurements. Perhaps his work with the pigeons had kept him far enough back to avoid some of the worst of the fighting.

"My name is Beryl Helliwell. I'm looking for Mr. Dennis Morley," she said, taking a step forward.

"Then you found him. Aren't you one of the detectives who found Lionel Cunningham's body?" Mr. Morley asked.

"As a matter of fact I am. I also happen to be acquainted with your wife," Beryl said.

"My Alice told me all about you and your business partner, Miss Davenport. She's all excited about getting the mining community involved with the May Day celebration. Are you here about that?" Mr. Morley asked. "Or are you here in your capacity as an adventuress? Do you have some new lark planned involving coal mines?"

"As intriguing as your suggestion is, I'm here to speak to you about your involvement with the long-distance pigeon racing club over in Walmsley Parva," Beryl said. "Do you mind if I sit down?" She pointed to an upturned milk crate. Mr. Morley nodded and she took a seat.

"What is it you want to know?" Mr. Morley asked. "Is this about Cunningham, because I already told that police constable everything I know about him."

"Actually, I'm far more interested in Mr. Scott's winning streak," Beryl said. "I wondered if you had any thoughts as to what explained his remarkable amount of success on the race course?"

Mr. Morley leaned back and crossed his

arms over his chest. The birds in their nesting boxes cooed and ruffled their feathers.

"I have a few thoughts as to what might explain his recent number of wins, but they aren't too flattering," Mr. Morley said.

"It sounds like you are a man with a story to tell. I make a very good listener," Beryl said. She reached into a pocket on the inside of her jacket and pulled out a silver flask. The flask had been a gift from one of her ex-husbands — she couldn't remember which — and it had helped her to make friends in many far-flung locations. Which was ironic, she thought, when one considered how unfriendly the state of most of her marriages had become. She waggled the flask at Mr. Morley who leaned forward and took it with a smile.

He unscrewed the cap and took a long swig before passing it back to Beryl. She capped it but left it out in open view in case he might need further encouragement to share his thoughts.

"I've been racing pigeons for a long time. My father raced them, short-distance, mind you, when I was a lad. I put as much stock as the next man in the value of a good diet for the birds, maybe even more, considering," he said.

"Considering what, exactly?" Beryl asked.

"Men like Gareth Scott haven't sacrificed for their birds the way workingmen and their families have done down through the years. Many's the night the family went to bed hungry so that my father would have enough money to buy food for his birds," Mr. Morley said.

"And your mother let him?" Beryl asked. It wasn't a criticism; not really. She hadn't any real maternal instinct herself but she was well aware she was an anomaly and that most mothers were quite insistent that their children should be fed. Everywhere in the world she had traveled she had noticed the same behavior, women doing without to make sure their children had all that they needed and quite often things they simply wanted. She had seen cases of abuse, naturally, but she had never encountered pigeons getting a meal when the children were forced to do without.

"Do you know anything about the mines, Miss Helliwell? Anything besides what you read in the newspapers about strikes and coal shortages?" Mr. Morley crossed his arms over his chest. She was in danger of offending him. If she wanted the investigation to stay on track she would have to shore up the rapport. Sometimes she had found the sharing of a confidence was required to cement a new connection. "Do you know about what a life in the mines does to a man's soul?"

"I confess, I know very little about them. I shouldn't like it to get around but I have something of a horror of going into spaces below ground and I cannot bear thinking about it. Cowardly, I know, especially when speaking with a man such as yourself who has served his country bravely." Beryl reached for the flask and took a long tug before setting it down once more.

"But you're known for your steely nerves and risk-taking," Mr. Morley said. He dropped his arms down from their defensive position and leaned forward with an astonished look on his face.

"I like to go fast and I like to go up. I have no interest whatsoever in descending underground. So I am absolutely certain that you will have my respect no matter what the state of your soul," Beryl said. Considering the surroundings and the whiskey, she felt the conversation had taken an unexpectedly ecclesiastical turn.

"I shan't burden you with the details of the dark or the damp or the sense of panic many miners feel until they become accustomed to the conditions. What matters most to understand is how it changes the

251

heart to be so cut off from the natural world. No grass, no insects, no sunlight or refreshing breeze," Mr. Morley said.

"It sounds bleak beyond measure," Beryl said. She felt a trickle of perspiration slither down the back of her neck and beneath her collar.

"That isn't the worst of it," Mr. Morley said. "The life of a miner is filled with hard labor and uncertainty about his wages and his health. What isn't uncertain is that he will spend his days covered in coal dust and has no claim to distinction in his own eyes or that of anyone else. He's just another strong back, just another pair of hands. And he is made to remember he should be grateful for the job despite all that."

"It sounds like a sort of a prison," Beryl said.

"It is. The men all need a manner of escape and for many of them it is found in the pub where they drink the grocery money and then return home to beat their wives and children."

"Was your father such a man?" Beryl asked.

"No, that's just it. My father took a notion to try racing pigeons. It gave him something to think about, to plan. It gave him a way to be a winner in a world that did not generally see him as one. My mother, and all of us children too, were willing to do whatever it took to help him to have that chance." Mr. Morley smiled. "Mother said if it meant missing a meal a few times each week to keep him out of the pubs she was more than happy to oblige."

"It sounds as though you were fond of your parents," Beryl said.

"I still am. My father taught me everything I know about keeping birds healthy under harsh conditions and about racing them, too."

"Is that one of the reasons you ended up in charge of a mobile pigeon loft during the war years?" Beryl asked. It was a touchy thing talking to a man about his time in the service. Some of them were eager to share their stories. Others clammed up so tightly you couldn't have pried their lips open with an iron bar. Or a flask, no matter its contents. She held her breath waiting to see what sort of man Dennis Morley was.

"That's right. The pigeons were a vital part of our communication system and they needed people who were familiar with keeping them to serve in that unit. In a lot of ways I was very lucky. I got to keep doing something that reminded me of home, but I still felt as though I was contributing an important service to the effort," Mr. Morley said, reaching for the flask again. Beryl obliged.

"So you are in a position to have a trustworthy opinion on what goes into making a champion racer?" Beryl said.

"That's right. It might sound like bragging but it simply is the truth." Mr. Morley reached over to a window well and laid hold of a pair of small books. Beryl squinted across the loft to read their spines. *Pigeon Husbandry and You* and *A Breeder's Guide to Champion Racers* both looked well thumbed. "Anything I don't already know, I read up on."

"Very commendable. And you feel capable of offering an opinion on Mr. Scott's chances of winning with such regularity?" Beryl asked.

"I know birds and I know when something just doesn't add up. Gareth Scott's claims that his birds keep winning because of the feed is one of those things that just doesn't make sense," he said.

"You don't believe what the birds eat has anything to do with performance?" Beryl asked.

"I'm not saying the feed makes no difference. Everybody wants to provide their birds with the best that they can afford. But no amount of fruits and vegetables explains his recent string of wins. I venture to say my birds are just as well fed as his but I keep coming in second or third place most of the time."

"I heard that second and third place almost always went back and forth between you and Mr. Cunningham," Beryl said. "Was Mr. Cunningham just as suspicious of Mr. Scott as you seem to be?"

"He was. The two of them argued about it at the last meeting. I think that's the reason Gareth accused Lionel of fiddling the books."

"You think that Mr. Scott was feeling defensive and wanted to change the scrutiny to someone else?" she said.

"That's the impression I had, yes. He wanted to take the spotlight off his own behavior," he said. "It worked, too. Everybody took a keen interest in what Gareth had to say." One of the pigeons took a notion to leave its nesting box and fly across the loft to a roost on the opposite side. It soared just above her head and Beryl thought fleetingly of Cyril the parrot.

"Mr. Scott told Miss Davenport and me that he questioned Mr. Cunningham's bookkeeping. Even if you suspected him of trying to point fingers elsewhere, do you

255

think there was any truth in his concerns?" she asked.

"Maybe I am blinded by envy, but to tell the truth, I wouldn't believe a thing Gareth Scott had to say. If he told me water was wet I'd check it out for myself."

"Did you know that the funds for the pigeon racing club disappeared at the same time Mr. Cunningham went missing?" Beryl asked. "Surely that has to make you wonder if Mr. Scott was right."

"It also might mean that Gareth set the whole thing up on purpose. He might've planted the seed of accusation at the meeting and then taken the money himself," Mr. Morley said.

Beryl had not considered that Mr. Scott might have helped himself to the club funds. It was possible, she supposed, considering he was in a position of leadership in the organization. She would have to ask Edwina what she thought of that possibility. Surely she would have an opinion as to the quality of Mr. Scott's character and the likelihood that he would take money that did not belong to him. Another thought occurred to her.

"Do you think it's possible that not only did Mr. Scott take the money and make it appear that Mr. Cunningham had stolen it, but also that he killed Mr. Cunningham to cover up the theft?" Beryl said.

"I wouldn't put anything past Gareth Scott. I haven't liked him since I first laid eyes on him. I know he's cheating somehow and I know he's eager to be in charge of the club. I met guys like that during the war. People who just couldn't get enough of bossing others around and being in charge. As the war went on, people who never would have been considered for leadership in the early days ended up promoted. Some of them were able to rise to the occasion and lead the men beneath them in ways that everyone appreciated. Then there were others, like Gareth Scott, who made things worse for everybody," Mr. Morley said.

Beryl had heard things like this from other soldiers. But she had also heard that leadership was often inept at the beginning of the war, too. So many things were different before the fighting had broken out. The old class structures automatically made people of the upper classes favored by those in charge for leadership positions. Many of them had no qualifications whatsoever outside of the accident of birth. While Beryl was willing to believe most had the best interests of their men at heart, she had no illusions that meant they were capable of seeing to those interests. There were no two ways about it; the entire war had been hell on earth. It was no wonder Mr. Morley had no patience with reminders of those dark days. Beryl had things she'd rather forget herself and her own memories of people of a sort she'd never like to encounter again.

"It sounds like you really despise Mr. Scott," Beryl said.

"He doesn't like me either. He made it very clear from the beginning he thought my presence in the club was bringing the whole thing low," Mr. Morley said.

"What do you mean? I should've thought the club would benefit from having an expert of your caliber as a member," Beryl said.

"You'd think so, wouldn't you? But I'm not the right sort. I come from a working-man's background and that's just not good enough to mix with the likes of him," Mr. Morley said.

"You're not good enough to mingle with the man who sells turnips and potatoes to his fellow villagers?" Beryl said. Truly, she would never understand the nuances of the English class system. How anyone would come to the conclusion that being a shop-keeper was more worthy of respect than helping to keep the country fueled with coal she would never understand. She certainly would have thought Mr. Morley's service to his country would have leveled the social playing field.

"No, I am not, according to him. Nor the pinched-faced woman at the post office neither," he said.

"Prudence Rathbone?" Beryl asked. Mr. Morley nodded and rolled his eyes. "I shouldn't have thought she would have had anything to do with racing of any sort. She doesn't strike me as the sporting type."

"Nor me, but she has the most important job of anyone in a race as far as some people are concerned," Mr. Morley said. "She's the keeper of the keys."

"The keeper of the keys? What a romantic-sounding title for such a pedestrian sort of woman," Beryl said. "What does she do for the club?"

"It's all right there in the name. Miss Rathbone keeps charge of all the keys to the pigeon clocks. She makes sure no one can fiddle with the time their birds arrived back at the loft."

"I see," Beryl said. Although, truthfully, she did not. But she heard an edge slipping into Mr. Morley's voice, and he kept darting glances at the door. She might need to speak with him again and it would not do to be remembered as someone who droned on and on for too long. "You've given me a lot to think about. I appreciate your time." Beryl held out the flask a final time. Mr. Morley shook his head.

"It's the middle of the day and I've reached my limit. I hope you find out what happened to Lionel. He may have been one of the bosses, but he was always good to me." Mr. Morley stood and Beryl took the hint that it was indeed time to go.

She got to her feet and gave a final glance round the small shed. Mr. Morley kept things tidy. Bins with lids and bales of clean straw stood neatly pressed back against the far wall. A wooden workbench ran along the end that had been behind Beryl's back while she had been seated. A tin lunch pail and a pocketknife sat on the bench. Next to them she spotted what looked to be a stack of leaflets.

Hoping not to appear too curious, she took a step forward to get a better look at what was printed upon them. Sure enough, there was a line drawing on the front of a man hanging by his necktie from a rafter in a mine shaft. It was just as Alice Morley had described. She wondered if Mr. Morley had collected the leaflets to help ease his wife's concerns and had simply not disposed of them. Or, she wondered, was he the one responsible for passing them out in the first place?

Mr. Morley cleared his throat loudly and startled the birds that fluttered and flitted about the room. She was quite certain he had done it on purpose. He yanked open the door and held it for her. His expression was just a touch less friendly than it had been only moments before. She headed back to her automobile with a great deal more to think about than when she arrived.

CHAPTER 23

Beryl had taken her usual spot in the comfortable chair closest to the drinks tray. Edwina sat on the sofa with her knitting needles clicking soothingly through some smooth soft wool. She found that the rhythm of the knitting helped her to think. And the conversations of the day had given her a great deal to think about.

"Months ago I never would've suspected Gareth Scott of being involved in anything more nefarious than passing off produce that was days older than he said it was," Edwina said. "Now I feel much more jaded about the character of all my neighbors. The events of last autumn pulled my rose-colored glasses from my eyes and crushed them underfoot."

"So you agree it's possible that Gareth Scott stole the club's funds as well as the birds and then murdered Mr. Cunningham?" Beryl asked. She took a sip from her half-empty glass.

"I'm sorry to say that I think we must consider him a suspect. And a strong one at that. During my conversation with him at the teashop I came to realize he is a fairly accomplished liar. And it sounds as though your conversation with Mr. Morley sheds an even more unflattering light on his character and his motivations," Edwina said.

Crumpet raised his head and bolted from his wicker basket and ran down the hall barking loudly. Edwina started to get up but Beryl waved her off and headed out the door to see what the fuss was about. She returned a moment later with Miss Chilvers in tow. Mr. Ecclestone-Smythe's secretary looked far less sure of herself standing in Edwina's parlor then she had ruling the roost at the colliery office.

"I'm sorry to interrupt your evening, Miss Davenport, but I felt as though I couldn't sleep tonight if I didn't speak with you and Miss Helliwell," Miss Chilvers said as she took a seat in the second overstuffed chair. Crumpet seemed to sense Miss Chilvers was not Edwina's favorite person and he came to sit by his mistress's feet. Edwina reached down and patted him on his loyal head. Then she took her knitting needles back up, determined to look at ease.

263

"It is our business to expect the unexpected," Edwina said. "How can we help you?"

Miss Chilvers cleared her throat and looked down at her lap as though looking for the answer in her clasped hands. She lifted her gaze and directed it at Edwina.

"I have not been entirely honest with you about the relationship between Mr. Cunningham and myself. The fact is we were utterly and completely, hopelessly in love. Only two days before he disappeared he asked me to marry him and I accepted. I could not let him go to his grave without doing everything in my power to assist with finding who killed him," Miss Chilvers said. She gave a sniff and fished a lace-trimmed handkerchief from her pocket. She dabbed daintily at her eyes before glancing at Beryl.

"The last few days must have been very difficult for you," Edwina said. "You have my condolences on your loss."

"Thank you very much. You are the only ones who know and it's been very difficult keeping up the pretense that we were nothing more than colleagues," Miss Chilvers said.

"Do you have any information to share with us that you think may identify who killed him?" Beryl said.

"I should not like to cast suspicion un-necessarily but I feel that it would be wrong for me to withhold something I know," Miss Chilvers said. "You see, the fact is, Mr. Ecclestone-Smythe lied to you when he said that he and Lionel were on good terms." She dabbed at her eyes again with her hand-kerchief.

"So Mr. Cunningham and your employer did not get along as well as we've been led to believe?" Edwina said.

"They had been on very good terms when I first came to work at the colliery. But in the last month or so things have become very tense. The two of them would lower their voices or stop talking altogether when-ever I came into the room," Miss Chilvers said.

"Did they seem to be arguing?" Beryl asked.

"As they were whispering, it was difficult to make out the content of their conversa-tion. But from their facial expressions and hand gestures I would say the exchanges could not be described as friendly. There was definitely a change in the atmosphere in the office," Miss Chilvers said.

"Did you ask Mr. Cunningham about the alteration in their relationship?" Edwina asked.

"I hated to do so at first because I thought perhaps I was imagining things. When I finally did ask, Lionel became quite cross with me and said he didn't like to discuss work during what little time we had to spend together outside of the office. But the day before Lionel disappeared he and Mr. Ecclestone-Smythe had a tremendous argument right there in the office. At that point it was impossible to ignore that something was wrong," Miss Chilvers said.

"Why was it impossible?" Beryl asked. "Did the argument take place in front of you?"

"No, they were both in Mr. Ecclestone-Smythe's office with the door closed. But their voices kept escalating to the point that I heard the last thing Lionel said to Mr. Ecclestone-Smythe."

"And what was it they were arguing about?" Beryl asked.

"I don't know what the argument was actually about because as I said the door was closed. But I did hear Lionel shout just before he came out of Mr. Ecclestone-Smythe's office. There was a banging noise too although I'm not sure which man was responsible for that. When Lionel came out of the office he slammed the door behind him. I asked him what was wrong but he refused to tell me. He said he didn't want to put me in an uncomfortable position by sharing what he knew," Miss Chilvers said.

"So you have no idea what was said between the two of them," Edwina asked.

"All I know is that when I asked Lionel if he thought he was likely to lose his position on account of the argument, he just laughed. He said Mr. Ecclestone-Smythe could not possibly get rid of him because he knew where all the bodies were buried."

Beryl looked over at Edwina and cocked an eyebrow. It seemed their suspect list was growing by leaps and bounds. Considering what happened to Mr. Cunningham, she wondered if it was possible any of those bodies were literal rather than figurative.

"You certainly did the right thing in coming to us. I'm sure it was very difficult to cast suspicion upon your employer," Edwina said. "We will take your concerns into consideration as we pursue our investigation."

"You won't let Mr. Ecclestone-Smythe know that I'm the one who told you they didn't get along, will you?" Miss Chilvers said.

"We make it our policy not to share the source of our information unless absolutely necessary," Beryl said. "People would hardly continue to come to us if we went squealing every time we discovered something new. Isn't that right, Edwina?"

"Assuredly that is the case," Edwina said. Miss Chilvers stood and took her leave of them. As she laid aside her knitting and watched Miss Chilvers depart, Edwina felt a vague sense of disquiet. She could not help but wonder about the young woman's story. She was not sure if her hesitation in accepting it was founded in her excellent skills at detecting lies or in her dislike of the woman for other reasons. She was still pondering when Beryl returned with her coat draped over her arm.

"It's been quite a day for adding to our list of suspects," Beryl said.

"Did you believe her story?" Edwina asked.

"About which part of it?" Beryl said. "That she and Mr. Cunningham were in love? Or that he and Mr. Ecclestone-Smythe were on the outs?"

"About any of it," Edwina said. "It may have been the truth. And then again she may be interested in pointing suspicion elsewhere. As Mr. Ecclestone-Smythe's secretary she would be in a position to know a great deal about his business. I'm having trouble believing Mr. Cunningham was

268

more acquainted with any irregularities than she was."

"We shall have to do some more digging. Which is what I'm about to do right now." Beryl glanced at the clock on the mantelpiece then slipped her arms into her coat. "If I leave immediately I'll be just in time to meet with Simpkins." Edwina reached for her knitting once more. The idea of Beryl spending time at the pub was hard to accept. The notion that her friend intended to go out carousing with the gardener was best not to even consider.

CHAPTER 24

While Beryl had found many things about the slow pace of life in Walmsley Parva difficult to adjust to, she found that a walk to the pub was not one of them. The investigation had invigorated her no end and as she found herself filled with restless energy, she decided to walk into the village rather than to take her automobile out for an evening of gallivanting. Besides, while she intended to keep a clear head, she was well aware that Edwina had momentarily abandoned her knitting and was peeping out the window at her as if not convinced of her good intentions.

As she strolled into the village, she felt a certain connectedness to her surroundings she still found startling. After all the years she'd spent gallivanting round the globe looking for adventure, she was surprised to find the one that had eluded her for so long, the adventure of being part of the community, was finally within her reach. Although it had been a strange adjustment, she was very glad she had made it. Just as she was beginning to chafe a bit at the mundane routine in Walmsley Parva, the opportunity to begin a detective business provided an effective antidote for any restlessness stirring up inside her.

She pushed open the door of the pub and stepped inside. The low ceilings with their darkened beams and the long bar with the brass rail along its front proclaimed this to be an English country pub to anyone who entered. It was the purview, by and large, of men, and Beryl had long flourished in such environments. She looked around the room for Simpkins. He sat in a far corner tucked up in what she assumed was his regular booth. He gave her a nod of acknowledgment and lifted his mostly empty glass. She strode up to the bar and ordered a pint for Simpkins and a half pint for herself.

She carried the glasses to the table and slid in beside the elderly gardener. He took a long swig before wiping the foam that clung to his mustache with the back of his hand.

"So, is your bookie here?" Beryl asked. Simpkins glanced around the room and his gaze landed on a completely bald, wiry man sitting at a table close to the bar. Two other men sat at the table with him and Beryl noticed one of them pushing an envelope across the table.

"That's him. Chester White. He's not all that keen on doing business with strangers, but if you bought him a drink and told him your name he might make an exception," Simpkins said.

"I don't suppose you could make the introduction?" Beryl said. "After all, that's what I thought I was meeting you here for, to make things easier." Beryl reached over and tapped on Simpkins' glass of beer.

"So you weren't just being friendly-like when you invited me here?" Simpkins said.

"I'm always friendly with you, Simpkins, but business is business. And as this business was your suggestion in the first place, I should think you would be eager for us to succeed." Beryl took a tiny sip of her beer. She did her best not to pull a face. An ability to choke the stuff down was an asset in many circumstances and she had trained herself to do it. But beer had never been one of her pleasures.

"Of course I want you to succeed. There's nothing I'd like more than for Miss Edwina to be happy. That one's always had a fine head on her shoulders and it's been a cry-ing shame to see her shut up in the house, cleaning, cooking, and taking care of her mother. It's one of the reasons I argue with her about the garden. It riles her up and gives her something to think about. As soon as I heard about this problem of the vicar's I immediately thought it was just the sort of puzzle that the two of you could get your teeth into," Simpkins said.

Beryl noticed that his face looked a bit flushed as he took another long draw on his beer. She knew that Simpkins had a heart of gold underneath his grimy and wizened exterior. She just hadn't realized that he knew it, too.

"I see we are in complete agreement, Simpkins," Beryl said. "I've long thought it a travesty that someone like Edwina has been so discouraged from exercising her gifts and talents."

"Her mother and I, rest her soul, always got along on every subject except that of Miss Edwina. Mrs. Davenport treated me more like a friend than like a servant. We grew up together, you see. My father worked as a gardener before me at the Beeches and he'd take me with him to work. I knew Mrs. Davenport long before that was her name. That girl could climb trees like nobody's business. The things she got up to before her mother sent her off to finishing school would inspire admiration from even you, Miss Beryl."

"Have you ever told Edwina any of this?" Beryl asked.

"It seemed disloyal to her mother to tell her secrets. If Mrs. Davenport didn't see fit to tell her daughter about her wanton ways when she was a girl, it certainly wasn't for me to speak up about it," Simpkins said. "I think too much of her memory to do that." Beryl was not quite sure what to say. She had little practical experience with mothers and felt the silence stretch out between them. The two men that had been sitting at the table with the bookie scraped back their chairs and got to their feet. It was the opening she had been looking for.

"Are you going to introduce me or not?" Beryl said.

"I'll head on over to Chester's table while you fetch another pint," Simpkins said. She slid out of the booth and sidled up to the bar. She looked over her shoulder and watched as Simpkins took a seat at Chester White's table. She asked the publican for another round for Chester along with another pint for Simpkins. She carried the glasses to the table and Simpkins turned his gapped-tooth grin in her direction. She placed the drinks in front of the two men and sat in the chair next to Simpkins without waiting for an invitation.

"I was wondering if I was ever going to get around to meeting you," Chester said. "As it happens, I've been a little offended that you haven't placed a bet with me before now. Rumor has it that you're quite a gambler."

"Mostly I bet on card games because I prefer a sure thing. I'm a very good card player," Beryl said. Chester arched an eyebrow.

"So what brings you to me? I'm not in the business of setting up card games. I take bets on sporting events," Chester said. He turned to Simpkins. "I thought you said she was interested in doing a little business."

"I am. But as I said, I'm only interested in sure things. Simpkins tells me that placing a bet on Gareth Scott in the upcoming pigeon race is certain to pay off," Beryl said. "Or have I been misinformed?" Chester ran his finger along the column of the ledger in front of him. He paused about a third of the way down the sheet.

"You can place a bet on Gareth Scott. It's a pretty safe bet. It doesn't pay off very well though," Chester said. "You know that's how it works, right? The more certain the bet, the lower the payoff?"

"I am familiar with the concept of odds. Which wager has the best ones? I understood that there might be a change in the favorite for second place now that Mr. Cunningham won't be participating in the race," Beryl said. Chester nodded slowly up and down, the low light in the pub bouncing off the gleaming baldness of his head.

"You're well informed. There has had to be some adjustment this week over the previous ones. Dennis Morley is the favorite now for second place. That would be a pretty sure thing, too," Chester said. "The odds aren't as good as they might've been last week but they're better than putting your money on Gareth Scott."

"Are you suggesting that might be a good course of action?" Beryl asked.

"I never make suggestions, missus. I'm not in the business of helping you to win big. There must be something in the air," Chester said. He threw back the rest of the whiskey then banged the glass on the table. "That's why I don't like doing business with new people. You all ask the same foolish questions." Beryl signaled to the publican for another round for Simpkins and Chester.

"Have you had a lot of new customers

lately?" Simpkins asked. "I shouldn't have thought that was too likely."

Chester paused long enough that Beryl feared he wouldn't answer. At length he cleared his throat. "I've had a lot more new customers since the Hambley mine started employing all those men for the pits. To tell you the truth, I feel a little bit guilty every time I take their money. They're so poorly paid and they all seem to have multiple mouths to feed," Chester said.

"I think of you as more of a man who provides a friendly service than somebody who helps people get in over their heads," Simpkins said. A serving girl with a cascade of blond curls tumbling down her back arrived at the table and placed the fresh round of drinks in front of them.

"That's just it. That's how I think of myself. I make a little money at this business but mostly it's for the fun of it. It's not my only job after all," Chester said.

"Chester here is a farrier during the day. He just does this of an evening as a way to pass the time," Simpkins said.

"I was speaking with somebody over at the mining village today about the pigeon races and the conditions of the pit," Beryl said. "It sounds as though those guys really are having it rough. I can imagine that some of them would be desperate enough to put all the money they could get their hands on down on a sure bet."

"You were over at Hambley?" Chester said. "Who were you talking to?"

"Why do you want to know?" Beryl said.

"You said you were talking to them about the pigeon races. Did you pick up any hot tips? Is that why you're in here for the first time asking to place a bet?" Chester asked.

"Maybe. I was over there speaking with Dennis Morley," Beryl said. "He had some very interesting things to say about getting the best out of his birds."

"You sure do get around, don't you?" Chester said. He whistled. "Anything you like to tell me about what he said?"

"I suppose that depends on whether or not you have anything to share with me."

"What did you have in mind?" Chester asked. "I can't go giving out the sort of information that would give you an edge on my other customers."

"I just wondered if you had any reason to believe there might be something a little fishy about how sure these bets were," Beryl said. Chester's eyes widened and he drained his glass in one fell swoop once again. Beryl wondered how long he'd been at it before she arrived at the pub.

"Constable Gibbs was in here asking the same question earlier this evening," Chester said. "Why are so many women interested in wagering all of a sudden?"

"I suppose the police think Mr. Cunningham's murder may well be connected to his participation in pigeon racing. If anything is not on the up and up with the betting, it might help to explain what happened to him," Beryl said.

"I don't want to have anything to do with something like that," Chester said. He got to his feet. "I gotta go see a man about a horse." Beryl watched him as he staggered towards the back of the pub and disappeared through a small door. She reached across the table and started to pick up the ledger.

"Don't let anybody else see you looking at that," Simpkins said. She nodded and slid it across the table towards herself without lifting it. She spun it around and quickly perused the list of names and the bets placed written in small neat handwriting in the ledger.

"It looks like Gareth Scott likes to bet on himself. So did Mr. Cunningham. I don't see Dennis Morley's name anywhere," Beryl said. She turned back to an earlier page in the ledger. Look at this." She pointed to an entry dated the day of Mr. Cunningham's disappearance.

"What's so special about that bet?" Simpkins asked.

"It's placed on the day Mr. Cunningham disappeared. Does Chester only take bets at the pub in the evening?" Beryl asked.

"As far as I know. Like I said, he works as a farrier during the day and wouldn't have time to do it unless he happened to run into somebody, while he was shooing a horse, who wanted to place a wager. I suppose that's possible," Simpkins said.

"Would he have been likely to be taking bets first thing in the morning? Would he have been taking them before Mr. Cunningham would have been heading off to the race?" Beryl asked.

"Not bloody likely," Simpkins said. "You see the way the man drinks. You're lucky to see him away from his cottage before noontime any given day. I'd never be willing to bet on him being awake and on the move as early as Lionel Cunningham would have gone missing. Why does it matter?"

"This bet is for the exact amount that's gone missing from the pigeon racing club treasury. And it was placed on the day Lionel Cunningham disappeared," Beryl said. "And look who is the one who placed it." She placed her finger beneath the name written neatly in the ledger.

"Martin Haynes," Simpkins said. "Who's that?"

"Martin Haynes just happens to be the man seen arguing with Lionel Cunningham down by the river the day before he died. He's one of the miners over at the Hambley pit," Beryl said.

"That doesn't look too good for him, does it?" Simpkins asked. "Most miners wouldn't have that kind of money." Beryl shook her head and then another thought occurred to her. She flipped back through the ledger quickly and spotted other bets placed for much smaller amounts by Martin Haynes. She felt her heart beginning to pound and her ears beginning to buzz. Excitement always made her feel as though a hive of bees had taken up residence in her skull. She turned the ledger towards Simpkins and called his attention to Martin's wagers.

"He didn't, generally. Not only that, there is something else that is different about this particular bet." Beryl pointed at the name on all his previous bets. "Until his last bet he only wagered on Mr. Cunningham." She turned the ledger back to the page with Martin's most recent bet.

"His last one is on Dennis Morley," Simpkins said.

"What do you think made him switch? He had done fairly well over time by betting on Mr. Cunningham." Beryl asked, "You don't suppose he knew Mr. Cunningham's racing days were over when he put down his money, do you?"

"If he was the one who killed him it would explain it," Simpkins said.

"That's just what I am thinking," Beryl said. "But we still have no idea why he would have reason to want to kill Mr. Cunningham in the first place. Surely not to steal from him and place a safer bet?"

"A man with the type of financial trouble most of the miners face might be sorely tempted over such a sum. I can't say no one would do such a thing. Besides, a lot of these young fellers came back from the war with a different outlook on right and wrong. And even more of them have temperaments that have been severely altered. He may have simply lost his temper over something and lashed out violently. He wouldn't be the only one." Simpkins elbowed her in the ribs and Beryl noticed Chester staggering back towards them, tucking his shirt into his trousers. She quickly turned the ledger around to face Chester's chair and slid it across the table.

"So are you ready to place your bet?" Chester said, easing into his chair. "I have other clients waiting." He gestured towards a group of men clustered around the bar.

"I should like to put five pounds on Dennis Morley to win," Beryl said. She was gratified to see the look of surprise upon his face. She had always believed in making grand gestures.

"Five pounds? Are you sure you want to do that?" Chester asked.

"I thought you weren't in the business of giving advice," Beryl said.

"It's your money. I'll put you down for five pounds," Chester said. Beryl reached into her coat pocket and pulled out the bills. She slid them across the table and watched as he added them to his greasy envelope already bulging with cash. She got to her feet and Simpkins followed.

When they were out of earshot Simpkins took hold of her elbow and leaned towards her ear. The smell of his beer breath reached her nose and made her glad she had a great deal of practice in encountering a wide variety of harsh conditions.

"You're not going to tell Miss Edwina what you just did, are you?" Simpkins asked.

"Why would I not?" Beryl asked.

"Miss Edwina doesn't think much of

283

wagering under any circumstances. Even in a friendly game of bridge she only wagers with matchsticks. She won't be any too happy to find you've spent so much of your company's earnings on something so foolish as a bet on a pigeon race," Simpkins said.

"I would not dream of keeping something like this from Edwina. Besides, Simpkins, like I said, I only place bets on sure things," Beryl said. "I have a feeling before the next race, Mr. Scott will find his comeuppance, leaving Mr. Morley in a fine position to win."

CHAPTER 25

Edwina still was not used to the sound of the telephone ringing in the front hallway. It happened rarely, and to her ears it seemed very shrill. Her father had refused to have one installed during his lifetime and it wasn't until after he had passed away that her mother had found the one consolation for her grief by having it put in. She hurried towards the source of the ringing and found Beryl had gotten there first.

"Certainly we can do that. Where would you like to meet?" Beryl asked. "Ten o'clock it is. We'll see you there." Beryl replaced the receiver and turned to Edwina.

"Who was it?" Edwina asked.

"Mrs. Ecclestone-Smythe. She would like a status update on the case. I agreed to meet her this morning on the village green. She would prefer that it looks as though we simply ran into each other there," Beryl said.

"But that's out in the open. Won't she be

concerned about her husband hearing that she was meeting with us?" Edwina asked.

"That's the genius of it. Who would expect us to be conducting a secretive meeting in public view?" Beryl said. "Our client is far cleverer than I have given her credit for."

"I suppose I could take my marketing basket and Crumpet as though I were going about my usual business," Edwina said. "I had intended to stop in to do a little shopping this morning anyway."

"Excellent. I'll join you as if we were simply out running errands. But we should hurry if we are to arrive on time. It's nearly nine-thirty already," Beryl said.

They arrived on the village green a few minutes before the appointed time. Edwina had had the foresight to add some dried bread to her marketing basket. She and Beryl stood scattering crumbs for a flock of ducks that made the pond in the center of the green their home when Mrs. Ecclestone-Smythe approached, appearing to be surprised to encounter them.

"Good morning, ladies," their client said. "What a lovely day to take a stroll. Would you care to join me for a walk around the pond? I see a little bench on the other side." Edwina picked up her basket and she and Beryl accompanied Mrs. Ecclestone-Smythe to the far side of the pond. They were still within sight of everyone who might pass by, but Edwina was pleased to note they did not seem to be conducting an assignation.

Mrs. Ecclestone-Smythe dropped onto the bench impatiently. "What news do you have about my jewelry?" she asked.

"We have searched Mr. Cunningham's desk drawers at the office and found nothing. The jewels were not found upon his person according to Constable Gibbs. We also know that they were not in his boardinghouse room," Edwina said. "Additionally, we thoroughly searched Mr. Cunningham's pigeon loft. The jewels were not there either."

"So what you're telling me is you know all the places my jewels are not?" Mrs. Ecclestone-Smythe said. The scowl on her face said it all. They were not making a favorable impression on their new client.

"What we have done is to eliminate the obvious possibilities," Beryl said. "We have also turned up some interesting bits of information as the investigation has gotten under way. We have a possible lead on someone who may have either harmed Mr. Cunningham to take money from him, which could indicate that person also helped himself to your jewelry."

"Who is this person?" Mrs. Ecclestone-Smythe said.

"It would not be in your best interest to be burdened by such knowledge. If this person is not involved in any wrongdoing it could make your interactions with him quite uncomfortable in the future," Edwina said.

"I suppose you're right," Mrs. Ecclestone-Smythe said. "Are there any other leads you are following? I'm getting quite desperate to retrieve my property. I'm sure that my husband is going to be wondering what happened to the jewelry before long. He's not the sort of man who doesn't take notice of such things."

"Are you in the habit of wearing them all the time?" Edwina asked. "I should think jewelry that is worth as much money as yours is would be something one saved for special occasions rather than for trips to the market or the bookshop."

Mrs. Ecclestone-Smythe shook her head. "I'm not in the habit of wearing them on a daily basis. In fact, I find them a bit cumbersome and ostentatious. But Ambrose is rather obsessed with them. If I believed in such things I would think he'd been a jewelry designer in a former life." Mrs. Ecclestone-Smythe slumped slightly on the bench and looked a bit defeated. "I hate to consider the scene that will ensue if he discovers that they are missing."

"Aren't the jewels something that you brought into the marriage?" Beryl said. "Does he really have the right to be so upset about what you do with your property?"

"My husband thinks of himself as an extremely savvy businessman and someone who would never be caught being taken advantage of. If he discovers that the jewels are missing I shall have to fake a robbery. There is absolutely no way I could admit what I've done," Mrs. Ecclestone-Smythe said.

"Surely falsifying a crime is a bit extreme," Edwina said. She wondered if Mrs. Ecclestone-Smythe was one of those nervy, high-strung women. In Edwina's opinion, if there could be said that there was any upside to the tragedies the war had wrought it was that the fashion for fainting spells at the least sign of emotional distress had faded out of favor. She much preferred the more modern approach to life in which women appeared capable of shouldering their burdens as stoically as men, even in the upper classes.

"You don't understand at all. Ambrose values loyalty above all else. He's quite a maniac about it. In all honesty, I fear for my safety should he find out. That's why Lionel and I were sneaking off instead of telling him that I was unhappy and asking for a divorce. He can be somewhat violent when he loses his temper," Mrs. Ecclestone-Smythe said.

Edwina noticed dark circles had appeared under their client's eyes since the last time they had met. Truly, the woman did not look well. Edwina's heart went out to Mrs. Ecclestone-Smythe. She well remembered the nights she'd spent tossing and turning in her narrow bed thinking about how to pay the accounts that had become shockingly past due at all the village shops.

Before Beryl had appeared last autumn to take up lodgings at the Beeches, she had begun to worry that she would lose her home. Her eyes had been equally marred by bluish looking bruises beneath them every morning when she looked in the mirror until Beryl had come up with a way to solve her financial difficulties. Perhaps she was not simply behaving dramatically but rather was terrified of her own husband. She wouldn't be the first woman to feel that way. Regrettably, she wouldn't have even been the first in Walmsley Parva.

"Please rest assured that we've done nothing to expose the purpose of our questioning. Your secret is safe with us," Edwina said.

Beryl crossed one trouser leg over the other and cleared her throat. Edwina just knew she was about to ask an impertinent question. Edwina's stomach clenched. She felt she had just done a decent job of smoothing things over with Mrs. Ecclestone-Smythe. Unless she missed her guess, Beryl was about to rile things up again.

"In the course of our investigation it has come to our attention that Mr. Cunningham may have had a romantic entanglement with another woman. Did you ever suspect him of seeing anyone else?" Beryl asked.

"Absolutely not," Mrs. Ecclestone-Smythe said. "My Lionel was certainly not carrying on with another woman. His heart was entirely devoted to me. Of that you can be absolutely certain." Mrs. Ecclestone-Smythe sat bolt upright once more and crossed her arms over her chest. She gave Beryl the sort of glare one reserves for an undisciplined scullery maid traipsing through the front parlor when guests are visiting.

"You seem surprised to hear such a thing might have been possible," Beryl said. "I assure you the information comes from a very good source."

"Who is this person? Who is it that lays claim to Lionel's affections or has insinuated that someone else does?" Mrs. Ecclestone-Smythe said.

"I'm afraid that much of what happens during the course of an investigation must be kept in the strictest of confidence," Edwina said. "Miss Helliwell means no offense. It is simply important that we ask the questions that will get us to the truth. If Mr. Cunningham had been involved with another woman, it does open up the possibility that he gave her your jewelry."

"He most certainly did no such thing," Mrs. Ecclestone-Smythe said. She struggled to her feet, her face suffused with red and her breath coming out in small pants. "I have hired you to find my jewelry, not to cast aspersions on someone I esteemed. I'm expecting a result sooner rather than later. I'll bid you good day." She hurried off without a backward glance across the green and onto the high street. Edwina heard a honk from a motorist forced to swerve to avoid hitting her.

"Oh dear, I do think you could have handled that differently, Beryl," Edwina said. "I think we're quite lucky that you haven't lost us our only paying client. I fear it was unkind of you to take her so completely by surprise." She turned to face Beryl who was looking thoughtfully at Mrs.

Ecclestone-Smythe's retreating form.

"I'm not so sure I believe she was surprised. She may have suspected him of being unfaithful to her all along," Beryl said.

"Do you really think so?" Edwina said.

"I think anything is possible at this point. For all we know our client is in fact the murderer," Beryl said. "She may have discovered his infidelity herself and killed him in a fit of rage. She may have already looked in all the places we have for her jewelry and come up with nothing. That may be why she hired us in the first place. She wishes to look like the victim, not the perpetrator." Edwina followed Beryl's gaze and wondered if the reason for the alteration in Mrs. Ecclestone-Smythe's appearance really did have more to do with guilt than with grief.

CHAPTER 26

Edwina suggested it would be best to give Mrs. Ecclestone-Smythe time to complete her shopping in the high street before approaching the shops themselves. She mentioned that should they encounter their client, it might be impossible for her to feign civility in their presence. They waited near the pond, feeding the ducks and basking in the spring sunshine for a quarter of an hour before making their way to the post office. Beryl was in need of stationery with which to write to her ex-husbands who were in arrears with their alimony payments. Edwina expressed an interest in purchasing a box of lemon drops. Beryl had noticed it was one of her friend's few dietary weaknesses.

The sweetshop cum post office cum stationer was empty when the pair pushed open the door and stepped inside. The proprietress, Prudence Rathbone, stood behind the counter buffing the wooden countertop with a polishing cloth. She looked up and gave Beryl and Edwina one of her famous long-toothed smiles. Prudence, Beryl uncharitably thought, always put her in mind of a meerkat. With her long skinny neck, her slightly bulging eyes, and her ever-wary ears, trolling for the slightest bit of gossip, she was a dead ringer for the small animal.

"Are you ladies here doing some shopping or are you here on a case?" Prudence asked.

"We have shopping to do today. Do you have any airmail stamps?" Beryl asked. Prudence nodded and whisked her cleaning supplies out of sight beneath the counter.

"I have some right here," Prudence said, pulling a tray of stamps from a drawer. "Of course you're here doing some shopping since the case has been solved. There isn't anything else for you to do now, is there?" Beryl heard a small squeak escape from Edwina's lips from somewhere over near the confectioner's case. Prudence must've heard it too because her already enormous smile stretched so far, it looked painful.

"It seems that you are in possession of some information we have not yet heard, Prudence," Edwina said. "Has Constable Gibbs made an arrest?"

Prudence Rathbone took her time in answering. She fussed and fidgeted with the tray of stamps, appearing to have difficulty in locating those meant for airmail. "Here they are. You must have so many people overseas with whom you correspond, Miss Helliwell," Prudence said. "So many admirers. Especially the gentlemen, I daresay." Prudence made a brisk tut-tutting noise. Beryl thought how quickly Prudence's tune had changed from ardent admirer to sly critic. Beryl still found novelty in what it meant to be settled anywhere long enough for people to become so accustomed to a celebrity that they no longer found them awe-inspiring. It seemed that it was only yesterday when Prudence fell all over herself to ingratiate herself with Walmsley Parva's most famous resident. Prudence's attitude would simply not do.

"I count myself fortunate that there are quite a number of people who esteem me in some way or other," Beryl said. She turned to Edwina. "People I have a great deal of interest in too, like Minnie Mumford. I suggest we go straightaway to Minnie's tearoom to get the story on what Prudence is happiest keeping to herself. Minnie has always stood out as someone upon whom we can rely to be in the know about such things." Beryl reached into her pocket and pulled out exact change for the postage and handed it to Prudence.

"An excellent suggestion. I always find Minnie to be remarkably well informed where truly useful information is concerned," Edwina said, stepping towards the door. Beryl lifted the stamps from the counter without waiting for Prudence to bother slipping them into a cellophane packet.

"Minnie Mumford most certainly does not know the details of this particular incident. I happened to see it with my own eyes." Prudence reached out and plucked the stamps from Beryl's hand. She rattled the cellophane envelope open as if it had done her a personal affront. "I just so happened to be looking out my bedroom window yesterday evening when Constable Gibbs could be seen marching a suspect into the police station." Prudence slid the stamps into the envelope and held them hostage.

"Well, that does seem as though you might know a little bit more than Minnie about what transpired," Edwina said, easing away from the door and back towards the counter.

"You don't happen to know the identity of the suspect?" Beryl said. Prudence leaned conspiratorially across the counter.

"I don't know his name as I do not associate with his sort of people. I do know that he appeared to be grubby and coarse. My immediate impression was that he was one of those miners. Which supports my opinion that it does no good to encourage them to attend the Walmsley Parva May Day fete," Prudence said. "So many of the working class are criminally inclined. It is such a relief not to be counted amongst them." Beryl and Edwina exchanged a glance.

"Just last year I seem to remember reading a lengthy article on crimes committed by tradespeople and even members of the gentry," Edwina said. "I distinctly remember mention of a postmistress over in Beddingstowe being caught helping herself to postage without paying for it and then selling it to family and friends at a reduced rate all the while pocketing the profit. I should hate to think all postmistresses were the same any more than I would think all members of the working class are the same."

Prudence's face crumpled and she took a step backwards. Beryl could see that Edwina's remarks had hit home. Beryl liked to think she had been something of a good influence on her friend on the subject of thwarting traditional class structural constraints. It did the heart good to see Edwina sticking up for the miners and all working-class people. Although, if Beryl were to be entirely honest, it was also good to see Prudence feeling so utterly uncomfortable.

"Thank you for the information, Miss Rathbone," Beryl said. "Based on your description, Edwina and I know exactly who it is Constable Gibbs has arrested. You've been most helpful." Beryl reached across the counter and plucked the envelope of stamps from Prudence's grip. She took Edwina by the arm and the two of them strolled out of the shop. She could hear Prudence coming around the counter and opening the door to shout after them, but they just kept going without a backwards glance.

They hurried out of sight and out of earshot. "Martin Haynes," they said in unison.

"Do you think he has the jewels?" Edwina said.

"I have no idea, but we're going to have to get in to the police station and ask some questions," Beryl said. "And I think I know who's going to help us to do it."

299

CHAPTER 27

Edwina left Beryl in search of Archie Harrison. Beryl would not tell her exactly what she was up to, which left Edwina feeling uneasy. Beryl had insisted they would be best served to leave Archie to her while Edwina paid a second call to Mrs. Plumptree, the boardinghouse landlady. Edwina steeled her nerves to the idea of heading back into the boardinghouse and encountering Cyril once more. His uncanny ability for mimicry reminded her most uncomfortably of Mr. Plumptree. Edwina had seldom found herself the subject of any male attention, let alone that of the persistently unwelcome variety. Mr. Plumptree had been an exception. In fact, just hearing Cyril's voice took her back to a few harrowing encounters with the bird's original owner at the Walmsley Parva reading room. It made Edwina blush with shame just to think of the liberties he had attempted to take. In fact, it had been so unpleasant she had stopped making use of the reading room entirely until word spread that Mr. Plumptree had run off in the night leaving both Mrs. Plumptree and more surprisingly, Cyril, behind.

Despite her discomfort, she told herself, she was a professional and it was important for her to do what needed doing, regardless of the cost to herself. She walked along the high street until she reached the lane to turn off for Shady Rest Boardinghouse. She knocked upon the door and Mrs. Plumptree answered almost immediately. Edwina wondered if the landlady was a bit lonely since she seemed so eager to welcome Edwina into her sitting room. Cyril stood perched on Mrs. Plumptree's shoulder and he leaned forward to greet Edwina with a bawdy welcome.

"You're a fetching lass," Cyril said. Mrs. Plumptree turned and waddled down the hallway with Edwina trailing in her wake. Edwina took the same chair she had sat in before. It maximized her distance from Cyril and minimized the distance to the doorway. Cyril lifted one foot from Mrs. Plumptree's shoulder and began grooming one of his claws. Edwina felt a shiver run up her back.

"So what brings you here today?" Mrs. Plumptree asked. "I heard that poor Mr. Cunningham had been found." Mrs. Plumptree reached up and scratched Cyril's head. The bird nestled its beak into Mrs. Plumptree's hair and began absentmindedly plucking at the wisps of grey threading through it. Edwina felt her own scalp crawl at the sight of him.

"I am here about Mr. Cunningham and I hoped you would be able to answer some delicate questions," Edwina said. She had a sense that the gossipy landlady would be thrilled to be asked about something slightly unsavory. After all, she had been, by all accounts, happily married to the unsavory Mr. Plumptree for many years. Mrs. Plumptree stood up and carried Cyril to his perch. She leaned forward and urged him onto it before returning to the couch. Clearly she did not want any distractions. Or perhaps she was concerned about developing a bald patch.

"I'd be more than happy to help you in any way that I can. Of course what happened to poor Mr. Cunningham was a tragedy and I'm eager to help bring his murderer to justice," Mrs. Plumptree said. She shifted forward in her seat.

"I knew you were exactly the person to help. I said as much to Miss Helliwell just this very morning. I'm wondering if you could tell me a little bit about Mr. Cunningham's personal relationships. You don't know of any special connection he had to any women here in the village, do you?" Edwina asked.

"Mr. Cunningham had no special lady in his life as far as I could tell." Mrs. Plumptree drummed her fingers on her knee and looked thoughtfully at the ceiling. Edwina snuck a glance upward herself and noticed a cobweb stretched across the ceiling fixture. Her fingers itched to pull out a duster and remove it. "In fact, I took a special interest in such matters. Although I would have been more than happy, as I believe I mentioned before, if Mr. Cunningham had been interested in becoming my second husband, I did not take offense when it was clear he was not open to that idea." Mrs. Plumptree shrugged as if to say who could blame him. Edwina most certainly could not, given the state of the housekeeping and the landlady's devotion to her parrot.

"So as far as you knew, there was no one?" Edwina asked. "Would it surprise you to hear that one of your other boardinghouse tenants, Miss Chilvers, claims to have formed a serious attachment to Mr. Cunningham?"

"I would find it absolutely astonishing," Mrs. Plumptree said. "In fact, when it became clear that Mr. Cunningham had no interest romantically in me, I suggested to Miss Chilvers that perhaps the two of them would make a good match."

"Did she say that she did not agree?" Edwina asked. Edwina pulled her notebook from her pocket once more and began to jot down the pertinent bits of their conversation.

"She said she had not the least interest in pursuing a relationship with Mr. Cunningham. She said that her employer, Mr. Ecclestone-Smythe, was very strict on the subject of office romances and would not continue to employ her should she become involved with Mr. Cunningham," Mrs. Plumptree said.

"But why should Mr. Ecclestone-Smythe find out about it?" Edwina asked. "They certainly could have continued to be discreet at the office, could they not?"

"I said much the same thing. I said they both would be busy at work and had no reason to let on the details of their private lives. After all, it wasn't as though Mr. Ecclestone-Smythe spent his time outside of the office socializing with the employees. I said it would be an easy thing to have her cake and eat it too so to speak," Mrs. Plumptree said. Cyril squawked from his perch as if in complete accord with his mistress.

"What did she say? Did she simply not find him to be an attractive young man?" Edwina asked. Edwina found that hard to believe. There was such a shortage of young men after the war that most young ladies were willing to consider every available option. In Mr. Cunningham's case he had all four of his limbs, both of his eyes, and a good paying job. She also had claimed that the two of them were in love. Why in the world would she have led her landlady to believe she had no interest in Mr. Cunningham whatsoever?

"If you can believe it, in these modern times, Miss Chilvers said that she had been raised in a very religious home and that it was unseemly for her to be romantically entangled with a man to whom she was not married whilst living under the same roof," Mrs. Plumptree said. "I could say nothing else on the matter. After all, who's to rebuke a thing like that?"

"Of course you could have said nothing," Edwina said. "Although it does seem unusual. Young women these days tend to be far less concerned about the appearance of that sort of thing."

"I was astonished," Mrs. Plumptree said. "In my business, you are most usually concerned with quite the opposite sort of behavior taking place under your roof. You have to maintain a state of constant vigilance in order to be sure that the reputation of your establishment does not become sullied. One would hate to be known as the sort of place where such things went on." Edwina could not help but notice a wistful look pass across Mrs. Plumptree's face. She was quite certain that in her heart of hearts Mrs. Plumptree was a romantic and not one bound by the strictest sense of morality.

"I've never heard a whisper of malicious gossip concerning the morals of your establishment," Edwina said soothingly. She did wonder if it would be best to let Mrs. Plumptree in on the sort of malicious gossip that she had heard from Minnie Mumford and Prudence Rathbone on the subject of Shady Rest Boardinghouse. If Mrs. Plumptree knew exactly what was being said, perhaps she would be more disturbed by the cobwebs clinging to her front parlor ceiling. Then again, Edwina decided it was not her place to tell another woman how to conduct her business. After all, Edwina would not care for someone doing the same to her.

She decided to take her leave of the landlady before she said something she would later regret. Mrs. Plumptree and Cyril escorted her back down the narrow corridor. As Mrs. Plumptree waved good-bye, Edwina thought again that the other woman really did look quite lonely. Despite the fact she personally did not like him, she was rather glad Mrs. Plumptree had Cyril.

CHAPTER 28

If Edwina had known what Beryl and Archie had been concocting as a plan, she would never have gone to the boardinghouse and left the pair of them to put their heads together. She knew she was in for something unpleasant when Beryl met her in the front hallway holding Edwina's camera bag in her outstretched hands.

"We've come up with the perfect plan," Beryl said. "Isn't that right, Archie?" Beryl elbowed Archie in the ribs. He looked just as excited as she did. Honestly the pair of them were like devilish children. Edwina could easily imagine how no long-term romance could have survived between them. They were simply too much alike.

"You best tell me what it is then since obviously I am involved. Unless Archie has taught you how to use my camera in my absence," Edwina said.

"Archie is going to tell Constable Gibbs

that he is writing an article on women constables and that she, with all of her success, and her groundbreaking position, has come to his attention," Beryl said. She turned excitedly to Archie who nodded enthusiastically in agreement. Edwina thought if he nodded his head any more vigorously he was in danger of shaking his freckles from his boyish face.

"I don't see how this involves my camera," Edwina said. She took her treasured possession from Beryl's grasp and held on to it tightly. Beryl tended to talk with her hands and Edwina could imagine her camera flying from her grip and shattering to bits upon the floor. She clutched it soothingly to her chest and waited for Beryl to deliver her bad news.

"You are going to pose as his photographer. She will be all the more willing to grant an interview if she thinks her picture will be in the paper," Beryl said.

"Why would she believe that I am a photographer for a newspaper?" Edwina asked.

"I plan to tell her that I always hire local talent when I travel on special assignments. I thought I would say that this is an exclusive scoop and that we don't want any of the other papers to get a whiff of it so I am traveling alone in order not to attract any unwanted attention to my activities. I thought I would tell her I'd come all the way from Australia in order to interview her," Archie said.

Edwina had to admit it would be difficult for Doris Gibbs to resist such flattery. While Edwina did not like the constable, or even respect her particularly, she did understand how much pride the other woman took in her position. It had been difficult for Doris to be taken seriously during the war years when there were no men to police the village. The fact that she had managed to hang on to her job when so many men were without work was a testament to either her tenacity or the unpopularity of the position.

"But why is it that she would believe that I am the qualified person to serve as your photographer?" Edwina asked.

"I plan to tell her the truth," Archie said with a huge grin. "That I'm an old friend of Beryl's and that when I asked her about local photographers she immediately suggested you. Naturally, I hired you at once."

"Why will my presence help us to find out if Martin Haynes is guilty or if he has Mrs. Ecclestone-Smythe's jewelry?" Edwina asked.

"Archie is an ace reporter," Beryl said,

giving the younger man's arm a firm squeeze. Edwina felt slightly uncomfortable with the lingering glance Beryl cast his way. "But it must be said; he's not actually a detective. One of us needs to be there on-site to pick the constable's brain and find out what's going on. We certainly can't let Prudence Rathbone be the source of our information in the case. I do not take photographs so you are the obvious choice. And we need to question Martin Haynes if at all possible."

Edwina sighed. It was obvious there was no way of getting out of it. She was going to have to encounter Constable Gibbs. She did not look forward to what was sure to be a confrontational visit to the police station.

"When did you plan to conduct this interview?" Edwina asked.

"Immediately," Beryl said. "Why do you think I met you in the hall with your camera all packed and ready to go?" Beryl spun Edwina's shoulders around and pointed her towards the door. Archie stepped up and took her elbow.

It was a testament to Beryl's affection for the reporter that she had allowed him to use her motorcar to drive them to the police station. Beryl said it would look more like they were telling the truth about Archie knowing her if she allowed him to take the wheel. They parked in front of the station, drawing glances from up and down the street. Edwina could see Constable Gibbs peering through the large window at the front of the police station. Her perpetual scowl was fixed firmly on her face as they entered the small building.

"I told you that you were not supposed to be involved with anything further to do with this investigation," Constable Gibbs said, placing her fists on her hips.

"Hello Constable Gibbs," Archie said, stepping forward. "It's a real pleasure and an honor to meet you again, ma'am." Constable Gibbs dropped her fists and the furrow between her brows deepened.

"You're that man who came to tell me about finding Lionel Cunningham's body," Constable Gibbs said.

"That's right. But today I'm here as a reporter on special assignment all the way from Australia. I'm currently filing my stories with one of the newspapers up in London. I'm here especially to humbly request that you grant me the favor of an interview," Archie said. Edwina noticed he had broadened his Australian accent as if to highlight the distance he had come in order to speak with the constable.

"An interview? With me? What about?" Constable Gibbs said, her scowl deepening even further.

"It is come to my attention, all the way over in Sydney, that there were a few superior sort of women in your fair land taking on the job of policing their communities. Your name was the first one mentioned," Archie said.

"You want to write an article on women police constables?" Constable Gibbs asked.

"Indeed I do, ma'am. It's a human interest story but one with real drama to it. I know that folks would like to see what it's like for you brave ladies who have done such a bang-up job of things without the credit you deserve," Archie said. With that, Edwina knew he had Constable Gibbs in the palm of his hand. If there was one thing Edwina knew about Doris Gibbs it was that she never felt she got enough credit. The idea of having her name splashed across a paper in London was something she could not possibly have dreamt of in her wildest fantasies.

"I suppose I could spare you a few minutes. We are quite busy here in Walmsley Parva despite being such a small police station, but considering how far you've come, I suppose I could make the time," Constable Gibbs said.

"Your busyness is one of the reasons you've come to my attention," Archie said. "It's not every village constable who's been instrumental in solving two murders in their small community. Which is why Miss Davenport has accompanied me. The newspaper has made it clear that not only do they want a front-page story, they require a photograph of you to accompany it." Edwina watched as Constable Gibbs' hand crept up to her head. She hurriedly patted her hairpins back into her untidy bun. She straightened her constable's hat and turned to Edwina.

"Did you want to take the photographs straightaway?" she asked, turning her attention to Edwina for the first time since they entered the police station.

"If you don't mind, I'd rather conduct the interview first. I find it makes the people I interview appear more relaxed and natural in the photograph if they've warmed up by telling me their story beforehand," Archie said, turning to give Edwina a wink.

"You're the expert," Constable Gibbs said. "Come on back here. We might as well sit and be comfortable."

Archie and Edwina followed Constable Gibbs behind the counter that divided the unwashed public from the sanctity of Constable Gibbs' private domain. There was a small table ringed by four chairs at the back of the room. A half-filled cup of tea sat in front of a pile of paperwork. Archie and Edwina took chairs at the table and waited for Constable Gibbs to settle into what was clearly her own favorite spot.

Archie gestured towards the stack of papers. "It looks like we interrupted you while you are hard at work. I expect that concerns the case you've been investigating recently," he said.

"That's right," Constable Gibbs said. "I suppose Edwina and her famous friend have been filling your ears with a lot of speculation."

"They mentioned a bit about it, but I told them I'd much rather hear about it from you," Archie said. "A good reporter always gets the story from the best possible sources."

Constable Gibbs' posture straightened as her chest swelled visibly with pride. She gave Edwina a mocking glance. "I see that the Australian standard for truth is at least as high as that here in the British Isles," Constable Gibbs said. "What is it that you wanted to ask me?"

Archie started the interview with the sorts of questions Edwina would have expected if his article had no hidden purpose of assisting in her investigation. He asked questions about Constable Gibbs' background, age, marital status, and whether or not she had been trained in any sort of police work prior to taking on the job. By the time they'd spent only a few minutes together, Edwina could tell that Constable Gibbs' frosty exterior was melting. Truly, Archie had a gift for flattery. He was the sort of man who knew exactly what to ask to get the information he needed. Edwina was surprised that he had lost his job at so many different newspapers. But perhaps the sorts of charms he had exhibited on Beryl were amongst the reasons for his need to move from city to city.

After complimenting Doris on her strict adherence to the local ordinances concerning the proper screening of pigsties, Archie turned the conversation ever so slowly and subtly to the current investigation. After the way he'd warmed her up, Constable Gibbs was happy to tell him anything he wanted to know. She had been deftly reduced to a twittering schoolgirl within fifteen minutes. In fact, it was not only surprising, Edwina found it rather nauseating.

"So I understand the case you've just cracked was quite a knotty puzzle," Archie said. "I'm sure our readers would be thrilled to be able to hear firsthand account of capturing a cold-blooded murderer."

"It's not the sort of thing the average individual encounters, now is it?" Constable Gibbs said. "It took a fair bit of investigatory expertise to get to the bottom of it. This was not just a straightforward case," she said.

"You must need to know a great deal about the community you serve in order to get to the bottom of something like this, don't you?" Archie said. "I mean an outsider couldn't simply step into your role and solve a crime in a village, could they?"

"Well, an outsider certainly wouldn't have known who to ask about unusual sums of money appearing in town. You have to know who has money and who doesn't before you can be following that sort of clue," Constable Gibbs said. "It was just that sort of thinking that led me to Chester's bookmaking scheme," Constable Gibbs said.

"You have a bookie right here in little Walmsley Parva?" Archie asked.

"I'm sorry to say that we do," Constable Gibbs said. "But in this case it ended up being a help rather than a moral blight on our community. I made enquiries about all sorts of unusual money being spent and turned up nothing in the usual places. No one bought an unexpected round for everyone down at the pub or went about throwing money away at the village shops."

"So that led you to check with the bookie?" Archie said. "That was clever thinking. You really have a gift for this job."

Constable Gibbs straightened her shoulders and smiled. "I'd like to think that's why I've kept my position for so long," she said. "You have to know the population you serve and where to ask the right questions. Chester needed a little convincing but I managed to get him to tell me about an unusual bet placed for just about the same amount that had gone missing from the pigeon racing club's treasury at the same time Mr. Cunningham disappeared. He was the club's treasurer, you know."

"And so you put two and two together?" Archie asked.

"Exactly. As soon as I was certain the office would be open, I telephoned down to the colliery to check on Mr. Haynes' schedule and it turned out he wasn't on shift when we believe Mr. Cunningham met his end. I've got him dead to rights, so to speak," Constable Gibbs said, glowing with pride.

Edwina felt a tingle of excitement. She

managed to keep herself from asking questions in order to allow Archie to extract the information from Constable Gibbs. She knew that any interruption from her would stop the flow of conversation.

"His work schedule?" Archie said. "Is that the sort of deductive reasoning and dedication the public has come to expect from you?"

"I'd like to think so," Constable Gibbs said. She began waving her hands round him passionately as if to make her point. "I consider myself a public servant above all else and it is that belief that guides my relentless pursuit of justice."

"Tell me, do you believe this was a cold-blooded premeditated act or was it an opportunistic crime of passion?" Archie asked.

"I am completely convinced Martin Haynes behaved with malice aforethought," Constable Gibbs said. "I suggested that Mr. Cunningham foolishly made some sort of display of the money in front of Martin Haynes who was overcome with temptation. Clearly he decided to follow the victim to his pigeon loft early on the morning of the race. I surmised that he killed Mr. Cunningham and helped himself to the contents of his victim's billfold. End of story," Constable Gibbs said.

"Did he admit he did that?" Edwina asked. She knew she should remain silent but the question just slipped out unbidden.

"He hasn't admitted anything other than placing a bet with the bookie. But mark my words, I'll manage to get a confession out of him one way or another," Constable Gibbs said.

"Do you believe him to be a first-time offender?" Archie asked. He leaned towards Constable Gibbs, his face flushed with interest.

"In my considerable experience, criminal types get their start early in life. Most start out nicking sweets at the village shop," Constable Gibbs said. "It isn't long before they graduate to housebreaking and worse. Murder is a final rung on a ladder they've been climbing for years."

Archie scribbled something furiously in his notebook and then he turned to Edwina.

"Constable Gibbs has just the right look on her face. Do you think you could take her photograph now?" Archie asked. Edwina nodded and busied herself with her camera equipment. She positioned Constable Gibbs this way and that and snapped several photos in order to look convincing.

"I have a few more questions I'd like to ask the constable," Archie said. "I think that you're free to go as I no longer have need of a photographer." Archie gave the constable a wink and made a point to look as though he were dismissing Edwina. She took it as a good time to go looking for Martin Haynes herself.

"Shall I wait for you in the motorcar to finish the interview?" Edwina asked.

"I think that would be best," Archie said.

"Will you be long?" Edwina asked.

"The constable is full of so many fascinating details that I'd like to pick her brain a bit longer. You don't mind, do you, ma'am?" Archie said, turning to Constable Gibbs.

"I would consider it a public service," she said.

"I should like to avail myself of your WC," Edwina said to Constable Gibbs. "That is, if I'm going to need to wait much longer." Constable Gibbs waved her off and Edwina found herself free to explore the back of the police station without supervision.

CHAPTER 29

Edwina made her way quietly along the corridor towards the holding area at the back of the police station. A heavy lock kept the door firmly shut. But a window with bars across it allowed her to see in. Peering into the gloom she saw Martin Haynes, sitting on a wooden bench placed along the far wall. She stretched up on tiptoe to get a better look through the window.

"Mr. Haynes, may I speak with you for a moment?" she asked in a low voice. He looked up in surprise and left the bench to join her at the window. Edwina thought he looked somewhat scared. She imagined that Constable Gibbs had been quite descriptive about the process of hanging. Doris Gibbs always did like the lurid and unpleasant. When they had been children Edwina remembered an occasion when Doris had stopped by the side of the road and pointed out a frog that had been trampled under the wheels of a passing cart. She ghoulishly and gleefully described the scene before her despite the fact that all of the other girls were horrified by what had happened to the small creature.

"What do you want?" Martin Haynes asked. He wrapped his soot-encrusted hands around the bars of the window.

"I wanted to ask you a question," Edwina said.

"I've already spent all night being interrogated by that other woman," he said. "I got no sleep whatsoever. Unless you are a newly minted member of the constabulary I'm in no mood to answer any more." Edwina thought his tone sounded defiant but as she stepped closer she decided the look in his eyes said he felt more frightened than he was attempting to show.

"It won't take long. I am quite certain I only have a moment before Constable Gibbs becomes suspicious of my absence and comes looking for me," Edwina said.

"I have already talked until I am hoarse. What good has it done me?" The haggard man looked over his shoulder at the narrow cot and unsanitary-looking chamber pot on the floor beside it.

"It can't make things worse, can it?" she

said, pointing to the bars on the door window.

"I don't know about that. After all, I wouldn't be a bit surprised to find you and your famous friend were the ones who hurried to tell the constable that you had seen me arguing with Cunningham by the river. That doesn't make me think you are on my side," he said.

"Beryl and I did not say anything to Constable Gibbs about your conversation with Mr. Cunningham. Even if we had, she wouldn't have believed us. She warned us off the case and we have not had any contact with her about it since we found Mr. Cunningham's body." Her hopes grew as he leaned towards the bars once more.

"So what did you want to ask me? I think I should warn you that I won't answer if I don't like your question."

"I am not convinced you are the one responsible for Mr. Cunningham's death," Edwina said. "The constable has a tendency to leap on the easy answer. She did that even as a girl in primary school. She said she checked with the colliery and you were not on shift when Mr. Cunningham was killed."

"That's not a question," he said.

"What I wanted to know was whether or

not you have an alibi for the time of Mr. Cunningham's death. Can anyone else vouch for your whereabouts?"

Martin Haynes' jaw muscles tightened and Edwina noticed his knuckles whiten as he tightened his grip on the bars. "I can't tell you anything other than that I didn't have anything to do with Cunningham's death."

"So no one saw you at the time of his death? You spoke to no one? Saw no one with whom you are acquainted?" she asked.

"I didn't say that. I simply said I can't tell you about where I was or whom I was with at the time of the murder. I can only say I had nothing to do with any of it," he said. "I'm going to hang, ain't I?"

Edwina heard a noise at the end of the hall and took a step back from the window. Constable Gibbs appeared at the far end of the corridor, a scowl on her face.

"I thought you said that you were heading for the WC," the constable said. "You do not have permission to speak with the prisoner. It's time for you to leave." Edwina took one last look at Martin's pinched and tired face. She hurried back down the hallway, gathered up her camera equipment, and headed out the door.

CHAPTER 30

While it was not her favorite thing to do, Beryl was capable of sitting in one spot for hours on end awaiting whatever was meant to transpire. In fact, she was surprised to discover she had far more patience for the tedium than had Edwina. Perhaps it was all the hours spent in the bush awaiting the appearance of big game. Not that she ever enjoyed shooting at the majestic creatures, but she did find she was willing to sit for as long as it took to catch a glimpse of a lioness and her cubs or a herd of elephants. Perhaps the excitement of sneaking into the back of the police station had still not worn off. Even though a couple of hours had passed since Edwina had been unceremoniously shown the door by Constable Gibbs, Beryl could not help but notice an unusual degree of restlessness in her fellow detective. Edwina had brought her knitting, a novel, and a flask of tea to keep herself occupied while they awaited their quarry, but still managed to shift almost continually in her seat. She seemed ill at ease with the practicalities of a surveillance mission.

The birds overhead were singing sweetly and the sun was just beginning to dip in the sky although it still gave off a gentle warmth through the windscreen. It seemed impossible to believe that anything as nefarious as a murder investigation could possibly be taking place on such a fine spring evening in the English countryside. She was almost ready to suggest that her friend walk home and leave the job to her when Edwina dropped her knitting needles into her lap and pointed at the colliery gates.

"There she is," Edwina said, pointing at the figure heading towards them along the road. Miss Chilvers was dressed for the office in a trim skirt suit and a neat little hat. Beryl opened her window and called cheerily to the secretary, "Can we offer you a ride back home?"

"I like to breathe in some fresh air every evening so I'd rather walk. Thank you very much anyway," Miss Chilvers said.

"We have a few questions we'd like to ask you and we didn't think you'd like to be overheard at the boardinghouse. But if you'd rather walk we can go on ahead and meet you there. Mrs. Plumptree seems the sort to enjoy all manner of persons dropping by for a chat without a moment's notice." Beryl sounded slightly menacing, even to her own ears. She was pleased to see Miss Chilvers turn on her heel and head straight for the vehicle. The younger woman yanked open the back door with ill grace and slid across the bench seat. Beryl and Edwina turned simultaneously to face her.

"We wanted to ask you about your claim that you and Mr. Cunningham were involved in a romantic relationship," Edwina said.

"What about it? I told you everything there was to know," Miss Chilvers said.

"You told us you were involved with him but no one else seems to know anything about it," Beryl said.

"And don't forget about Mrs. Plumptree," Edwina said. "She's absolutely certain that despite her determined matchmaking, you were completely adamant that you had no interest whatsoever in Mr. Cunningham." Beryl noticed Miss Chilvers shifting uncomfortably in the seat.

"Mrs. Plumptree is a nosy old woman who would have given us no rest if she had any idea about our private business," Miss Chilvers said. "I couldn't stand the thought of her prying and asking questions and giving us little glances every time we entered the room."

"Are you saying that you kept it from her simply because you couldn't stand for her to know?" Edwina asked. "That seems like an extreme reaction."

"You've met her. Can you imagine having her cooing at you and asking when you were planning to post the banns? It's hard enough living under the same roof with that woman when she knows almost nothing about your private business. It would have been absolutely intolerable to have been the focus of her constant, nagging speculation," Miss Chilvers said. "Not only that, but we decided not to tell her because not only would she have chattered about it nonstop to us, she would have spread gossip throughout the village."

"Would that have mattered so very much?" Beryl asked.

"It would have to my employer," Miss Chilvers said. "Mr. Ecclestone-Smythe is the sort of man who wants an unmarried, completely unattached secretary. He wants to imagine that he is the only man of any importance in her life. It's a harmless fantasy but one that makes it impossible to remain in his employ if he hears reports of

any sort of romantic involvements whatsoever. It would make it all the worse if the
object of my affection were also in his
employ. That would have made it impossible for him to ignore the relationship."

"Did Mr. Ecclestone-Smythe actually tell
you this was a condition of your employment?" Beryl asked.

"He implied as much," Miss Chilvers said.

"I noticed Mr. Ecclestone-Smythe looked
as though he had eaten some bad prawns
when we were at the colliery office and it
came to light that you and Mr. Cunningham
lived at the same boardinghouse," Edwina
said.

"Indeed. When he hired me he asked
about my personal life and told me that he
had terminated the employment of his last
secretary because she had become involved
with an unsuitable young man. He then
went on to say that he couldn't think of any
sort of man that would be suitable for
someone worthy of being his secretary,"
Miss Chilvers said.

"It seems rather unfair," Beryl said. "Did
he make any unpleasant advances towards
you?" Beryl noticed Edwina dropping her
eyes to her lap as though the topic made
her uncomfortable. It would be best for Ed,
Beryl thought, if she could soon get over

such scruples.

"Mr. Ecclestone-Smythe comported himself no better and no worse than any other employer I have ever had. The best I can say is that he never actually chased me around my desk. Not that he could have kept up with me had he tried," Miss Chilvers said. Beryl was inclined to agree with her assessment of Mr. Ecclestone-Smythe's fitness for frolicking. He was sadly encumbered by a bushel basket-sized belly and disproportionately short limbs. She doubted if he had caught up with Miss Chilvers his arms could have extended far enough past his rotundity to do much damage to her person.

"Do you think it's possible that that is what Mr. Ecclestone-Smythe and Mr. Cunningham were arguing about the day before your fiancé went missing?" Edwina asked. "Could Mr. Ecclestone-Smythe have found out about your relationship?" Miss Chilvers leaned back against the seat with a pensive look on her face.

"I hadn't considered our engagement might be the source of the row. I had assumed that they were arguing about something to do with the business itself. But now that you mention it, I suppose that could also make sense," Miss Chilvers said.

"Do you think it's possible that Mr. Cunningham tried to blackmail Mr. Ecclestone-Smythe into turning a blind eye to your relationship by telling him he knew his business secrets?" Beryl said.

"A week ago I would not have thought him capable of such a thing. But then, a week ago I would not have thought he could have gone and gotten himself killed over anything whatsoever," Miss Chilvers said. "At this point, I have no idea what to think about anything at all. Except for the fact that Mrs. Plumptree will have even more questions for me than usual if I arrive late for dinner."

"Would you like for us to give you a ride?" Edwina asked.

"Certainly not. Then I would be early and that would lead to even more questions," Miss Chilvers said. She slid across the back seat and wrenched the door handle with a slim hand. Miss Chilvers paused as she opened the door to get out. "You don't really suppose Mr. Ecclestone-Smythe is the one that murdered Lionel, do you?" Miss Chilvers asked.

"I would say it's decidedly a possibility," Beryl said. "If I were you I would keep on the good side of your employer for the time being," Beryl said before turning back around in her seat. She lifted a hand in farewell to Miss Chilvers then started the automobile and pulled out onto the main road.

"I think there just might be another possibility," Edwina said. Despite her rather sheltered existence Beryl had found her friend to have a keen understanding of the motivations of others. Perhaps it was an innate skill or one she had developed over the years spent tending to a tyrannical mother. Or perhaps it was the way that all of life in a village was conducted under a microscope and Edwina, having been there so long, had seen a great deal with her eye pressed to the eyepiece, staring at the contents of the petri dish that was Walmsley Parva. No matter what explained it, Beryl was always glad when Edwina put forth her own theories about a case.

"Which is?" Beryl asked.

"I shouldn't be a bit surprised if Miss Chilvers found out that her fiancé was seeing another woman and she killed him in a fit of jealous rage," Edwina said. "Although I do wonder if she was capable of stabbing him in the chest. She isn't a very large person, after all."

"In my experience a successful stabbing is more a question of either skill or luck rather than brute force," Beryl said. Edwina turned to her friend with a look of amazement on her face.

"How would you come to know a thing like that?" Edwina asked.

"When one spends much time rattling around by oneself in the depths of unknown parts I have found it best to be skilled with a knife as well as a firearm. I'll tell you all about it on the way back to the Beeches."

CHAPTER 31

Charles arrived promptly at eight. It was just like him, Edwina thought, to arrive for an evening of bridge at a friend's home dressed as though he was headed for a day in court. His shoes gleamed, his hair lay tidily upon his head courtesy of some manner of odiferous cream; he even wore a necktie knotted neatly at his throat. She ushered him into the sitting room where a card table and four chairs sat cozily near the fire. Beryl presided over the drinks tray mixing up some sort of American-style cocktail.

"Charles, so glad you could join us and make up a fourth for the rubber," Beryl said. "What can I fix you? Edwina has recently discovered she is partial to gin fizzes. I'm having a dry martini." Edwina was surprised when Charles took a step towards the drinks tray. It was a rarity for him to imbibe.

"I've always wanted to try a martini," Charles said. "I think I should like to have one if it's not too much trouble to make."

"But Charles, you almost never drink anything stronger than a lemon squash," Edwina said.

"Somehow, Edwina, it seems as though I should venture into new realms. After all, if you two ladies can start yourselves up in a new business, and one as adventurous as a private enquiry agency, surely even a stuffy old solicitor like myself could manage to try an American cocktail," Charles said with a smile.

"That's the spirit, Chaz," Beryl said, giving Charles the benefit of one of her most winning smiles. "How many olives?" Beryl asked, holding up a jar.

"However many you recommend. I put myself completely in your hands," Charles said.

"I knew I liked him," Beryl said, turning towards Edwina and winking extravagantly. "Always go with three. All the best things come in threes." Beryl turned back to her cocktail tray and began to measure and add quantities of clear liquids to a silver shaker. Much rattling ensued and Edwina did not hear the knock on the door. Fortunately Crumpet did. He went racing down the hall barking and alerting everyone within that another visitor had arrived.

"That must be Archie," Beryl said. "Will you get the door while I finish up with Charles' drink?" Edwina hurried down the hall and popped open the door. Archie stood on the stoop looking nothing like the other gentleman that made up the foursome. If he had ever been wearing a tie he had lost it somewhere along the way. His shirttail flapped in the slight breeze and his shoes looked more built for calisthenics than for polishing.

"I hope I'm not late," Archie said. "I got so lost in the story that I was writing up about Constable Gibbs that I completely forgot the time."

"Are you really going ahead with the article about Constable Gibbs?" Edwina asked. "I thought that was simply a ruse to get me in to speak with Martin Haynes?"

"That's what I thought it was at first," Archie said. "But it turns out your Constable Gibbs is a fascinating woman. I think it's exactly the sort of human-interest story that will sell to a London paper. Frankly, I'm surprised no one thought to interview her before now. It's turning out to be an extraordinary story."

Edwina was not entirely sure what she

thought about the idea of Constable Gibbs appearing in a London newspaper. In her opinion the constable was far too conceited about what her job entailed without the sort of accolades a newspaper article would heap upon her head. She didn't suppose she had anything she could say about it however. Besides, if Archie were able to sell the article to a London newspaper, it might help him to secure a permanent position. He was quite a nice young man and it would be good to see him succeed.

Archie followed her down the hall to the sitting room. Introductions were made all around, and in only a matter of moments the four of them were seated around the card table each with a drink of their choosing and a hand of cards in front of them. It became obvious from the start that Archie was an excellent card player. Beryl had suggested that Archie and Edwina pair up and that she and Charles do the same. Edwina felt that Beryl had gotten the shorter end of the stick. She had played bridge with Charles many times and had always found him to be surprisingly erratic at the card table. He tended to overplay his hand or to be far too cautious in his betting. His instincts were entirely off no matter which direction he leaned. Edwina had never played a rubber, partnered with Charles, which had turned out triumphantly.

After the first rubber and one or two more rounds of drinks, Edwina noticed Charles' bridge playing had improved considerably. She found herself surprised by the number of tricks Beryl and Charles had accumulated. He had even managed a grand slam. Edwina looked at him in shock. At first she considered it was Beryl's influence that was bringing out the best in his play. Then a far more interesting thought occurred to her. Perhaps Charles had always dialed back his abilities in order to make her feel more at ease. Edwina considered herself a decent player and perhaps Charles had not wanted to outshine her.

Beryl had been telling her for months that she suspected Charles Jarvis would like nothing better than to convince Edwina to become his wife. Edwina had dismissed the notion out of hand partly because she had known Charles for so long and he had never given any indication to her of any sort of romantic feeling. If she were to admit the truth, to herself, if no one else, she would also have to say that Charles had always seemed just the teensiest bit stodgy.

Edwina's life had always seemed to her to have been a small one and in her heart of hearts she really did wish for a bit of adventure. What finer adventure could there be than a tumultuous romance with an exciting stranger? Charles never seemed the sort to provide that kind of experience. And no one could argue he was not a stranger. Although this evening his bridge playing had improved to such a degree that he might well have been one. The thought flitted through her mind that had she seen him in fancy dress she would not have been able to recognize him from his playing alone.

The game became quite heated as the pairs kept overtaking each other for a lead in points. Edwina felt her face flush and her pulse racing. There was nothing like a rousing game of bridge to remind you that you were alive, even if the stakes were only matchsticks. By the time they completed the second rubber Edwina felt she required a bit of a break. She had prepared some light snacks for their guests and went to the kitchen to fetch them. Just as she lifted a damp tea towel from the platter of sandwiches, a knock landed on the scullery door and Simpkins hurried in without being invited to enter.

"Simpkins, I cannot imagine which jobs need doing in the garden at this time of night. What are you doing here?" Edwina

340

asked. More than likely he hadn't yet had his tea. Honestly, that man had an unnerving sense when it came to refreshments on offer at the Beeches.

"Nothing in the garden, miss, but I am here on business. Your business. Miss Beryl will be wanting to hear it, too. She's in the parlor cozied up next to the fire with a drink in her hand, I expect," Simpkins said. He didn't wait for an answer or even offer to carry the tray laden with crustless fish paste sandwiches and an assortment of pastries, but rather barged on ahead into the parlor where the other three were discussing the case. Although Edwina couldn't help but notice Simpkins seemed a bit unsteady on his feet to be safely trusted with the tray. She knew he was getting on but hadn't really given a great deal of thought to how much the passing of years might impact his balance. He had always seemed old to her, having been a member of her mother's generation rather than her own. She felt a strange pang when she considered for the first time that the day might come when Simpkins would not be there to argue with her about the proper way to transplant lupines or how best to divide dahlias.

"Hello, Simpkins. Pull up a chair. Archie was just telling Charles all about the adventure he and Edwina had at the police station," Beryl said.

"I only wish we had made more headway on the case. The constable bent my ear for an eternity and I don't think we learned anything new," Archie said.

"I wish the information I shared about Martin Haynes had been more useful," Charles said.

"It's a sort of headway we never would have made if you hadn't made that sketch of Martin Haynes," Beryl said. Edwina noticed that Beryl seemed to be looking at Charles with new admiration.

"Martin Haynes is what I've come to tell you about," Simpkins said. "Constable Gibbs had to release him from custody. Someone gave him an alibi for the time of the murder. Two someones, as it happens."

"Who?" Beryl, Edwina, and Archie all asked at the same time.

"A man by the name of Dennis Morley and his wife, Alice. They said he had dropped by for a bit of a chinwag that very morning. They said they invited him to breakfast and that after that the two men went off for a spot of fishing down at the river," Simpkins said as he reached for a sandwich.

"So he isn't in any trouble after all?"

Edwina asked.

"I wouldn't go so far as to say that. It looks like Martin Haynes is likely to be out of a job no matter what." Simpkins lowered himself gingerly into a nearby chair.

"Why would that be?" Beryl said.

"Because Martin Haynes isn't his real name. It's something altogether different. I just heard down at the pub from Douglas Gibb, that before the Morleys vouched for his whereabouts, Constable Gibbs had discovered his real identity while searching his rooms." Simpkins smiled then reached out and helped himself to another sandwich. Edwina could not help but notice that his fingernails were still grubby from a day spent in the garden. She resolved to content herself with what food was already on her own plate rather than expose herself to whatever Simpkins might add to whatever he touched.

As far as Edwina could tell, Beryl paid no mind to such things. She reached for a sandwich and held it to her face, giving it a slight sniff before peeling back the bread and glancing at the filling. While she never complained, Beryl still had not become entirely accustomed to the differences in cuisine on the other side of the Atlantic from her own. Things that Edwina took for granted as common, everyday fare, struck Beryl as exotic on occasion. Edwina never would have considered a fish paste sandwich something to attract notice from anyone. She supposed it was one of the reasons she found her life to be so much more interesting now that Beryl had come to live with her than she had in the months preceding her friend's arrival. It made one think, to see life with fresh eyes, when someone so different from oneself was in one's orbit on a daily basis.

"Why did he need to use a false name?" Charles asked. "Was he in trouble with the law?" Of course Charles would be interested in the legal aspects of the case, Edwina thought to herself.

"According to Douglas, when the constable taxed Martin Haynes with it he admitted that he had been blacklisted from the mines in the north. He was concerned that he would not be able to get a job at the Hambley mine if Ecclestone-Smythe knew who he really was," Simpkins said.

"He was probably right. I've heard the colliery owners oftentimes share the names of undesirable employees with each other all across the nation," Archie said.

"I shouldn't think that they could possibly keep track of all the undesirable employees,"

Charles said. "I have trouble keeping track of the names of unsuitable parlor maids. How could they possibly keep all the miners straight?"

"They would have all heard about this one. It appears that Mr. Martin Haynes, or whatever it is that he calls himself, wasn't just someone who didn't give a good day's work for a good day's pay. He was a labor agitator and was involved with an incident that turned ugly up in the north. Constable Gibbs reckons that his was a name that the bosses would recognize," Simpkins said.

"Considering the unemployment rate, I can't say that I blame him for changing it," Edwina said. "I doubt very much he's well suited to other work. A life in the mines does not translate easily to other sorts of industries, does it?"

"I've frequently used an assumed name," Beryl said. "I find that it has often been of great use to me to travel in a way that attracted no attention. I don't blame Mr. Haynes one bit for wanting to start over. As far as I can see, all the power belongs to the colliery owners and the other wealthy people. A man like Martin Haynes would have absolutely no chance of getting a job at Hambley mine if Mr. Ecclestone-Smythe had had any idea of his real identity."

"I'm sure you're right," Charles said. "After all, Mr. Ecclestone-Smythe seems to have enough troubles without having any labor agitation added to it." He took another sip of his martini and leaned back in his chair with a creak. Edwina wondered if the martinis were having the same sort of effect upon Charles that the gin fizzes had had on her earlier. It wasn't like Charles to be so expansive with his knowledge. He was one of the most tight-lipped and cautious men she had ever met. And that was saying something as her own father had been cut from a similar cloth.

"What sort of difficulties has Mr. Ecclestone-Smythe been having?" Edwina said.

"What I've heard is that the mine and the colliery both have been experiencing a large number of stoppages due to sabotage," Charles said.

"Sabotage?" Beryl said. "We've been to the colliery several times lately and have heard nothing like that."

"It's not the sort of thing that Mr. Ecclestone-Smythe is eager to have get out. I expect that he would have dismissed any employee found to be the one carrying tales about what he considered to be damaging private business," Charles said.

"How did you find out about it then?" Archie asked.

"One of my other clients happened to bring it up at a meeting. As it didn't pertain to him, and as Mr. Ecclestone-Smythe has not seen fit to engage my services, it's not a matter of client confidentiality, and I felt I could mention it to you to assist with your case," Charles said. He looked at Archie over the rim of his glass. Edwina felt a frisson of tension crackle across the table. She was not sure exactly the source of it but would not be surprised to find it was Beryl herself. She did have a habit of acting as a lightning rod.

"What specifically did your nameless client say?" Beryl asked. "We would be very grateful for any help that you could give us. After all, your instincts were so good about Martin Haynes that I'm eager to hear what you have to say about this."

"My client said he felt it was a miracle that the Hambley mine had managed to stay open as long as it has done. Between the difficulty in the actual structure of the shafts and the financial repercussions of all the stoppages, they have not yet turned a profit. My client is related to someone who is heavily invested and is frankly worried about his relation's money."

"That sounds serious," Edwina said.

"Indeed it is. As a matter of fact, it's my understanding that this is not the first time Mr. Ecclestone-Smythe has owned a business that found itself in dire circumstances. In fact, it is rumored that he is being investigated on account of his potentially unscrupulous practices," Charles said. "Although I don't know the specifics on that. It could just be stuff and nonsense or even wishful thinking on the part of my client." Beryl turned to Archie.

"That's just the sort of thing that would make a great newspaper article to sell to a London paper, isn't it?" Beryl asked Archie. He leaned back in his chair and drummed his fingers on the table.

"I could do some digging around. I don't suppose you would be willing to lend me your fine motorcar to run up to London with in the morning?" Archie asked.

"I expect I could do that as long as you report back anything you find about Mr. Ecclestone-Smythe or the problems at the Hambley mine as soon as you find out anything," Beryl said.

"It's a deal. If you all will excuse me I'm going to head for my room and finish up the article on Constable Gibbs. I can drop that off tomorrow in London while I am there," Archie said. "Unless there's some reason you'd like me to stay?" Archie said, looking pointedly at Beryl. Edwina felt decidedly uncomfortable. Not only had she witnessed a scene she would not prefer to know about between the reporter and her friend, she was not altogether pleased with how such a question seemed to have affected Charles. His cheeks suffused with color and he seemed unable to stop blinking.

"I wouldn't dream of keeping you from your work," Beryl said. "In fact, in order to make sure that you can get it all accomplished, why don't you take the automobile this evening back to your room? You'll get there faster tonight and be able to make an even earlier start in the morning," Beryl said.

CHAPTER 32

Beryl caught up with Prudence Rathbone just where she was certain she would find her, in her shop. Prudence was scowling at a small sticky-looking boy who held out a half pence with an eager look upon his face. Prudence might have been in the sweets business but that did not mean she got on well with children. It was clear to Beryl that Prudence had never cared for children. From the way she scowled at the small boy who left his sticky finger mark on her glass case, it was simply not a match. It was most unfortunate that her parents had left a sweetshop to her instead of something more suitable like a vinegar dispensary or a medical supply store.

Beryl waited until the child had exited the shop before turning her attention to Prudence. She had busied herself keeping her hands behind her back, as not to leave any finger marks of her own, while the boy had finished up his shopping. Now that Prudence was the only one there she wished to extract as much information from her as possible in the least amount of time. Prudence Rathbone made her skin crawl.

"Back again so soon?" Prudence said. "My, my, my, you certainly do go through a lot of correspondence. Letters to your fans? Former husbands? Something about your current investigation?" Prudence asked.

"Actually, I'm here for a box of chocolates. I think there's nothing like a box of chocolates to look forward to enjoying in the evening. Wouldn't you agree?" Beryl asked.

"I'm afraid I don't often indulge. I wouldn't have been able to keep my svelte figure all these years if I made too much of a practice of eating sweets," Prudence said, looking pointedly at Beryl's robust figure. If Prudence had meant to aim a barb at Beryl it would not have worked. Beryl prided herself in her statuesque appearance and knew the value of laying down a reserve of fat for those times when one found oneself out in the bush with nothing whatsoever to eat. Not a tin of beans, not a box of biscuits. Beryl found from hard-won experience that she could in fact live for some weeks on what she had prudently stored upon her person ahead of time. It served her in good stead and she had never had any trouble attracting admiring glances despite a bit of well-placed excess.

Beryl leaned over the case and pointed, deciding she would in fact leave a finger mark on the glass. She was not in any way insulted but she was certain there were other women who would be and she told herself she was acting on their behalf. "Then I shall just have to have enough for the both of us," she said. "I think I'll take three pounds please."

"Business must be very good then," Prudence said. "Chocolates are very dear now, you know."

"They certainly are and business assuredly has been brisk. We have investigations rolling in every minute of the day. It's no wonder I need to feed myself with chocolates in the evening," Beryl said. "It's a miracle I have time to tear myself away in order to do a bit of shopping."

"I know just what you mean. A competent woman's work is never done. So many people find things to fill her time, do they not?"

"Indeed they do. Actually, I had recently heard that you have a very important job that you've been doing as a volunteer here in the community," Beryl said.

"Which job is that?" Prudence asked. Her voice was tinged with a bit of restraint and wariness had crept in.

"I heard from Mr. Dennis Morley, over at the Hambley village, that you've been entrusted as the keeper of the keys for the long-distance pigeon racing club. What an honor that must be," Beryl said.

Beryl noticed Prudence's shoulders slowly slip back down from around her ears. The woman positively glowed with pride.

"Well, I shouldn't like to put on airs about it but it is a position of some trust," Prudence said.

"Have you been doing it for long?" Beryl asked.

"As a matter of fact, I've been doing it for several years," Prudence said, lifting a white box from beneath the counter and lining it with tissue paper.

"Tell me, exactly how does it work? I feel a bit uncertain as to how the results of the race are tallied," Beryl said. Prudence lifted chocolates into the box as Beryl pointed at each sort she desired.

"It's really very simple. Each of the racers has a wooden clock box in their loft." Prudence paused from her box filling to turn all of her attention on Beryl.

"I noticed a strange wooden box with a

clock on its face at Mr. Cunningham's pigeon loft. I wondered what it was for," Beryl lied. She could not remember seeing any such thing in the pigeon loft but Prudence needn't hear she had missed what could prove to be a vital piece of information.

"Did you see it the day that you found his body?" Prudence asked. She practically goggled with her desire for the lurid details. Beryl could see her longing etched on her face. It might be best to toss her a tiny little bone.

"Yes, that was it exactly. I found the clock just before I noticed an unpleasant smell coming up from below the loft," Beryl said. Prudence's mouth flapped open and then snapped shut once more. Beryl could see the wheels turning in Prudence's mind as she considered how she would spread that bit of knowledge around the village. "So what does the clock do exactly?"

"It serves as an official timer. When the pigeon flies into the loft the racer removes the band from its pigeon's leg and slips it into the hole at the top of the box. The cylinder of the band stops the clock at exactly the moment they placed the band into the box," Prudence said.

"How does that make you the keeper of

the keys?" Beryl asked.

"The box is locked so that the owner does not have access to the interior and cannot tamper with the time the clock was stopped. As the person with the keys I am the only one who can open it, retrieve the bands, and reset the clocks after the results from the race are registered and verified," Prudence said.

"Do you go to them or do they come to you?" Beryl asked.

"They all bring their clocks to the village hall. I have no intention of traipsing about to every one of the lofts and I certainly don't want them bringing their pigeon boxes into a place that sells food," Prudence said. "I bring my ledger to record the official results along with all the keys to the village hall and mark down everyone's time."

"So it really is a job that is prestigious," Beryl said.

"I shouldn't like to put on airs, but I will admit you are not the first to say such a thing," Prudence said. "I am responsible for calling in the official results to the racing board as well. They tally them from all the different districts and determine the overall winner." Prudence resumed filling the chocolate box. Beryl took that to mean she felt she had divulged as much information about her importance as she had to share.

"Is it at all possible that someone could tamper with the clocks and cheat?" Beryl asked. Prudence paused, her hand holding a chocolate hovering above the box. Without thinking she popped the chocolate into her mouth and began to chew, gazing at the ceiling in a thoughtful way. So much for not indulging in sweets, Beryl thought to herself. Beryl watched as Prudence swallowed hard.

"I shouldn't think so," Prudence finally said. "Unless someone had a second set of keys to their own box. That would be able to do it I suppose. What makes you ask such a thing?" Prudence leaned across the counter. Her gossip detection was in full force. Beryl wasn't sure if Gareth Scott deserved what was about to happen to him, but solving the case was more important than maintaining his reputation. Besides, she told herself, other people were already speculating as to his extraordinary winning streak. Prudence was unlikely to do much more harm than had already been done. In fact, given her propensity for spreading malicious gossip, it might do him some good. People might be inclined to disbelieve the rumors if Prudence was the one who was spreading them.

"In the course of our investigation it has come up that Gareth Scott almost always wins the races. I wondered if there might be another explanation for that extraordinary set of circumstances outside of his claims that he feeds his birds a superior diet of fruits and vegetables," Beryl said.

"I shouldn't think Mr. Scott would be the sort of man who would cheat," Prudence said. "Although I would say I've noticed from time to time that the vegetables he sold me seem to be a few ounces lighter than the price he has charged me. Sometimes I wonder if a pound is not quite a pound at Mr. Scott's establishment." Prudence drummed her long bony fingers on the glass counter, leaving a few finger marks of her own.

"So you think it is possible that he has been cheating?" Beryl asked.

"I suppose anyone could be tempted to cheat. These gentlemen take their pigeon racing extremely seriously and it would be remarkable if the idea had never crossed any of their minds," Prudence said. "But other than a second set of keys to his box, I can't think how he would have managed it."

"You've been very helpful," Beryl said. "I

think I'd like to take a box of licorice for Edwina as well please." Prudence nodded absentmindedly. Beryl could see that Mr. Scott was in for a good dose of the spotlight. She collected her parcels, paid for her purchases, and hurried out the door before Prudence began to speak to the next customer. She felt a little guilty about what Prudence might say and did not want to overhear it.

CHAPTER 33

Edwina was finishing off the lunch dishes and turning her attention to sweeping the kitchen floor when a freckled face appeared at the window of the back door to the scullery. She opened the door and Archie Harrison tromped in with an excited look on his youthful face.

"I raced back from London just as fast as I could," he said breathlessly. "And I've returned Beryl's automobile. There's a bit of a ding in the front bumper so I pulled it round back hoping she wouldn't see it. Is she here?" Archie asked. Edwina felt her heart sink. If there was one thing Beryl loved, it was her motorcar. It wasn't the first time it had seen some damage. Beryl herself had inflicted a horrendous dent in the bonnet on the day she had first arrived at the Beeches. Still, she wouldn't be happy to hear it needed more repairs. And their finances were not so robust that such a thing was easily absorbed into the budget. Hopefully whatever it was that Archie found out in London would justify the expense as well as the heartache.

"I suppose I had best see how it looks," Edwina said. Archie nodded and she followed him out the back door of the scullery and into her beloved garden. Archie had pulled Beryl's motorcar back behind the house and tucked it around the side of a clump of rhododendrons. It had been a valiant effort to hide it but the cherry-red of its paint job showed between the leaves and made it easy to spot. Archie and Edwina approached it and he pointed to the back fender.

"Tell me you think it's not so terribly bad," Archie said.

"Tell me you found out something incredibly important in London," Edwina said, eyeing a dent the size of a cottage loaf in the back of the motorcar. The paint was scraped away and the damage to the fender looked almost like a crime on such a beautiful piece of machinery. Even someone as firmly committed to a more sedate means of transport as Edwina could see that.

"That's it exactly," Archie said. "I was reversing out of a parking spot and into traffic to hurry back here to tell you what I'd found out when I rammed into another motorist. Considering what I discovered, I think Beryl will believe it was all worthwhile despite the damage."

"Well, then you best get on with telling me what it is," Edwina said. "Come sit on the bench and tell me your news." Edwina led him to her favorite spot in the garden, a wooden bench that overlooked a small pond filled with brilliant flashing goldfish and the occasional frog. A willow tree bent its graceful branches over the bench and provided just the right amount of dappled shade on a spring afternoon. Birds twittered and chirped in the branches above and it seemed a surprising place to be sharing the progress of a murder investigation. Edwina thought briefly how much her life had changed in the last few months. She never would have guessed that her garden would be a place in which she would be conducting business of anything but an herbaceous variety.

"Mr. Jarvis was right about the rumors concerning Mr. Ecclestone-Smythe's colliery. In the whole mine in fact," Archie said. "It's unbelievable that the man is still in business at all."

"Do you think the mine will be forced to close?" Edwina said.

"I think that it will take a miracle for it to

remain open. The mine itself is basically worthless. Not only are the shafts unstable, the quality of the coal is very low, and it's being said that what veins there were have been played out," Archie said.

"Played out? Does that mean they've finished extracting as much coal as there was?" Edwina asked. She wished she had her notebook but hadn't thought to put it in her pocket as she had only been doing some housework when Archie arrived.

"Exactly. And since the cost of setting up the shafts was astronomical because the ground is so unstable and inclined to flood, there is no capital left to sink new shafts in order to look for new veins. Not only that, sabotage has been constantly plaguing the entire operation," Archie said.

"Why do you think we haven't heard about it?" Edwina asked. "Shouldn't that sort of thing be very difficult to keep quiet?"

"The miners want to keep their jobs. It's a terribly bad time for all of them. They've managed to keep it hushed up because nobody wants to talk about it. It's a wonder no one's been killed yet in the course of some of the damage," Archie said.

"What sort of sabotage are you talking about?" Edwina asked.

"According to my sources in London

there are rumors of damage to the equipment, hobbling of the pit ponies, even fraying of the ropes and conveyor belts used to transport the coal up and out of the mine and on to its final destination in Dover," Archie said. "One person I spoke with said that he has it on good authority from different tradesmen making the repairs that Mr. Ecclestone-Smythe's bad luck has been a boon for them. Their businesses have had a steady stream of new work because of it."

Edwina sat back against the back of the bench and laced her fingers together.

"How has Mr. Ecclestone-Smythe managed to stay in business so long if everyone knows he has so much trouble financially? I should've thought it would take a great deal to keep his creditors off his back," Edwina said. While it had been extraordinarily unpleasant at the time to deal with the tradesmen and their dunning notices, Edwina suddenly realized that her own precarious financial position of the past few years had given her much more insight into the desperation one felt when one could not pay one's bills. Somehow it still did not seem worth it.

"He's got something very valuable that he can always cash in should he need to. The creditors seem willing to accept a delay in payment because they know they can more than get their money back should he be forced to sell his valuables," Archie said.

"Do you know exactly the nature of his valuable property? It isn't the land that mine is on, is it?" Edwina said.

"No, certainly not," Archie said. "The land, at this point, could be considered a liability. It's something far more stable in value than a played-out coal mine. Apparently his wife owns an extraordinary collection of jewels given to her upon her marriage by her parents. Mr. Ecclestone-Smythe has used them as collateral all over the country. It's the only thing of value he still owns."

Edwina felt her breath catch in her throat. Here was an extraordinarily good reason for murder. Did Mrs. Ecclestone-Smythe know that her husband had promised her jewelry as collateral for his loans? Did she understand the sort of trouble he would be in once he realized they were missing? Was that why she was so desperate for them to be recovered before he discovered their loss? Did anyone else understand their true value? Did someone take them in order to cash them in themselves or did they take them to ruin Mr. Ecclestone-Smythe? Edwina's head swirled with the possibilities and she desperately wished that Beryl would return to discuss the case, despite how she would likely react to the damage to her motorcar.

"Are you quite certain of your sources, Archie?" Edwina asked. "You would absolutely trust them that this information is true concerning Mr. Ecclestone-Smythe's finances?"

"I am absolutely certain. I may be a bit rough around the edges, but if there's one thing I'm good at, it's getting to the truth," Archie said. "I would stake my life on it. Mr. Ecclestone-Smythe is stony-broke."

CHAPTER 34

Beryl was not in the least bit surprised to
see the dent in the back of her automobile.
She knew when she had acquiesced to
Archie's request that it was a distinct possibility. In fact, she had never been in an
automobile with him when she was not
concerned for its safety, and even, it could
be said, for her own. Besides, his reckless
driving did not usually turn up such useful
information. She had been delighted with
his findings in London and felt that they
were making real progress on the case.

After reassuring Edwina that she and
Archie would still be friends despite the accident, she decided to kill two birds with
one stone and to head down into the village
once more to confirm Mr. Gareth Scott's
alibi for the time of the murder. She first
stopped off in the center of Walmsley Parva
so Edwina could do a bit of shopping.
Edwina said she needed more wool for a

project she was working on. Beryl could not believe how much yarn her friend could go through in a week. She was even more baffled at how much Edwina seemed to enjoy pottering about in the yarn shop, considering the merits of the various skeins and patterns available. Beryl was more than happy to have an errand of her own that would excuse her from accompanying Edwina and feigning interest in any of it.

She left Edwina at the front of the yarn shop then motored down to Blackburn's Garage and pulled to a stop right in front of the open garage doors. Michael Blackburn slid out from beneath the automobile he was working on, sat up, and smiled at her. His sister, Norah, glanced up from underneath the hood of the vehicle and gave her a wave. Beryl had met the Blackburns when she first arrived in Walmsley Parva and had admired their ability with automobiles. They had restored her prize possession to its former glory once before. She was confident they would be able to do so again.

Michael approached the vehicle then walked around it, making a thorough inspection with his eyes. "I see you've gotten yourself into some more trouble," he said.

"This time it wasn't me," Beryl said. "I lent my baby to a friend and this is what happened to it."

"Miss Edwina did this?" Norah said, coming up alongside her brother. "I should've thought she'd be a far more cautious driver than that."

"Edwina certainly would be far more cautious than this. But she still does not know how to drive. In fact, I had lent it to my friend Mr. Harrison, who took it up to London. He is still apologizing for what happened," Beryl said.

"It's a shame," Norah said.

"Yes, it is. I hate to see such a beautiful machine subjected to this sort of damage," Beryl said.

"Well, yes, that's true," Norah said. "But what I was in fact talking about was the fact that you have yet to teach Miss Edwina to drive. I think it would do her a world of good." Michael and Norah exchanged a glance. Beryl wondered what they were up to.

"I've been thinking the same thing," Michael said. "Did you know that we've decided in addition to the taxi service and the garage, to open a driving school?"

"You have, have you?" Beryl asked. The pair nodded eagerly up and down. Beryl heartily agreed that Edwina should learn to drive. She firmly believed that she should pay attention when the things that had been on her mind were mentioned by another, especially if it happened more than once. She felt as though the universe were giving her a sign that she was on the right track. And although she was pleased to think her plans were cosmically aligned, she was not at all convinced someone else should be entrusted with the weighty duty of teaching Edwina to drive. That was something she fully intended to do herself.

"What a wonderful idea," Beryl said. "I wish you every success with it. However, since I will be needing to pay for repairs to the car, I don't believe there will be any coin left in the coffers to pay for driving lessons. Besides, I think Edwina would be most comfortable learning from me anyway. But I do appreciate the suggestion."

"Maybe you could ask her for us anyway?" Michael said. He gave her one of his wicked grins. Despite the loss of one of his arms during the war, Michael gave off the impression of being an extremely attractive and completely able-bodied young man. Beryl would be lying to herself if she did not admit she had entertained the notion of putting her theory to the test. Although to do so in Edwina's house would present some difficulties. She imagined the look on

Edwina's face if she encountered any young man slipping out of Beryl's bedroom in the wee hours. Entertaining as they were, she pushed such thoughts to the back of her mind and returned her attention to the business at hand.

"Will you be able to attend to the repairs this week?" Beryl asked. She opened the door and slid out to join Michael at the back of the automobile. "I understood from Mr. Scott that you had his van here and I wondered if you might be too busy."

"We should be able to take care of it in a day or two. It's not so bad as it looks. A bit of hammering and some new paint should take care of it. It'll be good as new before you know it," Michael said. "Is that right, sis?"

"I should think so. We aren't all that busy right now," Norah said. "We finished up with Mr. Scott's delivery van and we only have two other vehicles to take care of before this one."

"That seems fast. When did Mr. Scott bring in the van? Wasn't it the other morning, on the day of the race?" Beryl asked. Norah motioned for Beryl to follow her into the garage and back into the office located behind a small door.

Norah opened the appointment book and

ran her finger down the columns. "It says here he booked an appointment that day, but I'm not sure exactly what time he was here," Norah said.

"He told me that he was here first thing that morning dropping it off," Beryl said.

Norah shouted to her brother, "Michael, what time did Mr. Scott drop off his van the other day?" Michael entered the garage, wiping his hand on a rag tucked into a loop on his coveralls.

"I'd say about nine in the morning," Michael said. "I was having my tea when he dropped by, and I always have a tea break around then if I am here at the garage."

"Are you certain about that?" Beryl asked. "He said that he was here far earlier. Perhaps as early as eight."

"That can't be right," Norah said. "I was just leaving our allotment when I saw him at his own patch. I saw him on the same morning but before he dropped off his van."

"Up at the allotments?" Beryl said. "Are you quite certain?" Beryl felt the buzz she had grown to recognize as a significant clue in a case. Gareth Scott had actually been on-site at the place Lionel Cunningham's body was found and on the same day he went missing. And he had lied about the time he had been there.

"I most assuredly am. I was up at our allotment watering the lettuces before the sun became too hot. They wilt so easily you know," Norah said. Beryl had no idea about the tendency of lettuces to wilt or to do anything other than to provide a bit of greenery on her plate at mealtimes. Nevertheless she nodded in agreement.

"So what time did you go about this watering?" Beryl asked.

"I was in our plot pulling weeds and thinning the carrots by seven. I kept at it until at least an hour before I decided to head on over to the garage to give Michael some help. I'd say I was back to the garage by quarter past eight," Norah said.

"So that would give Mr. Scott at least forty-five minutes between the time you left the allotments and when he arrived with his van?" Beryl asked.

"That seems about right," Norah said, looking at Michael for confirmation.

"Absolutely. I had finished my tea just about the time he came. That would make it just after nine," Michael said.

That would give Mr. Scott an hour, give or take a few minutes, at the allotment on the morning of the murder. Which would be plenty of time to have an argument with Mr. Cunningham, kill him, and hide his body beneath his own pigeon loft. Beryl needed to speak with Edwina immediately. She took her leave of the Blackburn siblings with the assurance that they would get to her automobile just as soon as possible. She hurried up the high street and burst into the yarn shop, surprising the owner and Edwina whose heads were bent over a ball of pale blue wool. A sunbeam shone down on the yarn, highlighting the colors as Edwina tipped the skein this way and that.

"What do you think of this one for a muffler?" Edwina said, holding up the yarn for Beryl to give an opinion.

"Could you put that on her account, ma'am?" Beryl asked. "Edwina, I don't think you'll be having much time for knitting today." Edwina seemed to sense from her friend's tone of voice that something was well and truly up. With a hurried exchange between herself and the owner of the Woolery, Edwina tucked the ball of yarn into her basket and followed Beryl out the door.

CHAPTER 35

Edwina was amazed at how much Beryl had unearthed in just the short time it had taken her to select yarn for two projects. And not even projects that had required a great deal of agonizing thought. Charity knitting and a muffler to send to an acquaintance she had met through a long-deceased aunt did not have the same import as a jumper she would wear for the next decade. She marveled at Beryl's skill in detecting as well as her good luck. She was grateful that she had had the foresight to don a stout pair of walking shoes when she left the house that morning as they hurried more quickly than could possibly be considered seemly through the village and on towards the allotments.

They arrived in record speed and stealthily made their way to the one tended by Gareth Scott. Edwina looked out over the other patches and spotted one she knew belonged to Norah and Michael Blackburn.

"It's right over there," Edwina said, pointing to a tidy garden filled with a variety of colorful lettuces and the soft fronds of emerging carrots. Quite a green thumb, Norah Blackburn has, Edwina thought approvingly to herself as she glanced over the neat rows and flourishing plants. "That's the one that belongs to the Blackburns." Beryl turned and looked in the direction Edwina indicated and then set off towards it.

"You stay here and we'll see how well we can see each other from one spot to the next," Beryl said as she strode towards the Blackburns' allotment. Edwina held her hand to shield her eyes and looked up and down the whole space. Much of it was open to view, but here and there, sheds and trellises and water barrels stacked one upon the next, as well as the odd chicken coop, blocked the view. She watched as Beryl stopped at the Blackburns' patch and let herself in through the small gate in the wire fencing. Beryl called out in her booming voice, "Can you see me?"

"Clear as day," Edwina said. "Can you see all of me?"

"Yes, as long as you are standing right there," Beryl said. "Move around a bit though to make certain I can see you from every spot." Edwina did as she was asked and tried angle after angle. After several moments the pair determined the only place it would be impossible to see Mr. Scott from the vantage point of Norah's allotment was if he had entered his own shed or stood directly behind it. Beryl returned to Gareth Scott's allotment.

"It isn't as though I didn't believe Norah, but it was best to check to be sure. It seems that she was entirely within reason to say she had seen him," Beryl said. "If he was here, and she had looked up at all, she couldn't have missed him."

"I agree. Now the next question is how easily do you think Mr. Scott could have seen Lionel Cunningham's allotment?" Edwina asked.

"We shall have to conduct same sort of test to find out," Beryl said. "This time you hide and I'll seek." Edwina picked up her skirts and headed towards the unfortunate Mr. Cunningham's allotment. It was farther from Gareth Scott's than Norah's had been but when she turned back around she could still see Beryl standing next to a trellis smothered in early peas. She waved and Beryl waved back.

"Move about a bit and I'll let you know if I can still see you," Beryl shouted. They conducted the same experiment they had between the first two allotments, and after a few moments time Beryl joined her at Mr. Cunningham's pigeon loft.

"Mr. Scott could absolutely have known Mr. Cunningham was here. There are more places to hide or to just be obscured from view, but on a quiet morning with very few other people here, he would have been likely to notice the movement of another person," Beryl said. "Especially one he disliked as much as he did Mr. Cunningham."

"While we're here I think we should take the opportunity to take a look inside Mr. Scott's own pigeon loft, don't you?" Edwina said. "After all, he isn't here and there's no one else to see what we are up to either."

"Wonderful idea," Beryl said. "I think it's a testimony to my good influence that you would consider breaking and entering."

"I'm not sure a good influence is what you would call it. But if we wish to solve the case and collect our fee, needs must," Edwina said. The two of them looked furtively around once more to be sure they were not observed then hurried to Mr. Scott's pigeon loft.

It was far more spacious than the one Mr. Cunningham had constructed. It was more like a toolshed than an elevated chicken coop. There were two steps leading up to a full-size door fastened with a sturdy latch. Edwina took the lead and Beryl seemed happy to let her. For all Beryl's adventures with creatures in the wild, Edwina was sure she was the better acquainted with animal husbandry.

Despite her experience with domesticated birds, she was surprised to find her heart hammering inside her chest as she pressed the door closed behind her. The warm air and gentle cooing of the birds gave her a sense of claustrophobia. The smell of straw mixed with dried corn feed and pigeon droppings made her feel slightly sick and dizzy. The sooner they could leave the loft, the happier she would be. Beryl also seemed eager to complete the job at hand as she methodically glanced around from pigeon nesting box to pigeon nesting box.

"While we are here I suppose we ought to take a look for the jewelry," Edwina said. "Perhaps Mr. Scott not only killed Mr. Cunningham but took the opportunity to rob him as well."

Beryl let out a sputtering sigh. "I can think of nothing I would rather do less than to grope about beneath all these birds. Still, I am sure you are right. We would be foolish not to check." Beryl took one side of the loft and Edwina headed for the other. Slowly, and carefully, they reached under the straw in each of the boxes before looking in the corners of the loft and peeping under tools and crates. After a few moments it became clear that no jewelry was there to be found.

Edwina realized that some little nugget of an idea was tickling away at the back of her head. She was an avid bird-watcher and had spent many happy hours observing the birds that flitted about her garden in the growing season as well as those that appeared at her feeders during the winter months. When she was a child her family had kept chickens and she had always been able to tell the members of the flock apart at a glance. She paused and looked more closely at the pigeons in the loft. One by one she looked them over carefully.

"Beryl, have you noticed something odd about all of these pigeons?" Edwina said.

"I can't say as I have." Beryl raised her shoulders in a shrug. "They just look like a bunch of pigeons to me."

"Take a close look around and see if you see similarities between them," Edwina said. "For instance, see that grey one over there with the two stripes below its eye?"

"What about it?" Beryl said.

"Look over in the corner," Edwina said. "Do you see another grey pigeon of approximately the same size with two black bands beneath its eye?" Beryl turned her head from one bird to the other then back again.

"Yes, as a matter fact I do see that. What about it? Don't all pigeons look grey and black or white and grey or some such thing?" Beryl asked.

"They do have similarities, but if you look, you'll see that there are pairs of birds that look almost identical even though there are all different sorts. There is a white one with grey speckles. And another white one with the same markings. From what I can see, the only pigeon in here that doesn't have a twin is that silvery colored bird with no markings at all," Edwina said.

"What are you suggesting?" Beryl said. "Are you saying there is a reason for that?"

"If Mr. Scott has been cheating in order to win so many races perhaps he's substituting one bird for another," Edwina said. "What if he has a second set of birds that he releases much closer to the loft with an identical band to the bird that is released at the official start of the race? And what if the reason that bird has no double is that Mr. Cunningham made off with its twin the day he disappeared?"

Edwina was gratified to see Beryl's eyes widen and her mouth drop open. It wasn't often that she was the one doing the shocking instead of finding herself the one being shocked. Although the feeling was novel, it was entirely gratifying.

"What a remarkable suggestion. But how can we be sure?" Beryl asked. Edwina walked softly towards a sleek white pigeon. She plucked it from its perch and tucked it under her arm. She grasped the pigeon by the leg and read the number on the band secured just above its clawed foot. She returned the bird to its perch and reached over a few feet for its twin. She glanced at the second bird's leg band then gave Beryl a wide smile.

"They have the exact same number on their identification bands. Didn't Prudence tell you the birds all have identification numbers officially registered with the club in order to prove their times?" Edwina asked.

"That is what she said when I asked her about her job as the keeper of the keys," Beryl said.

"Then I can't imagine there is any reason for Mr. Scott to have birds with duplicate number bands other than to cheat," Edwina said.

"Edwina, you are a genius," Beryl said, grasping her friend by both arms and shaking her slightly. "We must head to the vicar immediately and ask him if he thinks such a swindle would be possible."

Edwina looked about the loft and spied a rectangular, lidded basket used to transport pigeons to the races. She made short work of plucking two almost identical birds from their roosts, and stowing them carefully inside. "We'd best take evidence along with our suspicions. I shouldn't think the vicar will be in a hurry to accept our theory without proof."

With a backwards glance at the rest of the fluttering birds, Edwina hoisted the basket in her arms and followed Beryl quickly out the door. She pulled the door behind her firmly to be sure none of the evidence could escape and rushed along the street towards the vicarage.

CHAPTER 36

The vicar looked as doleful as ever sitting behind his wooden desk strewn and heaped with books and papers and bits of string. Beryl could not imagine living the sort of life she imagined Vicar Lowethorpe did, surrounded by dust and close air and the burdensome needs of his congregants day after day after day. Just stepping into his small office made her feel an itch to take off for parts unknown. If he had not been a man of the cloth she might have invited him to join her. But even she had some lines she had drawn for herself and vicars were on the far side of them.

"Are you here with news of the pigeon club's missing birds?" the vicar asked, with a hopeful glance at the basket. "Or are you in need of spiritual counsel?" He indicated the seats opposite his desk and Beryl waited for Edwina to settle herself and the basket of birds into the nearest before seating herself in the remaining chair. Beryl had decided not only were vicars more in Edwina's wheelhouse, but that as the person who had figured out the puzzle, Edwina should be the one to take the credit with the vicar for bringing the cheating scheme to light.

"Although we have not recovered your birds we are here about Mr. Cunningham and some irregularities in the pigeon racing world," Edwina said. "I hope you have some time to answer a few questions for us."

"You won't be charging me, will you?" the vicar asked. "My good lady wife has my finances on quite a tight leash lately." He leaned forward and lowered his voice. "Too many losses with Chester White lately. Although I ought to let you know you can stop concerning yourselves with the missing funds. Chester returned the exact sum missing from the club. He said that he suspected it rightly belonged to the club."

"I thought you were eager not to let anyone know about the missing money," Beryl said. "How did Chester know to give it back to you?" The vicar tugged at the collar of his shirt.

"I might have made mention of our difficulties when I was in the pub placing a bet. A bit too much imbibing, I'm afraid.

Still, the money is back in the club's coffers so no harm done," the vicar said.

"We have no intention of charging you, Vicar," Edwina said. "We are simply following up on behalf of another client." The vicar looked relieved and then curious.

"Another client. I see that your business is really taking off," he said. "I'd be happy to assist you in any way that I can so long as it does not compromise any confidences shared with me by one of my congregants."

"We understand. Our line of enquiry has more to do with confidence you have bestowed upon one of your pigeon racing club members," Beryl said.

"Then please, go ahead with your questions," Vicar Lowethorpe said.

"We have strong reason to believe that Mr. Scott has been cheating at the races," Edwina said.

"That sort of rumor has been floating around for quite some time, but I do say, ladies, that I have put it down to envy rather than any real evidence," the vicar said.

"I rather think it amounts to a good deal more than envy," Edwina said. "I believe that we have discovered how he's been doing it and that we have the evidence to back our assumption."

"Really? Then I suppose you had best tell

me what you think you figured out," the vicar said.

"How likely is it that he would have two birds of several sorts that look almost identical?" Edwina asked.

"To the untrained eye pigeons can look very much alike," the vicar said.

"While I am not a pigeon fancier, you know that I am an avid bird-watcher," Edwina said.

"Well, yes, you do have that reputation," the vicar said slowly. "What makes you think he has two birds that looked remarkably alike?"

"Because we've just seen them with our own eyes," Beryl said impatiently. She promised herself she would not take over the conversation but it was difficult to wait. She felt how close they were coming to the end of the investigation and it irked her to think they could not just get on with it. Edwina shot her a restraining glance and she took a deep breath.

"We were just up at Mr. Scott's pigeon loft having a look around. I happened to notice in the loft that he had several pairs of birds that each looked remarkably similar. The markings were the same, the sizes were approximately the same, and at a quick glance I don't know that anyone would have noticed that they weren't the same bird," Edwina said.

"Still, my dear lady, I cannot be a party to you bandying about such wild accusations without real proof." The vicar clamped his thin lips together tightly.

"We have the proof," Beryl said. "Show him, Ed." Edwina placed the basket on the vicar's desk.

"Go on and see for yourself," she said. Vicar Lowethorpe loosened the latches holding the basket lid in place and lifted it just enough to peek inside.

"These birds do look remarkably similar but it still proves nothing. It could be no more than a coincidence."

"Indulge us, Vicar, and inspect the leg band on each bird," Edwina said. The vicar slipped his hand into the basket and withdrew first one bird and then the other, inspecting the bands carefully. His pale blue eyes widened and he slipped the second bird back into the basket.

"I regret to say, I see what you mean. I assume you are suggesting Mr. Scott is in some way substituting one bird for another during a race?" the vicar asked.

"That is just what we decided he must be doing," Edwina said.

"That would be dashed un-sporting of

387

him." The vicar appeared distressed. His cheeks grew even paler and his voice cracked as he spoke.

"But it would explain how he kept winning much more easily than any amount of fruits or vegetables, wouldn't it?" Beryl asked.

"How do you propose that he's been making the switch? And how do you think it's helping him?" the vicar asked.

"We think he's releasing the second set of birds much closer to their own loft than where the start of the race would be. I think that he's placing the bands from the second set of birds into the official clock in front of witnesses. Those witnesses then go on to some other place before the second bird returns," Edwina said.

"But that's monstrous," the vicar said. "He would be banned from pigeon racing for the rest of his life should he be convicted of such a thing."

"But it would be possible?" Beryl asked.

"Yes, I suppose it would be, now that you come to mention it," the vicar said. "I should never have thought of something like that myself." Beryl thought that that said much more about the vicar's lack of ingenuity rather than his level of morality, but she prudently kept that thought to herself.

Edwina took another tactic.

"One would never expect a man of God to behave in such a devious manner. It's no wonder you did not think of it before. I shouldn't have myself if I hadn't seen the birds with my own eyes," Edwina said.

"I suppose he must be hiding the second set of birds anytime anyone visits his pigeon loft," the vicar said.

"That would make sense. Have you ever been inside his pigeon loft without an invitation?" Beryl asked.

The vicar cast his gaze up towards the ceiling as if searching his memory banks. "I can't think of a time that I have. Generally, we meet at the village hall or some location other than the vicarage, but not at the lofts themselves. Most racers prefer to spend their time with their own pigeons rather than someone else's," the vicar said.

"So you would agree that it is a possible explanation for his duplicate birds and for his unprecedented string of wins?" Edwina asked.

"It pains me to say it but I would have to agree that it is not only possible, but given the evidence of the identical bands, it is the only plausible explanation. While it would be an extraordinary coincidence for him to have pairs of identical birds, there is no legitimate explanation for the duplicate bands," the vicar said.

"I'm afraid that I agree with you," Edwina said.

"It looks like you're going to need a new vice president for your club," Beryl said.

"That makes two openings in less than a week," the vicar said. "I only hope we can find people willing to take over those positions."

Beryl thought it likely that if they had opened their membership to the miners from Hambley, they would have had plenty of takers for any of the positions the club wished to fill. But she kept her thoughts to herself and was glad she did so when the vicar spoke again.

"I suppose you came across this information in the course of your investigation into Mr. Cunningham's death?" the vicar asked.

"Yes, we did. While we are no longer investigating his disappearance we have been asked to look into something else connected with the case," Edwina said. The vicar opened his mouth as if to speak then closed it again. He looked back and forth between Beryl and Edwina as though he were trying to make up his mind about something.

"We are conducting ourselves and our

investigation with the utmost discretion," Edwina said. "If there's something you think we should know you can trust us to be responsible with the information."

"I shouldn't like to ruin anyone's reputation," the vicar said.

"You know that I am never a malicious gossip," Edwina said. She nodded encouragingly at the older gentleman and he seemed to reach a decision.

"It's just that I go out for a walk every morning, quite early. It's the only time I really have to myself every day, you see," the vicar said, glancing quickly at the door. Beryl thought he must have been thinking of the demands of his wife rather than the demands of his congregation.

"And you've seen something you think we should know about?" Edwina said encouragingly.

"I'm afraid that I have. I take a walk on a regular route every day and it takes me past Mrs. Plumptree's boardinghouse." The vicar paused as if gathering his resolve. "Two or three times each week, lately, I've noticed a young blond woman entering the boardinghouse at the crack of dawn. I should not like to speculate where she has been all night, but I can't say I can think of any good reason for her behavior."

"Thank you for sharing that information with us, Vicar," Edwina said. "We will be sure not to spread any gossip about the village but will look into it discreetly." Edwina slid forward in her chair and stood. She and Edwina took their leave of the distraught clergyman. She did not envy him the conversation he would be having with his other club members. But she was eager to go have a talk with one of them in particular herself.

CHAPTER 37

Edwina was of two minds on the subject of confronting Gareth Scott. On the one hand, she was excited about the possibility of making progress on the case. On the other, she was distressed to ponder the fact that the local greengrocer was a man of such low character. One didn't like to consider that one had consumed things that had been in such close proximity to someone of such base morals. In fact, the entire situation made her feel decidedly flushed and indignant. She tugged at the collar of her blouse as she and Beryl made their way swiftly from the vicarage to Mr. Scott's shop. In Mr. Scott's pigeon loft, and while visiting the vicarage, she had been too caught up in the chase to feel personally perturbed by the greengrocer's perfidy. But now she felt her agitation growing.

"Which one of us do you think should do the talking?" Beryl asked.

"Perhaps you should handle this one," Edwina said. "Honestly, I am so angry to think that I've been frequenting a tradesman of this ilk that I'm not sure I can control myself should I open my mouth to speak. To think of all the vegetables I have consumed that this man has handled." Bushels of them, Edwina thought to herself. She had always objected to her mother's insistence that one clean one's plate before leaving the table every night. Now she had even more reason to feel maligned by that practice.

"Just leave it to me, Ed," Beryl said, laying a reassuring and restraining hand on Edwina's arm as they approached Mr. Scott's door. Edwina cast a spurious glance over the bins of early peas and scallions flanking the door. She felt as though the poor things had been contaminated.

They pressed open the door and stepped inside, setting the bell to jingling. Beryl strode confidently up to Mr. Scott and poked him in the chest with a gloved finger. Edwina wanted to do much the same herself but would not have dared no matter how angry she was. One simply did not go about touching other people's husbands. Unless one was Beryl. She congratulated herself on having the presence of mind to turn the interrogation over to her far more outspoken friend.

"You aren't going to get away with it," Beryl said. "We have figured you out." Mr. Scott crossed his beefy arms across his chest and leaned against the counter behind him.

"I'm sure I don't know what you're on about," he said, looking down at the top of Beryl's head. Beryl was a tall woman, but he still had a few inches on her. Edwina suddenly wondered if it was such a good idea to confront him so boldly. His face was flushing with color and his body language signaled that he was on the defensive. Edwina was quite sure that after their last interaction with Constable Gibbs the police-woman would be in no hurry to rush to their aid should they have need of her.

"We have solved the mystery of your win-ning streak. Suffice it to say it's far easier to pull off with substitute birds than it is with quantities of fruits and vegetables. Wouldn't you agree?" Beryl said to the greengrocer. She tapped him in the chest again. "What's more, we've already told the vicar of our suspicions." Mr. Scott drew himself up to his full height and scowled at the pair of women.

"You're not saying the vicar agreed with such a ridiculous suggestion, are you?" Mr.

Scott said.

"We have and he agrees it's entirely possible," Beryl said. Edwina noticed her friend was widening her own stance in a most unladylike and confrontational fashion. Edwina would not have known how to begin such an exchange. She marveled at what was taking place before her.

"That's preposterous," Mr. Scott said. "The vicar trusts me implicitly. I'm his vice president and right-hand man. It would take more than a couple of nattering women to convince him that I'm doing anything I should not be. Besides, where's your proof?"

"We've been to your pigeon loft and have seen your duplicate birds with our own eyes," Beryl said.

"Since when are you an expert on pigeons?" Mr. Scott said.

"We didn't need to be an expert on pigeons to see that the bands on their legs were identical," Edwina said, adding her two pence worth. "I happen to be an avid birdwatcher so I noticed the similarities. All it took was a willingness to check their leg bands to know for sure that you are swapping one for the other during the races."

"You are correct when you say the vicar was not easily convinced of your unsportsmanlike behavior. Fortunately, Edwina had the forethought to take a pair of twin pigeons to Vicar Lowethorpe's office to show him the birds and the identical bands they each wear around their legs. He was easily convinced after that," Beryl said.

Mr. Scott looked as though he were about to speak when Beryl jabbed him in the chest once more. "The only real question here is whether you are simply a cheat or if you are also a murderer," she said.

"I didn't kill anybody," Mr. Scott said, lowering his arms and waving his hands before him. "I swear, all I did was fix the races a bit."

"Fix the races a bit?" Beryl asked. "You have consistently skewed the results with your cheating. I can't begin to imagine how much money you've bilked the other bettors out of over the years. How long have you been running this scam?"

"Only for the last few months, truly," Mr. Scott said.

"Whatever made you start?" Edwina asked. "I should have thought such a thing beneath you." Beryl was not entirely sure but she thought she heard one of Edwina's *tsk tsks.*

"I needed some extra money and it seemed a good way to make it. The opportunity came up to expand the business and I didn't want to let it slip away. Banks aren't lending money the way that they used to do, so I couldn't go to them for a loan. I was helping out my nephew who wants to expand his landholdings. He said he would give me a great deal on produce if I helped him with down payment money. It seemed the perfect way to make that happen," Mr. Scott said.

"It sounds as though you had an awful lot to lose. I suggest that Mr. Cunningham found out what you were up to and you killed him for it," Beryl said.

"I didn't. I can't prove it, but I didn't." Mr. Scott's posture deflated and left him looking shrunken. In fact, Edwina thought that he appeared as though he had lost six inches in height in approximately thirty seconds of time.

"What were you doing at the allotments that morning?" Edwina asked. "You lied about what time you dropped off your van at the Blackburns' garage. It seems likely to me you would have done so to cover up the time you were murdering Mr. Cunningham."

"I saw Cunningham that morning, it's true. He collected the birds from me that I was racing and then went on to his loft. I went back inside my own loft and didn't see him again. The truth is I was too busy inside preparing my duplicate birds to be released later to have time to kill him and dispose of his body," Mr. Scott said. "I swear."

"That's an awful lot of swearing from a man whose word cannot be trusted in the least," Edwina said.

"Did you see anyone else at the allotments that morning?" Beryl asked.

"I saw Cunningham and I also saw Norah Blackburn. She was busy doing some weeding and watering on her patch. I can't say that I saw anyone else and I don't believe that anyone saw me besides Cunningham."

"You are a most unfortunate man, considering your only witnesses are a dead man and someone who has accused you of lying," Beryl said. "You're absolutely certain you didn't see anyone else there that morning?"

"I was too busy worrying about anyone else seeing me. I made a point to stay hidden inside my pigeon loft until I was sure that Cunningham had left and that nobody would connect me being there with the race that day. It's become harder and harder to convince myself that I was not going to get caught fixing the races. In fact, it's almost a relief that it's over." Mr. Scott hung his head and Edwina considered how it would feel to be a prominent citizen who had been caught out on something as loathsome as cheating. She did not envy him the weeks ahead. She doubted his reputation would recover from it.

"I hope you realize that this means I will no longer be able to purchase my produce from you." Mr. Scott nodded. Edwina almost felt sorry for him. Almost. Perhaps it would not be necessary to tell anyone else what had transpired if they extracted a promise from him to retire from the sport forthwith. Before she could make the offer, Beryl spoke up.

"It won't be a relief to be investigated for murder," Beryl said. "At this point you're one of the few people with a very strong motive for killing Mr. Cunningham. If you stood to lose your reputation amongst the community members you might be desperate enough to kill him."

"All I can do is to reassure you for once and for all that I didn't have anything to do with Cunningham's murder. However, I can't prove that I didn't, and as far as I can see, you can't prove that I did. I understand if you want to take your trade elsewhere although there aren't many options here in Walmsley Parva. You may have to start growing all your own vegetables if you don't wish to trade with me," Mr. Scott said, gathering up his courage once more. Beryl could see the shift in his demeanor as he pushed off from the counter and stood up straight. "Now, if you'll excuse me, I have to make sure the shop is in readiness for those customers who would like to purchase from me." He pointed at the door and held his arm outstretched until they retreated. Edwina could feel his eyes boring into the back of her head as she strode out of the shop behind Beryl.

"That didn't go quite as well as I had hoped," Beryl said as they took a few steps down the sidewalk out of earshot of Mr. Scott. "I had sort of imagined that he would break down and confess. In my mind I had it built up into a very dramatic scene."

"You always have had a love of the dramatic, Beryl," Edwina said. "I'm afraid it's going to take more than that to get to the bottom of things. Let's go back to the Woolery and settle up my account. I would rather not have difficulties with all of the shopkeepers here in Walmsley Parva." Edwina thought she could manage without a steady supply of vegetables and even without fruits. After all, she could grow those herself at the Beeches. But unless she wished to start farming sheep, and she most certainly did not, she would be hard-pressed to supply herself with sufficient yarn for her knitting projects.

CHAPTER 38

The next day Edwina set off bright and early to help set up the May Day celebration. She and all of the other volunteers congregated near the village hall to take charge of their various assignments. Edwina was to oversee the raising of the tents and booths. She could only imagine she'd been given such an onerous task on account of her earlier, and most likely distressing, visit to the vicar. Mrs. Lowethorpe was not one to overtly hold a grudge. But she was one to make sure her retribution for any infractions was swift and merciless. Edwina headed to the center of the green where laborers of various sorts were struggling to lift up tent poles and wide swaths of canvas.

She checked her clipboard and consulted the map it held as to where each booth was planned to be erected. The coconut shy, the tea tent, the tombola booth were all marked on the map and she could easily see where those tents were being erected. Down at the end of the row was an unplanned gathering of laborers. Their tent did not match the others. In fact it was cobbled together with blankets and bits of tarpaulin. Edwina headed towards them, knowing that the vicar's wife would be most distressed indeed to see something so unattractive featuring in her festivities.

As she approached, Edwina suddenly felt uncomfortable at the idea of confronting the group. There were several men who looked like miners whispering and jeering. She was paused partway across the green to convince herself she ought to speak to them when she felt a restraining hand upon her arm. She turned to see Charles Jarvis standing beside her. He leaned towards her and spoke quietly in her ear.

"Best have a care there, Edwina," Charles said. "I have a feeling you don't want to tangle with those men."

She watched as they jostled and joked with each other as they hastily constructed a makeshift stage. "Whatever do you think they're doing?" she asked.

"I think they may be planning a speech," Charles said. Edwina glanced at her clipboard once more. She could see no indication that a stage had been planned at that end of the village green. In fact, the vicar's wife had mentioned at a committee meeting that she felt the occasion did not call for something as ostentatious as a stage and that it should be an altogether more informal event. The centerpiece for the May Day celebration, despite the fact that a member of the clergy was organizing it, was a maypole. And that had been set up in the center of the green. Edwina noticed the ribbons fluttering from its top despite them being held down with large rocks.

"The only speech slated is the one being given by Mrs. Lowethorpe to introduce the Maypole Queen. What sort of speech are they planning, do you think?" Edwina said. "And what's more to the point, who are they?" Simpkins appeared out of nowhere and joined them in staring at the group of men.

"You did say you were interested in including miners in the festivities. It looks like you may have gotten your wish," Simpkins said. "I'd say they are setting up a Labor Day demonstration."

"I'm very much afraid that you're right, Simpkins," Charles said. "This could turn nasty."

"Do you think they will become rowdy? Or violent even?" Edwina asked.

"Labor demonstrations are not known for their decorum," Charles said. "I think it would be best to let Mrs. Lowethorpe know that this is in the offing." Edwina nodded.

"She and I are not on the best of terms at the moment. Unfortunately, Beryl and I needed to deliver some upsetting news to her husband and I have reason to believe she is holding it against me," Edwina said. "I don't suppose I could persuade one of you to let her know on my behalf?"

"Well, I'm not going to go and tattle on them," Simpkins said disloyally. "My allegiance is to the workingman in all circumstances." Edwina could not say she was surprised. It was quite like Simpkins to prove unreliable when there was work to be done. After all, how many times had he left her alone to finish planting spring crocuses or pulling weeds in order to disappear into the potting shed to go about God knows what business of his own. Edwina turned towards Charles. While he was not a man who particularly liked confrontation, he could always be counted upon to behave as a gentleman.

"I would consider it a privilege to help shoulder your burden, Edwina," Charles said gallantly. "But I will only go in search of her if you will promise not to confront these men yourself while I am gone. I really think it will make things far worse if you do."

"I promise I will mind my own business and worry about setting up these tents and seeing to the items on my list. There's far too much to get done without adding to my responsibilities," Edwina said. She and Simpkins silently watched as Charles moved out of earshot before her gardener spoke again.

"That was a neat bit of work getting rid of your protective friend. I noticed you said that you would mind your own business," Simpkins said. "You didn't say anything about me minding mine."

"I see we understand each other perfectly," Edwina said. "I don't suppose you would be willing to take on the role of the working-man and go eavesdrop a little bit on them?"

"I planned to do just that even if you hadn't asked." Simpkins touched his cap and gave her a cheeky wink before striding off with an enormous grin plastered across his craggy face. Really, Simpkins was taking his part in her detective business far too seriously for her liking. It was almost as though he felt he was a detective himself. Still, it would be useful to know what he was able to find out.

She turned her attention back to setting up the tents but all the while a bit of her brain was considering what Simpkins was hearing. Every time she stole a glance in his direction, she saw him nodding and clapping the younger men on the shoulder with a gnarled paw. The other men seemed comfortable with his interest in their activities. Before long Simpkins headed back to where she stood pretending to be entirely engrossed in what was written on the pages attached to her clipboard.

"It's just as we suspected, there is a Labor Day demonstration planned for the festivities. But I think they're just a bunch of good lads," Simpkins said. "I don't think they want to cause any trouble to any of the villagers in Walmsley Parva. I think they just want folks to know what it's like down in the mines. They want folks to know that they aren't just a bunch of troublemakers planning to strike for the fun of it."

"Can they do that?" Edwina asked. "Can they just set up as though they were one of the official participants at the festival?" She glanced in their direction once more. She feared it would cause a great deal of fuss if anyone were to try to make them leave considering the amount of setup they had already done.

"I think that will turn what's planned as a peaceful demonstration of workers' rights into something far nastier," Simpkins said. "I think that likely the best thing to do would just be to leave them well enough alone and let them hand out their flyers. From what the lads were saying, that's all they're interested in anyway."

Edwina noticed that Dennis Morley had arrived to assist the other miners and she decided the best thing she could do for everyone involved was to go and speak with them before either Constable Gibbs arrived or worse, the vicar's wife, came on the scene.

"I'm going to head over and speak with them. I know Dennis Morley and his wife, Alice. Perhaps I will be able to have a conversation with him that gets us both what we want," Edwina said.

"I'll head on over with you. A fine lady such as yourself may not be equipped for the likes of them," Simpkins said. He fell into step next to her, and as much as it pained her to admit it to herself, Edwina was glad of his solid presence at her side.

"Good morning, Mr. Morley," Edwina said. "I'm pleased but a bit surprised to see you here." Mr. Morley looked her up and down in a way that left her feeling uncomfortable. She saw several of the other men elbowing each other and whispering. Their posture seemed defensive as if they were saying they had every right to be there and that they dared her to ask them to disband.

"I understood from my wife, Alice, that you were highly desirous of involving the people from Hambley in your celebration here today. Was she mistaken?" Mr. Morley asked.

"It's absolutely true. I just had no idea that your idea of participation would include handing out pamphlets," Edwina said.

"I had not understood that there was any sort of restriction on our participation. I thought that you were eager for us to come in so we accepted the invitation," Mr. Morley said. "I hope that's not going to be a problem."

Edwina took a deep breath. "I have no problem with you handing out pamphlets so long as they aren't something that's going to include things that would frighten children or turn this happy family occasion into something unpleasant," she said. "Would you say that the literature you wish to spread to the attendees is of that sort of a nature?"

Mr. Morley held out a leaflet. "Take a look for yourself. The statistics and the information written on these pamphlets may turn your stomach but there's nothing in here that's not the God's honest truth. It's one thing for us to complain to other people in our same situation about the problems we're facing. But real reform of labor laws won't happen until people who have things easier than we do understand what we're facing. The good folks here in Walmsley Parva are exactly the sort of people we need in the voting booths in order to make changes for the workingman." Edwina reached out and accepted the flyer. She read it over quickly. There were no objectionable line drawings depicting violence. Mr. Morley was right about the disquieting nature of the text but she couldn't say that any of it sounded like something that was untrue. If the country wanted to keep running on coal, they ought to know, in her opinion, what that cost their fellow citizens. The vicar's wife was not going to like it but Edwina was not going to say anything to dissuade them.

"I see no reason why you should not be allowed to have your say. But I do have a suggestion for you," Edwina said.

"What's that?" Mr. Morley said.

"I think you'd be best served not speaking from a stage but by spreading out to blend into the crowd. I would advise you to be as friendly as possible when you approach other people. If you want them to be open-minded about your message, you don't want to seem threatening or off-putting when you first encounter them. Looking like a hostile gang at the edge of the green is not going to help your cause. It's also going to make you more of a target for the local constable and the festival organizers," Edwina said. "Wouldn't you say so, Simpkins?"

"Yes, Miss Edwina, I'd say that's about right. Constable Gibbs is not someone who will take that sort of thing in stride. If I were you I'd fade off into the crowd and hand these out on the sly," Simpkins said.

"We're tired of hiding in the dark," said a man at the back of the group. "Part of the problem is feeling like we need to apologize for asking for what's due to us or that we need to make sure not to rile the feathers of those who think of themselves as our betters." Edwina noticed the heads nodding and the grumbling of the group.

"I have no authority to tell you what to do. I can only tell you what I think is likely to get the result that you want. That is if the result is to hand out your flyers for as long as possible to as many people assembled here as you can. If your real intention is to cause a scene and make a disruption then I have nothing further to say," Edwina said. She gave a curt nod to Mr. Morley and then turned her back and walked across the green. In the distance she noticed Mrs. Lowethorpe approaching, gesticulating wildly with her arms and pointing at the various tents. Edwina turned back to look at the miners. Simpkins had his head bent close to Mr. Morley's and the two seemed to be conferring. Within moments there was no evidence left of the makeshift stage and its tent. As quickly as they had appeared, the group of miners slipped off into the gathering crowd, each holding a stack of leaflets.

Simpkins made a beeline for her. "They took your words to heart and I think they will follow your advice about how to spread their message. That was just the way to speak to them. You do have a way with people, Miss Edwina," Simpkins said. Edwina felt astonished at Simpkins' words. She didn't think of herself as someone who was particularly good with people, just someone who knew from vast experience of life in the village how such things would tend to play out. Before she could thank him for his words, he gave her a nod and hurried off. Maybe he felt embarrassed at expressing a compliment. Or maybe he was not eager to interact with Mrs. Lowethorpe, who was speeding toward her like a woman possessed. With no evidence left in sight, Edwina regretted that she was going to have to tell the vicar's wife that she feared Charles Jarvis had been imagining things.

CHAPTER 39

Beryl looked around and thought that the May Day fete looked exactly how she expected that it would. The white tents billowed in the slight breeze. The sun shone down on the pond on the green and set the water sparkling. Children ran up and down the aisles bumping into their elders and chasing each other with sticky fingers wrapped around sweet rolls and lollipops. Beryl was glad she had decided to adhere to convention and to wear a wide-brimmed hat. The sun was warm and she was glad of the shade the head covering provided.

In fact it was so warm, she actually found herself desirous of a cup of tea. She raised a hand to shield her eyes and looked back and forth up and down the tent rows. The line at the tea tent seemed extraordinarily long. The heat must have gotten to everyone else too, Beryl decided. She made her way slowly along the back side of the tents taking advantage of the shadows cast by their canvas. She took her time as she walked. There was no need to exert herself only to find that she needed to stand in line.

She paused behind one of the tents when she heard the unmistakable sound of someone having an argument conducted in whispers. While Edwina would certainly have chastised her for the poor manners eavesdropping displayed, Beryl thought she recognized the sound of Mr. Ecclestone-Smythe's voice. It was no time for scruples. She leaned a little closer to the tent canvas and focused her attention on the muffled noise on the other side of the canvas.

"I want to know where they are and I want to know where they are right now," Mr. Ecclestone-Smythe said.

"I told you, Ambrose, I have no idea," Mrs. Ecclestone-Smythe said.

"You cannot possibly have no idea. You are the only one besides myself to have possession of them," Mr. Ecclestone-Smythe said.

"Well, I don't have them now and I don't know where they are," Mrs. Ecclestone-Smythe said. "If you must know, I gave them to someonc for safekeeping."

"You gave them to someone?" Mr. Ecclestone-Smythe's voice raised slightly in anger. "Whom the devil did you give them to?"

"I don't see how it's any business of yours to whom I give my jewelry or how I take care of it," Mrs. Ecclestone-Smythe said.

"It matters to me very much that my wife has done something so foolish with such valuable property. So I ask you again, to whom did you entrust the jewelry?" Mr. Ecclestone-Smythe said. Beryl heard Mrs. Ecclestone-Smythe give a slight shriek. The shadows playing through the tent and the silhouettes of the figures within made it clear that Mr. Ecclestone-Smythe had grabbed his wife by the arm. Beryl was torn between wanting to rush to her client's aid and wanting to hear how the argument would unfold. As Mrs. Ecclestone-Smythe seemed capable of continuing the argument she decided to refrain from interrupting.

"This is exactly the reason I gave my jewelry to Lionel," Mrs. Ecclestone-Smythe said, struggling to wrench her arm from her husband's grasp. "If you must know, I was leaving you. We were going to use the jewelry to start a whole new life together far from you, your bullying, and all the rest of it."

"You gave a vast fortune in jewels to my bookkeeper?" Mr. Ecclestone-Smythe said, his voice rising above a whisper. Beryl was able to hear every word as clearly as if she were perched on the colliery owner's shoulder.

"Yes. Unlike you, he loved me. We were going to run away together the day that he disappeared and you never would have found me," Mrs. Ecclestone-Smythe said.

"Did it ever occur to you he was only using you?" Mr. Ecclestone-Smythe said. "You always have been a naive, emotional, weak-minded woman. You can't possibly believe he planned to spend his life with you after he got his hands on your money."

"What I believe is that you found out what we were up to and you are the one who killed him," Mrs. Ecclestone-Smythe said. "I think you stole the jewels from him yourself and you are just asking me where they are to cover up for your crime." Beryl watched the shadows as Mr. Ecclestone-Smythe reached over and grabbed his wife with his other hand, pinning both her arms firmly to her sides.

"Do you think if I had done such a thing I would be asking you any questions about it whatsoever?" Mr. Ecclestone-Smythe said. "I need that jewelry and I had no reason to expect you no longer had it."

"Well, I don't. I've hired that detective

agency in town to look for it but so far they've turned up nothing. It wasn't with his body, it wasn't in his rooming house, it wasn't even in his pigeon loft. It has simply vanished," Mrs. Ecclestone-Smythe said. "It's just like you to be more concerned about the jewelry than the fact that I no longer wish to be your wife."

"Do you have any idea what you've done? The jewelry is the only reason I asked you to be my wife in the first place. You can't possibly think I would have wished to marry the likes of you for any reason other than what you could bring into the marriage financially," Mr. Ecclestone-Smythe said. Beryl heard Mrs. Ecclestone-Smythe began to sob. Her next words came out in stuttering gasps.

"I brought the jewelry with me into the marriage. It's my property and I have every right to do with it as I please. I can't see how any of it has anything to do with you. It's not as though you are going to wear it at a board meeting," Mrs. Ecclestone-Smythe said.

"You foolish, foolish woman. You've ruined us both," Mr. Ecclestone-Smythe said. "What you don't realize is that I have used your jewelry as collateral for the Hambley mine. It was the only thing I had left of any real value and now I find out I don't have it either. We are going to be utterly ruined," Mr. Ecclestone-Smythe said. He dropped his hands from his wife's upper arms, let out a loud groan, and stomped out of the tent. Beryl saw Mrs. Ecclestone-Smythe turn and leave, headed in the opposite direction.

Both Charles Jarvis and Archie had been right about the rumors concerning the Hambley mine. Mr. Ecclestone-Smythe was far over his head in his business practices. Beryl had to consider the possibility that what she had overheard made it seem far less likely that Mr. Ecclestone-Smythe was the one who killed Mr. Cunningham. Although it was still possible that Mr. Cunningham did not have the jewels on his person at the time he was killed. She hurried off in search of Edwina to tell her what she had just heard.

CHAPTER 40

Edwina passed Beryl half of a cucumber and cress sandwich before helping herself to one as well. Beryl's news about Mr. Ecclestone-Smythe's reliance on the jewelry, as well as her efforts all morning, had left her famished. She swallowed a bite of sandwich and was about to take another when Alice Morley appeared before them. Alice looked flushed and slightly disheveled, as though she had been running, and the expression on her face was one of distress.

"I'm so glad I found the two of you," Alice said, dropping onto the picnic blanket beside them. "I desperately need some advice."

"What seems to be the matter, Alice?" Edwina said. She tried to hand Alice a piece of sandwich but the younger woman shook her head. "You look frantic."

"I'm very worried about my husband, Dennis. You may remember that I mentioned before that there have been leaflets circulating around the mining village calling for labor reform," Alice said.

"Your husband was here this morning with some other men handing out just such pamphlets," Edwina said. "But the leaflets were not as gruesome as the ones you described to us that day when you came to lunch so I didn't see anything objectionable about them. Is that what's worrying you?"

"No, that's not it. Dennis has been spending a lot of time with people who are unsatisfied with the working conditions and I wasn't at all pleased that he wanted to come and hand out the leaflets here at the May Day festival. As a matter of fact, I begged him not to. I said that we were not going to make the sort of changes we wanted by making disruptions and making ourselves unwelcome. We actually had a flaming row about it this morning," Alice said.

"So you need some marital advice?" Beryl asked. "I've been married more times than I like to recall so I expect I'm qualified to speak on that subject." Beryl leaned towards Alice and gave her an encouraging smile. In Edwina's opinion, Beryl was far more qualified on the subject of dissolving a marriage than remaining in one. But as she had no practical experience of either, she wisely decided to remain quiet on the subject.

"It's not the leaflets really, it's the other things. It started out with mere conversations about the working conditions, but it's escalated. What I haven't told you is that there's been sabotage at the mine and I'm worried that Dennis knows more about it than he has let on," Alice said. "In fact, after our argument today he confirmed it."

"What sorts of things did he say to you?" Beryl asked. "Do you think that he's involved in the sabotage?"

Alice nodded. "I've tried to convince him to stay away from the people who are involved in violence but his dissatisfaction at work has been growing steadily lately. When I told him that I thought that the leafleting was going a step too far, he laughed in my face and said I really wouldn't like what he actually had planned. He was at a meeting earlier in the week with the saboteurs. From what he hinted at I think it is likely they've planned an attack on the mine. The shifts don't run today since it's Sunday, which would make any sabotage easier. Besides, as far as I know, most of the miners are here at the celebration," Alice said.

"What sort of attack on the mine?" Edwina asked.

"I don't know. Dennis wouldn't tell me the specifics and maybe he doesn't even know. He's not really in the inner circle. At least I don't think he is. I believe he's just being used by the people organizing it because he has a foot in each community. His involvement with the pigeon racing club has given him access to people that most of the miners don't have. He knows things that they don't know because of conversations he had had with Mr. Cunningham and even with Mr. Ecclestone-Smythe."

"Where is your husband now?" Edwina asked.

"That's just it. I haven't seen him since we quarreled. After the argument I went in one direction and he headed off in another. I haven't laid eyes on him since and I'm concerned that he's gone back to the mine with some of the others to put whatever they planned into action," Alice said. "I don't want to carry tales to the authorities but I'm really worried that someone's going to be hurt. The sabotage keeps escalating. It started as small things like missing equipment or jammed machinery. The last sabotage involved a fire that they barely managed to put out before it spread into the village. I hate to think what they have planned for today but I'm convinced that it's far more serious than anything they've done before."

"I think we'd better head over there immediately," Beryl said, standing and tossing the remains of her sandwich towards a passing flock of ducks. They swooped down on it and Edwina scrambled to her feet and sent them the remains of her meal as well.

"We have to tell Constable Gibbs. Something like this is beyond our experience, Beryl," Edwina said. She turned to Alice. "I'll try to keep your husband's name out of it but we do have to tell someone in authority." Alice's shoulders slumped and tears rolled down her cheeks but she nodded in agreement.

"How long ago did you have this argument with your husband?" Beryl said.

"About an hour ago. I should have come to find you sooner but I kept telling myself I was not being a good wife if I did so. In the end it seemed foolish not to ask your advice," Alice said.

"That's long enough for them to have gotten back over to Hambley if that was their intention," Beryl said.

"I think we should also speak to Mr. Ecclestone-Smythe," Edwina said. "He has the right to know that his business is in danger."

"I'm not sure if we will find him here or not," Beryl said. "After the argument he had with Mrs. Ecclestone-Smythe, he could be anywhere."

"Why don't we split up? I'll go looking for Mr. Ecclestone-Smythe and you see if you can find Constable Gibbs," Edwina said. "I'll meet you back in front of the tea tent in fifteen minutes." Beryl nodded.

"I would tell you not to worry, Alice, but I'm sure that you're going to anyway. The best advice that I can give you is to stay away from Hambley until you hear from one of us," Beryl said. Edwina nodded in agreement and they both raced off in search of someone who could stop whatever was planned at the mine.

Beryl found Constable Gibbs trying her luck at the coconut shy. After a moment of watching her during her approach Beryl had decided it was a good thing that the constable was armed with a billy club rather than a pistol. She certainly would not have struck terror into the heart of any criminal perpetrator with the sort of aim she was displaying to the masses there at the May Day fete. If she were not on an important errand, Beryl would have been sorely tempted to give the constable a display of her own prowess with a firearm if only to get back at her for all the harassment she and Edwina had endured during the course of the investigation. Fortunately for Constable Gibbs, time was something she was sure she did not have to spare.

"I'm sorry to interrupt you but I must speak with you immediately," Beryl said, stepping up beside the constable and removing a wooden ball from her hand.

"I wasn't done with that," Constable Gibbs said. Beryl raised the ball and effortlessly hurled it at a coconut perched upon a slender base. The target toppled to the ground. Beryl turned to the constable and lowered her voice below earshot of the rest of the queue.

"Now you are. I'm here to report a crime, or rather a crime that's about to take place," Beryl said. "I thought you were eager to be the voice of law and order in the village rather than leaving such things to Edwina and myself." Constable Gibbs turned and faced her, seeming to forget entirely about winning a prize.

"I'm glad to see you've come to your senses," Constable Gibbs said. "It's high time the two of you realized who's in charge here and what the boundaries are. What do you have to report?"

Beryl inclined her head toward the spot a bit away from the crowd assembled in front of the coconut shy tent. Constable Gibbs took the hint and followed her to where they could speak privately.

"I have it on good authority that there is some sort of major sabotage incident planned for the Hambley mine while so many of the miners are here at the May Day festivities. I thought you should know in order to stop it before it happens," Beryl said.

"You say there's a problem about to take place over at the Hambley mine?" Constable Gibbs said, her eyes straying back over towards the coconut shy tent. Constable Gibbs' husband, a man with great aim, had knocked over three coconuts in rapid succession and Beryl noticed the constable wince as the person in charge of the tent handed over a pouch of tobacco as a prize.

"That's right. If you hurry you might get there before whatever trouble is planned breaks out," Beryl said.

"I have no intention of hurrying anywhere," Constable Gibbs said. "I'm not even going to amble over there at a leisurely pace."

"Whyever not?" Beryl asked. Surely winning a prize was not more important than her policing duties. While Beryl did not particularly care for Constable Gibbs or even respect her abilities, she had come to believe that the constable took them seriously and could not understand her reluctance.

"Because the village of Hambley is not my responsibility. Walmsley Parva is my sole purview and I intend to stay here keeping an eye on its citizens rather than haring off to someplace where I have no authority in order to stop a crime you say has not yet been committed," Constable Gibbs said.

"Who is in charge over there then?" Beryl said.

"That's Mr. Ecclestone-Smythe's problem, not mine. I think he hired some sort of private detail to keep an eye on things, but there were rumors that he had cut back on that several weeks ago. At this point I'm not sure that anyone's in charge of the security at the mine," Constable Gibbs said.

"And you don't feel like you want to take a look, as a good citizen?" Beryl asked, trying to appeal to the police officer's better nature.

"One of the ways in which I behave as a good citizen is to know my place. I've been trying to tell you and Edwina to do the same. But you two just don't listen. Now if you'll excuse me, I'm going to go back to my game and to my responsibilities here in Walmsley Parva." With that, Constable Gibbs strode back to the coconut shy tent, pushed to the head of the line, and picked up a wooden ball once more. Beryl was delighted to see her aim had not improved during their conversation. While she expected Edwina would be sorely disappointed in the constable's attitude, Beryl found that she was not. She was happy to see they would have no interference from Constable Gibbs or from anyone else in authority. As far as she could see, it provided them with the perfect opportunity to solve the case themselves.

CHAPTER 41

"Constable Gibbs has absolutely no interest in assisting us with anything that happens over at Hambley," Beryl said. Edwina was not surprised to hear the constable had no desire to stretch herself to assist others outside of her purview. In the many years Edwina had known her, the constable had not been someone she would have described as overly generous on any front. Unless one counted the way she exercised her authority with her citation pad.

"I wonder if they have their own police force of a sort over at Hambley," Edwina said. "Someone we could contact with this information?"

"According to Constable Gibbs, whatever force they had was a private concern and one for which Mr. Ecclestone-Smythe paid for himself. Constable Gibbs said rumors have it that he cut back on their services some time ago," Beryl said. "I should think that there's very little help to be had."

"The person who seems to know the most about what's going on at the colliery is Miss Chilvers," Edwina said. "Perhaps we should ask her if there is someone to notify."

"She should be at the tombola tent, shouldn't she?" Beryl asked. Edwina nodded and the two of them took off for the far side of the green. The tombola booth was always amongst the most popular at any sort of fete. It had been Edwina's suggestion to set it down at the end so that fete-goers would need to pass all of the other booths on their way to try their luck at winning a prize. She had been prepared for a line in front of the tombola booth but she was surprised to see quite how large the throng in front of it had become. As they reached the crowd, one of the festival-goers turned and pointed an accusing finger at Edwina.

"Aren't you one of the people on the committee for this fete?" the woman asked.

"I am. Is there something the matter?" Edwina asked.

"There's no one here operating the tombola. That's what's wrong. We've been waiting for at least twenty minutes to try our luck. Isn't that right, Frank?" the woman asked of the portly gentleman standing next to her. He nodded his head silently, his beefy arms crossed over his barrel chest. Edwina struggled through the crowd to the front of the throng, Beryl following closely behind.

"Miss Chilvers is not in there," Edwina said. "Where can she be?" She turned to Beryl as a sense of dread filled her.

"You don't think she's had reason to return to the mining village, do you? Or the colliery itself?" Beryl asked.

"If she did, she may be in danger. Who knows what is planned at the mine and what could happen to her if she interrupts them," Edwina said. "We need to get over there right away." The two women hurried away from the tombola booth as quickly as the crowds would allow. Edwina flagged down Prudence Rathbone on her way and asked her to take over at the booth. It would not do to lose all the fundraising money because it was unstaffed. Edwina heard Prudence calling after her with questions about what had happened to Miss Chilvers but she waved her off and continued on her way.

"We'll go to the garage and fetch my automobile," Beryl said. "As long as it's not up on blocks with all of its wheels removed, we can drive it over."

Beryl's motorcar was most fortunately parked outside of Blackburn's garage. The dent was still there but the vehicle was in working order. They jumped in and Beryl roared off at a terrific rate of speed. Clouds of dust billowed up all around as they sped out of Walmsley Parva. Edwina kept one hand clamped upon her hat and braced herself against the dashboard with the other in order to not be flung forward. But she issued no recriminations concerning the speed. In fact, she found herself in the unusual position of wishing they could proceed even faster.

They squealed to a stop in record time and tumbled out of the vehicle. All around them the village of Hambley lay silent. It seemed that the efforts on the part of the May Day committee to interest the miners in attending had been wholly successful. Not even a stray cat or an unfriendly dog wandered past as they stood surveying the village.

"Do you think we should have stopped at Miss Chilvers' boardinghouse first?" Edwina asked.

"No. Whatever is planned is planned for here, not for Shady Rest Boardinghouse. We did right to come, but I think whatever we were looking for we shall find in the mine itself or over at the colliery office," Beryl said.

"Let's try the office. I have no fondness for tight spaces and dark places. If we can avoid entering the mine that would be my preference," Edwina said.

"Believe it or not, Ed, it would be mine as well. I'm much more comfortable with heights and speed. I've always wanted to go up. I've never been interested in heading down. In fact, it makes my head go all swimmy," Beryl said. Edwina was astonished at the expression she saw on Beryl's face. She never thought of Beryl as having any sort of fears or circumstances in which her courage would falter. Beryl was absolutely dauntless in the face of every sort of thing Edwina most dreaded. Still, Edwina knew that look. It was the one that so many of the young men would suddenly have flit across their faces. Something had bubbled a scorchingly terrifying memory to the surface. Edwina didn't know what had caused the memory in the first place but she was certain the possibility of descending into the mine had triggered it. To find that Beryl had a weak spot made Edwina feel protective and braver somehow.

"Then that's settled. We will head for the mining office," Edwina said. She strode off with what she hoped looked like confidence in the direction of the small building at the edge of the mine.

As silently as they could manage Beryl and Edwina entered the mining office. The doorknob turned silently in Beryl's hand and the floorboards most accommodatingly refrained from squeaking under their feet. Beryl tilted her head to one side to listen for footsteps or voices in the rooms beyond the front office. The inside of the colliery office seemed to be as silent as the center of the mining village had been.

Beryl moved farther into the office for a better look. She stepped around the side of a potted palm and almost tripped over a pair of suitcases and a small valise perched on top.

"Edwina," Beryl whispered, beckoning with her hand. "What do you make of this?" Beryl pointed to the two pieces of luggage. They weren't a matched set but both were made of leather and were altogether unremarkable.

Edwina joined her and looked where Beryl indicated. "It looks like someone is planning a trip," Edwina said. "I wonder to whom they belong."

"Perhaps there is something inside that will tell us whose it is," Beryl said. She reached down and unlatched the valise, pulling it open widely. She rummaged about inside, somewhat surprised not to hear Edwina admonishing her for taking such liberties. Instead her friend had leaned forward to get a better look inside the handbag herself.

"What's that small bag?" Edwina said pointing to a drawstring pouch tucked into the corner of the valise. Beryl reached in and plucked it out. She crossed the room and placed the bag on Miss Chilvers' desk then loosened the drawstring. A beam of light streaming through the colliery office window landed on the contents making it look as though a small fire had started atop Miss Chilvers' desk. Beryl heard Edwina gasp as she reached out to run her finger over the pile of sparkling jewelry spilled out in front of her.

"It looks as though we've solved one part of the case," Beryl said. "Mrs. Ecclestone-Smythe will certainly be happy to see these once more." Beryl gathered the drawstring back up around the jewels and slipped the pouch into an inside pocket of her coat for safekeeping.

"Let's take a look into the suitcases themselves," Edwina said. "Someone's got to be around here somewhere if he or she has left something so valuable as that jewelry lying about in the office."

Edwina hurried across the office and loosened the straps on the larger of the two suitcases. She lifted the lid and riffled through the contents. A pair of trousers, two cotton shirts, and a few pairs of socks took up most of the space. Edwina removed a thin bundle of yellowed envelopes tied up with string. She tipped the stack towards Beryl.

"Does that name seem familiar?" she asked.

"Morris Howe was checked off on the list I found in Mr. Cunningham's pocket." Beryl said. "Do you think he is here working at the Hambley mine?"

"I can't see any other reason for someone to have these letters in their possession, can you?" Edwina said, "If there is sabotage going on in Hambley and he is here I would be willing to bet he could be the one spearheading it."

"It looks as though he's taking off for somewhere and doesn't plan to return," Beryl said. "He can't have left yet though if he hasn't collected his belongings and the jewelry."

"Who is he though?" Edwina said. "Dennis Morley? Martin Haynes? Even Ambrose Ecclestone-Smythe could really be Morris

Howe, couldn't he?"

"You don't really think it is Mr. Ecclestone-Smythe, do you?" Beryl asked. "He seems far too established and frankly too boring to be living under an assumed name."

"Once one has lost all faith in one's greengrocer, one finds it easy to entertain all sorts of outrageous notions," Edwina said. Beryl felt a tug of guilt. In many ways, Edwina was quite naive and she felt a pang at having involved her in a business that exposed her to the sordidness of humanity. Still, it was too late to give it much thought and there was still a case to close.

"The only way to know who he is will be to keep looking for him. Even if we have to go down into the mine itself," Beryl said. Edwina nodded.

"I suppose you're right although it is tempting to simply take the jewels back to Mrs. Ecclestone-Smythe and to consider our part in this case resolved," Edwina said.

"But that wouldn't be the right thing to do, now would it?" Beryl said. "After all, if we wish to be engaged in the private enquiry business we have to be willing to follow wherever a case will lead."

"Of course you're right, I'm simply pointing out that the idea of leaving immediately and avoiding a descent into the mine is hard to resist," Edwina said.

"I'm the one who is troubled by being tempted far more than you, Ed. You're quite a moral compass for me, you know," Beryl said. Beryl was gratified to see her friend color slightly. Edwina was really coming into her own.

"Off we go then," Edwina said. She strode out the door with Beryl close on her heels.

CHAPTER 42

At first glance the mine yard appeared as deserted as the rest of the complex. It was strange to see all the clamor of production halted. There was no clinking of machinery, no tumbling sounds of the coal as it moved along a conveyor belt, no squeak of pulleys lifting buckets aloft and sending them towards cargo train cars. No men called to one another and no horns blew, announcing a change of shift. The quiet was eerie and Beryl felt more nervous than ever at the thought of descending down into the pit. After all, she thought, they did not know the nature of the sabotage planned, only that the scale of it was intended to be crippling.

Still, she had a reputation to uphold as a swashbuckling adventurer. The fact that she had confessed trepidation to Edwina as far as underground spaces was concerned did not mean that she could give in to a case of nerves. Archie was a good friend but she was not entirely confident he would be able to resist writing a story that trumpeted the fact that they had failed to solve the case because she had been bested by something as commonplace as a coal mine. Such a report would reflect poorly on their fledgling business. Until they became more established they needed every ounce of proof that they were capable, and worthy, of pursuing their course in a man's profession.

She felt comforted by the heft of her pistol in her right-hand pocket. She had not thought it prudent to mention the firearm to Edwina when she had added it to her ensemble that morning. But she was relieved to think she had it with her now.

With more bravado than actual confidence Beryl threw back her broad shoulders and headed for the opening into the mine. Iron supports holding up a conveyor belt cast shadows on the ground and lent the entrance an even more menacing air. She asked herself how terrifying could it actually be considering all the workers she had seen coming and going from its depths during her visits to Hambley over the last week. Edwina stood so closely behind her that Beryl felt her bump into her back when she stopped short of the descent. Beryl looked to the side and noticed a row of well-used lanterns lined up on a girder supporting the mouth of the pit. Hanging on pegs above them was a long row of metal safety helmets. Edwina plucked two from the row and placed one firmly on her own head before handing the other to Beryl.

"We'd best take lanterns, too," Edwina said. "I don't suppose you have a box of matches in your pocket, do you?"

"I don't but I'm sure they must have some here with the lanterns." Beryl looked about and spotted a small metal tin. She pried off the lid and wished she had not found exactly what they needed. She tipped the tin towards Edwina and they each lit their lanterns before crossing the threshold into the mine.

The light bounced off the close walls and cast strange shadows as it angled off the irregular surface of the rock face. Beryl found she was holding her breath and forced herself to exhale slowly and silently. Even though they picked their way carefully along, every now and again she or Edwina managed to kick a pebble or a bit of debris along the path in front of them. The sound of it echoed through the gloom and increased her feeling of unease. Beryl thought she heard a noise from up ahead but wasn't sure whether her mind was simply playing tricks on her until Edwina grabbed her by the arm and held her back.

"Do you hear something?" Edwina spoke softly and directly into Beryl's ear. "I think whoever we are looking for is up ahead." Beryl simply nodded rather than speaking and risking being overheard. She turned down the flame in her lantern and motioned for Edwina to do the same. As soon as she did so Beryl felt certain the walls on either side of them were closing in even tighter. Her heart clattered and thwacked in her chest as the air became damper and far cooler than it had at the surface. It brought to mind the root cellar of the house where she grew up. But rather than being surrounded by crates of onions, burlap sacks of potatoes, and buckets of damp sand into which the family cook had packed carrots for winter storage, she was pressed on one side by a jagged, sooty rock wall and on the other by a line of coal carts set in line along a track.

The sound continued to bounce as oddly around the mine shaft as the light did and she became convinced there was indeed someone else in the mine. Reluctantly she turned the wick on her lamp so low it gave off no more than a small glow through the grimy glass. She hoped whomever it was that they could hear had a lantern of his own that cast sufficient light to make sure they wouldn't notice hers or Edwina's. The path bent slightly up ahead and so did the track the carts used to transport the coal up from the depths of the mine. She and Edwina pressed close to the carts rather than the rock wall. The path was well-worn below her feet along the track's edge and in the low light she needed all the help she could get to keep from slipping. As she rounded the corner she stumbled against something sticking out of one of the carts. It was all she could do to stay on her feet.

Edwina ploughed into her back and Beryl wished she had been wearing her sturdy expedition boots rather than the party shoes she had donned for the fete. Edwina was a small woman but her feet did a job on Beryl's Achilles' heels. The women lifted their lanterns simultaneously and Beryl heard Edwina allow a breathless squeak to pass her lips before she covered her mouth with her small hand. The dead-eyed gaze of Martin Haynes stared up at the ceiling of the mine. He lay on his back atop a load of coal and his feet overhung the side of the cart. Even in the low light Beryl could see a knife handle protruding from his chest.

"I think it may be safe to guess that Martin Haynes was Morris Howe, don't you?" Edwina said.

"I expect you're right. But I don't think he killed himself, do you?" Beryl asked. Edwina shook her head, but before she could reply, the sounds from deeper in the mine came louder and what Beryl thought were footsteps clattered towards them. She pressed a finger to her lips and pressed back against the wall opposite the body. Edwina followed her lead and they stood waiting for whoever it was that was on the way.

The sound of footsteps grew louder still and out of the corner of her eye Beryl detected a shadow moving along the wall. She squinted in the direction of the motion and despite the low light she made out the figure of a person hurrying in their direction.

Edwina seemed to see it, too. She gripped Beryl's elbow in a tight squeeze. Out of the shadows another lantern appeared and illuminated a familiar figure.

Beryl slipped the pistol from her pocket and stepped forward. The knowledge she did not need to go any farther down into the pit gave her a surge of confidence and renewed enthusiasm for their purpose. Edwina must have turned up the wick in her lamp because suddenly it seemed as if the tunnel was bathed in a warm glow.

"Stop!" Beryl shouted, aiming her pistol at Miss Chilvers.

"You don't understand," Miss Chilvers said. "We mustn't stay here." She lunged forward a few steps. Beryl squeezed off a shot and it landed just shy of Miss Chilvers' feet. She froze in place and Beryl thought from the panicked look on her face that the secretary must have some sort of phobia of firearms.

"Don't do that, Beryl. Any spark could set the coal dust alight. Even sparks from the cart wheels have caused disasters," Edwina said.

"I don't think telling our suspect that my weapon can't be used was the best strategy, Edwina. She could stay in here all day if that is the case," Beryl said, lowering her weapon. She felt a standstill was in the offing until she realized Miss Chilvers still looked terrified. "Or maybe she would rather not stay under any circumstances."

"We are all in danger," Miss Chilvers said. "Please, we must get entirely clear of the mine." Beryl waved the pistol at her again but it was more because she liked the feel of it in her hand rather than that she planned to use it. She had no intention of testing Edwina's assertion about sparks.

"You're not going anywhere until you explain what you are doing here," Beryl said. "And what you know about poor Martin Haynes, or should I say, Morris Howe." Beryl pointed the pistol back at the pair of feet dangling out of the coal cart directly behind them.

"If you don't want to end up like Morris, you have to get out of the mine. There won't be anything left of any of us if we don't move away from here immediately," Miss Chilvers said.

"You're the saboteur?" Edwina said. "What have you done down there?"

"I've rigged the mine with explosives. The timer is already set," Miss Chilvers said. "If we don't get away from here we will all be killed."

"How long until it goes off?" Beryl said.

"We may just make it to the colliery office if we hurry," Miss Chilvers said.

"All right," Beryl said. "But I'm right behind you and I promise you that I didn't miss your feet by accident. If I need to shoot you I won't have any compunction in doing so."

Beryl kept her pistol trained on Miss Chilvers' back as they rushed away from the mine entrance and towards the colliery office. She and Edwina followed closely. A deep rumbling sound came up from the mine as they burst through the door. Edwina pushed it closed behind them. Within an instant the ground beneath their feet trembled and shook. A giant blasting noise filled Beryl's ears and left them ringing. The windows of the colliery office exploded and shards of glass sailed through the air. A picture detached from the wall and tumbled to the floor, the frame shattering at Miss Chilvers' feet. Overhead, the ceiling splintered with jagged cracks and chunks of plaster rained down on their heads.

Beryl was grateful for Edwina's insistence on donning the miners' helmets. Out of the corner of her eye she noticed the brick wall behind her begin to buckle. She felt a tug on her arm and someone dragging her backward as the wall caved in. She lost her balance and landed in a heap on the floor next to Edwina. She was pleased to note she held tightly to her pistol but was discouraged to realize she had lost sight of her target in the fray.

When the shaking and rolling beneath her feet died away she looked at the spot where she had last seen Miss Chilvers.

"You don't suppose she got away, do you?" Edwin asked. Beryl, whose eyesight had always been remarkable, squinted through the swirling dust. Much to her relief a pair of feet clad in low-heeled sensible shoes stuck out from beneath the rubble.

"Her body hasn't gone anywhere. I cannot speak for her soul," Beryl said. She stood and Edwina scrambled to her feet, too. They reached out and began lifting bricks from the prone figure. A second rumble from the ground rolled beneath their feet.

"Aftershocks," Beryl said. Edwina nodded. A moan came from below the bricks and the pair lifted off debris from Miss Chilvers as quickly as they possibly could.

Edwina's ears still rang from the terrific noise of the explosion. She kept looking at Miss Chilvers' face, trying to see how the woman she had met days earlier could be the same person surrounded by piles of rubble before her now. How was the mine explosion tied to the theft of the jewelry? No matter how she turned it over in her mind she still had more questions than answers.

"You're the one who killed Mr. Cunningham, aren't you?" Edwina said. "We found Mrs. Ecclestone-Smythe's jewelry in your handbag and we know from its rightful owner that she had entrusted it to Mr. Cunningham. The fact that you have it tells me you're the one who killed him."

"Do you mind if I sit down?" Miss Chilvers asked. She pointed at a chair in the waiting area of the reception room. Edwina nodded and the younger woman sank into it as if her legs had lost their ability to hold her up. Edwina thought Miss Chilvers suddenly looked much older than her years. She almost felt sorry for her.

"Were you engaged to Mr. Cunningham and became jealous when you found out about his relationship with Mrs. Ecclestone-Smythe?" Edwina asked. "Is that why you killed him?"

"I was never engaged to Mr. Cunningham, or anyone else for that matter," Miss Chilvers said. "In fact, I don't even believe in marriage. It had absolutely nothing to do with romance and everything to do with Mr. Cunningham's bad character. If he hadn't been a blackmailer he wouldn't have lost his life."

"He found out about the sabotage, didn't he?" Beryl asked.

"He did. The man always was far too nosy. He was always sneaking around, taking notes about the miners coming and going. Were they late for a shift, what did the other

451

miners have to say about them, were their papers in order. He ended up stumbling across Martin damaging some of the equipment. If he was the sort of employee that Mr. Ecclestone-Smythe had believed him to be, he would've reported it to his employer immediately. Instead he started blackmailing Martin." Edwina noticed something had shifted in Miss Chilvers' face. It seemed determined, hardened almost, and the efficient but pretty secretary she had met earlier seem submerged beneath a completely different personality.

"What does Martin Haynes and his involvement with the sabotage have to do with you though?" Beryl asked. "You weren't romantically involved with Mr. Haynes instead, were you?" How like Beryl, Edwina thought, to continue to consider a romantic entanglement the key to the mystery. Edwina was glad she reserved her romantic notions for the pages of the novels she so loved to read. As far as she was concerned, real life was far less romantic.

"I thought I had already made that clear. I have no interest in that sort of thing whatsoever," Miss Chilvers said. "We were colleagues, comrades even."

"You're a Communist," Beryl said. Miss Chilvers nodded.

"Exactly. I wasn't here only because I was interested in mining reform. Although that's a huge part of it. If you stop the mines from producing coal you cripple a country. A crippled country is much more interested in reform than one where things are limping along however slowly," Miss Chilvers said.

"I had heard there were Communist operatives working all over England but I didn't realize they ever recruited young women such as yourself," Edwina said. "I thought it was just a rumor."

"I should have thought you and Miss Helliwell would be more willing to imagine equal opportunity for women in the Communist Party than the average person. Your own exploits" — she pointed to Beryl — "and the business you've engaged in indicate a willingness to think of women as equal to men in ways that the ordinary citizen is not."

"So you killed Mr. Cunningham to keep him from exposing your plans to grow the Communist Party?" Edwina asked.

"Martin was beginning to lose his nerve. Lionel Cunningham kept upping his demands for money and I knew from past experience with blackmailers that he was unlikely to stop. When Martin finally came to me and told me what had happened I knew something had to be done."

"Why would Martin tell you?" Beryl asked. "Why wouldn't he simply take care of the problem himself?"

"Because I outrank him in the organization," Miss Chilvers said. "In fact, I recruited him for the job. As I keep saying, Communism offers equal opportunities for women. The two of you should consider joining. You would find a great deal more support for your ambitions and respect for your capabilities with us than you have under the current system. Martin understood that I was the one in charge so he came to me to solve the problem."

"How long have you known what was going on?" Edwina asked.

"Martin told me about it the day before the pigeon race," Miss Chilvers said. "The timing couldn't have been better if I had planned it. Mr. Cunningham had had that terrific argument with Mr. Ecclestone-Smythe the day before he died, too. I lied when I told you I had not heard what they had said. I knew that the business was in trouble and I knew that Mr. Cunningham knew it, too. It didn't take a genius to notice that he and Mrs. Ecclestone-Smythe had been conducting an affair. They thought they were being so discreet, but it was written all over her face every time she came to the office ostensibly to visit her husband." Miss Chilvers gave a slight shudder.

"How did you know that the business was in trouble?" Edwina asked.

"It's my business to know such things. Not only was I well connected to sources of information through the Communist Party, but I'm also a very good secretary. And what secretary doesn't know everything about her employer?" Miss Chilvers asked. "He trusted me completely and sometimes even confided his troubles to me. All it took was a few encouraging words and some sympathetic clucking to get him to reveal that he was worried about the mine closing. The man was moving money from one of his corporations to another, robbing Peter to pay Paul so to speak. The entire thing was a giant shell game and there was only one piece propping it up," Miss Chilvers said.

"Mrs. Ecclestone-Smythe's jewelry?" Edwina asked.

"Exactly. It was a stroke of luck that I solved more than one problem at the same time that morning at Mr. Cunningham's pigeon loft. Not only did I get rid of the person who could expose Martin for who he really was, I got my hands on the one thing keeping the mine afloat. The sabotage was almost more of a creative flourish rather than a necessity," Miss Chilvers said.

"So you just stabbed him? That morning in the loft?" Beryl asked. Miss Chilvers nodded. "What did you use?"

"I took one of the knives from the kitchen at the boardinghouse. Because I had the element of surprise, it was an easy thing to overpower him. Mr. Cunningham never saw it coming. After he was dead, I noticed a bulge in his jacket pocket, and I found he was in possession of Mrs. Ecclestone-Smythe's entire jewelry collection. Naturally I helped myself to them," Miss Chilvers said.

"There was no knife with the body. What did you do with that?" Beryl said.

"I expect she took it back to the boarding-house, cleaned it up, and put it back in the drawer," Edwina said.

"You really would have been a wonderful fit for the organization," Miss Chilvers said. "It's not too late for you to join. All you need to do is let me go. I'd even be happy for you to keep the jewelry since I was never planning to gain from it personally anyway. Although if you keep it all to yourself, you wouldn't be a very good Communist."

"I don't think anything would make me a very good Communist even though I have no intention of keeping things that don't belong to me. I am happy just the way I am and will be happier still when you are safely behind bars," Edwina said.

"What about the birds Lionel Cunningham was supposed to take to the race? You haven't left them locked up somewhere to die have you?" Beryl asked.

"Of course not. If I wanted to make it look as though Lionel had absconded with them I needed to take them so I grabbed the basket and took them along to Martin. He secured them in his loft and had been taking care of them ever since," Miss Chilvers said. "Although, I suppose someone else will have to take care of all the birds in his loft now."

"That ties everything up then, doesn't it, Edwina?" Beryl said.

"It does except for one detail. If your motorcar is undamaged by the blast, Beryl, I suggest we use it to deliver Miss Chilvers to the police station in Walmsley Parva at once."

CHAPTER 43

Crumpet heard the visitor first and went scampering off towards the scullery to head off the intruder.

"That will be Simpkins with the evening paper, I expect," Beryl said, reaching for a second glass on the drinks tray and pouring in a generous tot of Scotch whiskey. She crossed the room and stood waiting at the door as Simpkins followed Crumpet into the parlor.

"How did you know he would be here?" Edwina glanced up from the comfort of her favorite wingback chair. She looked the very picture of feminine domesticity with her small slipper-clad feet propped up on a footstool and her hands busied with her latest charity knitting project.

"Because she asked me to fetch it for you, Miss Edwina," Simpkins said, trading the newspaper for the glass of whiskey.

"Archie telephoned yesterday while you

were out to say his article concerning our involvement in the Hambley case would be in this evening's edition of the paper. I wanted to be sure we read it as soon as it was available," Beryl said. She thought it best not to share with Edwina that she also wanted to be sure they read it in the privacy of the Beeches in case there was anything in the article that did not paint either their fledgling business or Walmsley Parva in a flattering light.

Beryl flipped quickly through the paper and found the article she sought. " 'Female Sleuths Solve the Case — A Tale of Murder, Sabotage, and Financial Intrigue by Archie Harrison,' " Beryl read aloud. " 'Intrepid sleuths Edwina Davenport and Beryl Helliwell have brought to heel a ring of labor agitators bent on murder and mayhem in the quiet Kentish countryside.' " She continued to read the rest of the article, pausing now and again for dramatic effect. Archie had done a remarkably fine job of presenting the pair of them as consummate professionals and ingenious detectives.

Beryl felt a warm glow of satisfaction that had long eluded her. She had spent years dashing about the globe undertaking one adventure after another, but at the end of each she always experienced a nagging certainty that something was lacking. She felt far more proud of what was written in Archie's article on their business than she had of any of the scores of other reports of her exploits. Perhaps it was that she was being valued for her brains as much as for her wit or her daring. She looked at Edwina whose knitting lay abandoned across her lap. It occurred to her that the real difference was that she had equally shared the accomplishment with a dear friend. A thoroughly uncharacteristic lump rose in her throat and she swallowed it down before continuing.

"He concludes the article with the words 'Reliable, effective and discreet, Misses Davenport and Helliwell are accepting new clients. Please direct your enquiries in care of The Beeches, Walmsley Parva, Kent.' "

"You'll have clients lined up at the door before you know it," Simpkins said. "I hope you'll remember who it was that suggested this to you in the first place." He winked at Beryl before crossing to the drinks tray to pour out an even more generous tot of Scotch.

"Well, Ed, surely you have something to say about all this?" Beryl said. "What do you think about seeing your name splashed about the paper?"

"I'm afraid such publicity leads me to conclude you've had a shocking influence on me, Beryl." Edwina picked up her knitting once more, a mischievous smile spread across her face. "I could not be more pleased."

ABOUT THE AUTHOR

Jessica Ellicott is the author of *Murder in an English Village,* the first book in the Beryl & Edwina Mystery series. She loves fountain pens, Mini Coopers, and throwing parties. She lives in northern New England where she obsessively knits wool socks and enthusiastically speaks Portuguese with a shocking disregard for the rules of grammar.

The employees of Thorndike Press hope you have enjoyed this Large Print book. All our Thorndike, Wheeler, and Kennebec Large Print titles are designed for easy reading, and all our books are made to last. Other Thorndike Press Large Print books are available at your library, through selected bookstores, or directly from us.

For information about titles, please call:
  (800) 223-1244

or visit our website at:
  gale.com/thorndike

To share your comments, please write:
  Publisher
  Thorndike Press
  10 Water St., Suite 310
  Waterville, ME 04901